The Unwanted Wife

THE UNWANTED SERIES

The Unwanted Wife

THE UNWANTED SERIES

NATASHA ANDERS

First published in 2012
This edition published by Montlake Romance, Seattle, 2014

www.apub.com

ISBN-13: 9781477818060
ISBN-10: 1477818065

Cover design by Laura Klynstra

Library of Congress Control Number: 2013919710

Printed in the United States of America

To my awesome friends and former colleagues at the Nagaoka Eigoshidoushitsu—for the unwavering support, the fabulous camaraderie, the laughs, and the never-ending movie games. I'll never forget you guys.

CHAPTER ONE

Theresa fell back onto the mattress, her body slick with perspiration and limp with pleasure. Spasms of her powerful release still violently racked her slender frame. Her husband, Alessandro, had disentangled, detached, and distanced himself from her within seconds of their mutual orgasm and lay on his back beside her, his breathing heavy and ragged.

Theresa turned on her side to lovingly trace his profile with her eyes, yearning to touch and caress the smooth and slightly tanned skin, but she knew her touch would be rebuffed. His words, the ones he always said after his climax, still hovered in the air between them and still, after all these months, hurt more than they should have.

"Give me a son, Theresa . . ."

With those five words, he killed the afterglow, destroyed the intimacy of the moment, and relegated the act into nothing more than a biological imperative. After eighteen months of the same, Theresa had finally accepted that it would never change. It wasn't an abrupt realization. No, it was one that had been growing steadily since the very first time he'd said them.

But Theresa had her own five words. They were words that had been on the tip of her tongue for months and should have been spoken long before now. They were words that she could no longer swallow; no matter how much it hurt her to say them. She sat up, naked, her body still trembling, and drew her knees to her chest. She wrapped her arms around her legs, pressed her cheek to her knees, and watched as his breathing steadied and his own shaking subsided. He lay spread-eagled, magnificently nude, his eyes shut, but she knew that he wasn't asleep. As usual he would take a few moments to compose himself before heading for the shower, where she always imagined him frantically scrubbing her scent and touch from his bronzed skin.

She could no longer contain the words, and they spilled from her lips in desperate earnestness.

"I want a divorce, Alessandro."

He tensed. Every single muscle in his body went as tight as a coiled spring before he turned his head to meet her stare. His eyes were hooded, and his upper lip curled mockingly.

"But I thought you *loved* me, Theresa," he taunted with exquisite cruelty, and Theresa closed her eyes, trying to mask the pain that his words caused. When she was sure she had her emotions under control, she opened her eyes.

"Not anymore." She hoped the lie sounded convincing.

"Hmmm . . ." he purred. "What happened to 'I'll love you forever, Sandro'?"

"Things change," she whispered.

"What things?" He rolled onto his side and propped himself up onto his elbow, resting his head on his hand. He looked so much like a Roman gladiator in repose that her throat went dry with desire. She swallowed painfully.

"F-feelings change . . ." she stuttered. Again he gave that husky purr of agreement, but Theresa wasn't fooled by his relaxed posture; he was as tense as a coiled snake. "I . . . I've changed . . ."

"You look no different," he said, his voice still terrifyingly tender. "Still the same Theresa I married. The one who claimed to love me *so* much she couldn't live without me. The one whose daddy made sure she got exactly what she wanted . . ."

And that was when he struck, without moving, without so much as changing his voice.

"The same timid little Theresa who can't even give me the only thing I've ever wanted from this pathetic excuse for a marriage." She flinched but she refused to divert her eyes.

"All the more reason for a divorce." She tried for blasé but failed miserably.

"Maybe for you." He shrugged. "But I told you from the very beginning, *cara*, there would be no easy way out of this marriage. Not until I got what I wanted from you, and that day looks to be a long way off. Unfortunately, cliché though it may seem, you've made this bed and now we *both* have to lie in it!"

"I can't live like this anymore." She buried her face in her knees and fought to keep the tears at bay.

"Neither of us has much choice . . ." He sat up and stretched languidly before getting up to walk to the en-suite bathroom. Theresa heard the shower start moments later and took a few seconds to compose herself before swiping the hot tears from her face with the backs of her hands. She dragged on a gauzy peignoir and headed toward the kitchen to fix a drink of hot milk and honey. It was a concoction her mother used to make for her when she was a little girl, and she hoped that the comforting beverage would soothe her ragged nerves.

The familiar task of preparing the drink calmed her down significantly, and she had just eased onto a bar stool and taken her first sip when she felt Sandro's presence behind her. The hairs on the nape of her neck stood on end, and her hands started shaking again.

"You must be cold in only that skimpy little thing you're wearing," he observed idly, heading to the fridge for a carton of orange juice. His short black hair was damp and standing up in tufts where he had carelessly towel-dried it after his shower. He wore nothing but a pair of black boxer shorts. He looked as gorgeous as always, and Theresa hated him more than ever for that masculine perfection.

"I'm fine." She got up abruptly and headed toward the sink to rinse her mug, but he grabbed her elbow to halt her movement. She tensed, shocked by the touch . . . Alessandro *never* touched her outside of the bedroom. In the eighteen months they had been married, this was the first time that she could recall him touching her without it being a precursor to sex. He leaned closer to her and lowered his lips to her ear. She felt his hot breath on the side of her face before he spoke.

"There'll be no more talk of divorce, Theresa . . . *ever*," he told her with a sickening air of finality.

"You can't stop me from divorcing you, Sandro," she responded bravely.

"You really want a divorce, *cara*?" he asked.

She nodded stiffly.

"If you get that divorce, your cousin loses her business, and she can't afford that now, not with a new baby on the way. She and her husband need all the capital they can get." Somehow she hadn't expected that. She *should* have, but she hadn't. Sandro had loaned her cousin, Lisa, the start-up capital for her bookshop. Theresa didn't know what the specifics of that loan were, but she had always assumed that it was done out of generosity. Staring up at him now, she couldn't believe her own naïveté. Sandro did nothing out of sheer generosity, and that loan was merely another weapon for him to use against her.

"You wouldn't," she responded. "Lisa has done nothing to deserve this."

"*Cara*, I will do whatever it takes to get what I want from you."

"I have money too, I can help her . . ." she began desperately.

"No, *you* have a rich father, and he had the opportunity to help Lisa, but he made his contempt of the idea more than obvious to everyone at the time, and you know that he would *never* support you through a messy divorce, Theresa."

"I still don't believe you would do it! You have a reputation to uphold. You're an honest businessman, and you wouldn't destroy a small business just to prove a point. What kind of message would that send?" she asked.

"That I'm not to be trifled with." He shrugged. "Do you honestly think I care what people think of me, Theresa? Do you think I care what *you* think of me? I never have and I never will. You're weak and spoiled."

"I'm *not* . . ." She tried to defend herself, but he made a scoffing sound in the back of his throat before continuing as if she hadn't spoken.

"You'll get your divorce eventually, but there's something I need to get from you first. You wanted this marriage, remember? You begged for it, I'm sure. So if you want a divorce right now, it'll come with some heavy penalties. Are you willing to gamble with your cousin's future?"

Theresa wouldn't do it, and Sandro knew it. He had her exactly where he wanted her. There would be no divorce. Not when so much hung in the balance. But there *would* be changes . . . Theresa Chloe Noble De Lucci was done being a doormat! She said nothing, choosing to turn and walk away instead. He watched her go, and she could feel his eyes burning into her slender back but he did not call her back. She did not return to the bedroom they had shared since the first day of their marriage, opting instead to head for the library, knowing that she could not sleep another wink. Not in that room, not anymore.

~

Hours later, he came downstairs for breakfast. It was a Saturday morning, so he didn't have any early-morning meetings to rush off to and instead he tended to linger over his newspaper and coffee and largely ignore Theresa. That morning was no different. It was as if their earlier argument hadn't happened at all. They ate their casual weekend meals in the kitchen and the homey setting lent a false sense of domesticity to the scene. But while Theresa was uncomfortable and tense in the intimate setting, Sandro always remained as cool as the proverbial cucumber.

Then again, that was nothing new, as he rarely showed emotion. In fact the "discussion" of that morning was the most heated she had ever seen him. He kept his feelings under wraps but had always made his contempt for her more than clear. It was in the way he refused to meet her eyes, the way he could make love to her without kissing her on the mouth, the way he could talk past her when he had something to tell her, while eternally optimistic and *stupid* Theresa had never been good at hiding her feelings from him. Not from the very moment she'd met him, nearly two years ago. How hopelessly infatuated she had been! How quickly she had fallen in love.

~

She vividly recalled their first meeting. He had come to dinner at their house. Her father hadn't told her much about their guest except that he was the son of an old acquaintance. He had then left her to meet Sandro by herself so that he could make an entrance. It had been one of Jackson Noble's many "tricks" to keep his business adversaries constantly wrong-footed. He loved getting them on his own turf and had conducted many business deals in his home. He would let Theresa soften them up with her natural warmth, and then he would swoop in while they were still charmed and go in for the kill.

Theresa hadn't known about her role in her father's wheeling and dealing until she was nineteen; before that she had merely been grateful for the opportunity to help her father entertain his important friends. By the time she met Sandro, Theresa was the consummate hostess: charming, sweet, warm on the outside but completely disillusioned on the inside. Her father's little business parties had always left her feeling used and disheartened.

Alessandro De Lucci had swooped into their home looking grim and purposeful, like a man ready for battle. He had seemed surprised to see her standing in the huge entrance. She had been wearing a simple green sheath dress, her hair upswept into an elegant chignon, and she had chosen a simple emerald pendant with matching earrings as her only embellishments. He had faltered at the sight of her and frowned in confusion. Theresa, for her part, had been completely riveted by the unexpectedly splendid man who stood in front of her, and for the first time ever her poise had deserted her. She had been unable to utter a single word. He had been beautifully outfitted in a tailor-made business suit, but his windswept hair had contradicted that air of sartorial splendor, giving him a slightly wild appearance. His dark stubble and loosened tie reinforced that ruggedness. He had been like no other man she had ever seen before, and she wanted to know everything there was to know about him.

Sandro had recovered first. He had taken a step toward her, followed by another and then another, until he stood directly in front of her, so close that his every inhalation of breath caused his chest to lightly brush against her. Theresa had tilted her head back to stare at him in wonder, tracing every angle and curve on his face in fascination.

"Hello, *cara*." His voice, like dark velvet over gravel, had sent a shudder of awareness up her spine. "What's your name?"

"Theresa." She had been helpless to do anything but respond. He had smelled *wonderful,* and she had found herself leaning toward him to breathe in his scent.

Theresa remembered every word, every emotion, every sensation of the exchange that had followed.

"Theresa?" he repeated, his appealing voice going slightly husky. "*Bellissima.* I'm Alessandro."

"Yes," she said, not making much sense in that moment, and he grinned. It was a beautiful, warm, boyish smile that made him even more handsome.

"Can you say it?" he asked quietly.

"Say what?"

"My name. I want to hear my name on those amazing lips." He traced a finger over her lips and she stopped breathing completely and moaned. "Say it, *cara.* Four little syllables—A-les-san-dro. Please?"

"Alessandro," she whispered, and he groaned a little.

"Perfect. You're perfect, little Theresa." No one had ever looked at her and seen perfection before. No one had ever smiled at her with so much appreciation and warmth in his eyes before. Theresa had found herself staring back at this appealing stranger, and for the first time in her life, she had felt wanted. Between one heartbeat and the next, Theresa had fallen head over heels in love.

She shook herself, refusing to dwell on past events that she could not change and instead tried to focus on her present.

Breakfast passed with agonizing slowness, the silence broken only by the sound of his newspaper as he carefully perused the business section. She barely ate and hated him for being so unaffected by the tension that he could finish a hearty meal. She picked up her dishes and headed to the sink.

"You have to eat more than one slice of toast," his voice suddenly growled unexpectedly. "You're getting much too thin." The fact that he had noticed what she'd eaten, despite having hardly glanced at her over his newspaper, startled her.

"I'm not that hungry," she responded softly, and placed her dishes in the sink.

"You barely eat enough to keep a sparrow alive." He lowered his paper and met her eyes for a few seconds before diverting his focus back to the mug of coffee on the table in front of him. The direct eye contact was so unusual that Theresa barely restrained a gasp.

"I eat enough," she responded halfheartedly. Normally she would have let it go, but she wanted to see if she could goad him into meeting her eyes again. No such luck; he merely shrugged, neatly folded his newspaper, and dropped it onto the table beside his empty plate. He gulped down the last sip of his coffee before getting up from the table.

She watched as he stretched, his black T-shirt lifting to reveal the toned and tanned band of flesh at his abdomen. Her mouth went dry at the sight of that dark flesh, and once again she was disgusted by her reaction to his physical presence. She had spent the first year of her marriage believing that Sandro would come to love her. She had valiantly believed that if *she* loved him enough, he would go back to being the laughing, affectionate man she had known in the first few months after they had met. She still wasn't completely sure what had caused the change, but from the snide things he sometimes said in passing, she suspected it was her father's influence. After nearly a year of marriage she had been forced to face reality; he truly hated her. He hated her so much so that he couldn't bring himself to speak to her, kiss her, touch her outside of bed, or even *look* at her.

Theresa had finally realized that there would be no thaw; their marriage was a perpetual winter wasteland, and if she ever wanted to feel the warmth of the sun on her face again, she had to get out of it. Unfortunately, escaping would be trickier than she had thought. She would have to find a way out that did not include hurting her cousin. Lisa and Rick Palmer were expecting their first baby, and while Lisa was having a fairly easy time of it, Theresa was concerned that anything that would upset her could be potentially harmful to her or the baby. Also, while Rick's advertising agency was fairly successful, Lisa had always prided herself on the fact that she held her own financially in their relationship. Taking her bookshop away could put too much strain on their relationship, and Theresa didn't want that on her conscience.

She sighed heavily and started to do the dishes. She liked to do little household tasks despite the fact that her thirty-one-year-old husband, who had worked his way up from mailroom clerk to the president of the bank his father owned, "had more money than God," as her father had once put it. Theresa had even enthusiastically insisted on doing some of the cooking herself. They employed a housecleaning staff, as was practical when one lived in a ten-bedroom, five-bathroom monster of a house.

Because their marriage united two prominent families, the press avidly followed the intimate details of their marriage, yet Theresa tried to cling to what she believed was a semblance of normalcy. On Saturdays the staff had the day off and Theresa liked to pick up after herself and Sandro rather than wait for the maids to get to it later. She had never had a "normal" life, and she fondly imagined that these tasks kept her grounded in reality. Sandro didn't pretend to understand her need to have a hand in the everyday running of the house and had mockingly accused her of playing house once, shortly after their wedding. He had never seemed to notice it again after that. She stared down at the dishes she had ready to be placed in the dishwasher and quite abruptly abandoned the task halfway through before heading upstairs and leaving Sandro still in the kitchen.

She changed her clothes from sweat suit to jeans and T-shirt, dragging her vibrant, waist-length Titian hair into a ponytail and tugging on a denim jacket to ward off the early autumn chill. On her way to the front door, she passed by the den where Sandro had retreated with his laptop.

"I'm going out," she casually called through the open door, and his head jerked up while his eyes flared with some indefinable emotion.

"Where . . . ?" he began.

"I don't know how long I'll be gone." She dashed out before he could utter another syllable, grabbing her shoulder bag and car keys on the way out. She had her reliable silver Mini Cooper fired up by the time he eventually made it down to the front door. With a cheery little wave that she *knew* had to grate, she reversed out of the drive-way and headed out. She had *no* clue where she was going and knew that there would be hell to pay when she got back—Sandro liked to keep her in a little box labeled "wife," to be brought out only for social occasions when he needed someone to act as his perfect host-ess. Any sign of mutiny from her was bound to have unpleasant and unforeseen consequences. Still, it felt good just to do something so defiantly out of character. Her cellular phone started ringing seconds later and when she stopped at a red light she switched it off and tossed it aside.

It was still early, barely nine, and because it was Saturday, the roads were a bit congested. Still, she felt free and she headed from the relative tranquility of Clifton, one of the wealthiest and most beautiful suburbs in Cape Town, toward the city. Usually she would go to Newlands and spend the day with Rick and Lisa . . . but she knew that it was the first place Sandro would look. He knew how limited her social life was. She had never made friends easily; her father had kept her isolated throughout her childhood, and her only real friend growing up had been her cousin Lisa.

Her family had founded one of the first banks in the country in the 1800s and had always been leaders in the rarefied reaches of society. Jackson Noble maintained that someone of Theresa's "breeding and background" shouldn't be allowed to mingle with just anybody, which had left Theresa's options for companionship severely limited. She had grown up playing by herself, with Lisa, or—when her father wasn't around to see—with the housekeeper's children. The loneliness and isolation had carried over into her adulthood and even now, she spent most of her free time with Rick and Lisa or learning new recipes from Phumsile, her housekeeper. She spent more time chatting with Phumsile than she did speaking with Sandro. The loneliness was a cycle that Theresa didn't know how to break.

Now she found herself contemplating all the things she *could* do with this unexpected time and, deciding to stick with the trend of the day, opted for the most out-of-character thing she could think of: going to the movies. It was the purest form of escapism, and if there was anything that Theresa desperately wanted, it was to escape from her life. So she spent her day going from one cinema to the next—laughing, crying, cringing, or jumping, depending on the plot. It was the most unproductive day she had ever spent in her life and she *loved* it.

By the time the last show of the day finished it was after midnight and she had a throbbing headache from sitting in darkness and the flickering light of the projector all day and a slightly upset stomach from a diet of soda and popcorn. As she headed back to her car, the sudden reality of her situation sank in and she started trembling. She didn't know what to expect from Sandro. She had never seen him display anything other than icy control, even in bed, but it was the first time she had ever done anything like this. She always strove to be the perfect wife and perfect daughter, always putting Sandro or her father's wishes first, and something as innocent as going to the movies without telling Sandro seemed beyond reckless. While she knew he would never physically hurt her, his potential to hurt her emotionally was unlimited.

The house was ablaze with light when she got back, and the dread made her stomach heave. She swallowed down her nausea before parking her car and heading toward the front door, which was wrenched open before she even had the chance to get her keys out.

She gulped slightly at the intimidating form of her husband looming in the doorway and stifled a yelp when he grabbed her arm and yanked her inside. He slammed the door shut, gripping both her shoulders in his huge hands and backed her up until she was leaning against the door. It took her a few seconds to get over her disorientation and grasp that he wasn't hurting her. His eyes feverishly raked up and down her trembling body, until he was apparently satisfied that everything was in relatively good condition, and then he raised his eyes to meet hers full on.

His eyes, which she'd had so little opportunity to actually look into of late, were heartbreakingly beautiful. They were chocolate brown and set between incredibly thick, blue-black lashes and beneath sweeping brows, and right now they were smoldering with something that, in a less controlled man, might have been described as fury. His hands released her shoulders and crept up to her face. She flinched slightly at the contact, but they remained gentle, moving to cup her jaw, his large thumbs brushing over her cheeks. Her breathing became ragged when he leaned toward her, dipping his head closer to hers. He was so near she could feel his clean, warm breath on her face. He tilted her jaw slightly and she groaned, aching for his lips on hers, wanting it so desperately her legs had just about turned to jelly, and the only thing that kept her from falling to a puddle at his feet was his solidly muscled body braced against hers. She could feel his erection throbbing against her stomach and knew he wanted her as desperately as she wanted him. His lush mouth was centimeters away from hers, and when he spoke, his lips brushed against her mouth.

"You pull a stunt like this again, *tesoro mia,* and I swear to *God*, you'll regret it!"

She flinched as reality brought her back down to earth with a thump. He let her go and she slid down the door to land at his feet. He raked a contemptuous glance over her, the ice back and the fire gone.

"Where have you been?" he asked calmly. She staggered to her feet, humiliated that she had allowed him to affect her to such an extent that she would fall at his feet. She tilted her head back defiantly and refused to answer him. "Theresa, I'm warning you . . ."

"Warn away," she taunted shakily. "You want to stay married? Fine. But I refuse to let you walk all over me anymore. It's time you start showing me some respect!"

"How the hell am I supposed to respect someone who sold herself to the highest bidder?" he growled with tight control, and she gasped, stung. "I have no respect for you, Theresa, not even as the potential mother of my child, because, quite frankly, you can't even do *that* right."

She lost it, *completely*, and for the first time in her entire twenty-six years, Theresa resorted to violence. She launched herself at him, hissing, spitting, and scratching like a cat. In that moment she hated him so much that it felt like a living thing trying to claw its way out of her to get at him. When she came back to herself, she realized that he had her in his arms, her back to his front, her wrists in his hands, and her arms crossed over her chest. They were both out of breath. There were terrible mewling sounds coming from the back of her throat, the words of hate she had repeatedly hurled at him having long ago faded into incoherent sobs. His lips were in her hair, just above her left ear, and he was making soothing sounds, not hurting her, just restraining her with his superior strength. She went limp, hanging defeated from his arms.

"I'm sorry." She froze; the words were so quiet she wasn't sure she'd heard him correctly. "That was . . . cruel and wrong of me."

More words? She didn't know how to respond and so chose not to say anything. She felt him swallowing before he gingerly released her wrists and stepped away from her. She made a show of rubbing them, even though he hadn't hurt her at all. Instead *she* seemed to have inflicted most of the damage on both of them. A few of her nails were broken and her fists were bruised from the few angry punches she had managed to land against his hard body. She turned around to face him and was shocked to see that he was bleeding. He had scratches on his hands and face, including a deep, angry-looking one on his neck. He also had bite marks on his muscled forearms, and a darkening bruise on his jaw. He saw her eyes land on the bruise and ruefully rubbed at it.

"You pack a mean punch," he said sheepishly, before looking down at her hands and swearing softly. "You've hurt yourself." He lifted one and grimaced at the bruises and broken nails. She snatched her hand from his; she was not sure what this weird act was about and definitely did *not* trust it. His eyes darkened at her mistrustful glare, and he shoved his hands into his pockets. She pushed her way past him before heading toward the staircase.

"Theresa . . ." She stopped but didn't turn around. "I really am sorry about what I said. It wasn't true." She knew his apology was insincere. While he hadn't ever said so, she knew that he blamed her for the baby she had lost early on in their marriage. The fact that she hadn't conceived since had merely cemented his low opinion of her.

"I'm going to bed," she whispered, ignoring the apology and still not looking at him.

"Yes . . ." He moved out of her way and buried his hands in his trouser pockets. She was intensely aware of his eyes boring into her back as she walked away from him, and held her head up as she ascended the stairs to the second floor.

She made her way to one of the luxurious guest rooms and tears welled in her eyes; Alessandro's cruel words had struck a nerve. She had lost the baby after just five months of marriage and three months of pregnancy, and Theresa had always felt that the miscarriage was her fault. When she had discovered that she was pregnant, she had wished the child away—her relationship with her husband had been so cold that she had been unable to fathom bringing a child into such a loveless environment. Worse, after she had lost the baby, she had been ashamed to admit that relief was mingled with the heartbreak. She had hated herself for that, had felt that there was something wrong with her for wishing her own child out of existence. She had never shared what she had felt with Sandro, and they had mourned the tiny life's passing separately, never talking about it. Now she suspected he had known all along, and that it had increased his contempt for her.

Despite her extreme depression after the miscarriage, she had worked through it on her own. Rick and Lisa hadn't even known about her pregnancy. She had felt so terrible about her reaction to the baby that she had never told them, feeling that her behavior had been indefensible. But tonight, Sandro's cruel taunts had quite simply sent her over the edge.

She sighed, trying to shake herself out of her maudlin mood, and after a quick shower, she fell into bed wearing only the T-shirt and panties that she had quickly grabbed from her chest of drawers in the master suite. Despite the drama of the day, she fell asleep almost immediately. She didn't know how long she had been asleep before she heard the quiet knock on the door. She immediately awoke and sat up, pushing her tangled hair out of her face.

"Theresa! Open the damned door!" Sandro angrily thumped on the wood again, and this time it was loud enough to make her jump up and hurriedly unlock and open the door, for fear that he would wake the live-in housekeeper. Despite the fact that his voice had been only a grim whisper through the wood, she was in no doubt that he was absolutely livid. She stood staring up at him in the dim light and was surprised by the flash of hot fury on his face, which was so quickly masked beneath the more familiar mask of icy indifference, that she wasn't sure if she had imagined the emotion.

"What are you doing in here?" he asked stiffly.

"I've decided to move into this room," she informed him, not quite succeeding in keeping the anxiety from her voice, and his jaw clenched. She had not anticipated having this conversation until morning. Sandro was full of surprises today. She had known that he would be upset about her moving out of their bedroom. He enjoyed sex with her and seemed happy to have her conveniently within arm's reach. Still, it was completely out of character for him to actually come thumping on her bedroom door, demanding an explanation in the dead of night! She had expected a cold and controlled conversation about it over the breakfast table. The light from the landing was just bright enough for her to see the stormy emotion brewing in his eyes, and she swallowed a lump of disappointment when the emotion was doused in ice.

"I can see that," he gritted out. "I think the pertinent question is *why*?" And she could see that it just about killed him to ask it.

"I'd feel like a hypocrite if I stayed in the master bedroom with you." She shrugged again. "Just this morning I told you I wanted a divorce, so it wouldn't feel right if I continued to share your bed as if we'd never had that conversation."

"You're being ridiculous," he said dismissively.

"No . . . I think I'm actually making sense for the first time in nearly two years."

"My *wife*"—he placed sarcastic emphasis on the last word—"sleeps with me. You *will* come back to our bedroom, if I have to drag you there kicking and screaming!"

"I-I . . . m-may have to sleep with you, Sandro," she conceded, knowing that if he chose to do as he threatened, she would definitely lose to his superior size and strength. "But I won't be having sex with you anymore."

"You would deny me, your *husband*, this basic marital right?" He sounded frankly astonished by that, as astonished as Theresa felt for even daring to say the words.

"Yes."

His eyes narrowed and he took a threatening step toward her.

"What's to stop me from just taking what belongs to me?" he asked speculatively, his eyes raking dismissively over her thin, shivering, T-shirt-clad body. Theresa crossed her arms over her chest and hunched her shoulders defensively.

"I don't belong to you," she said softly.

"Well, I certainly forked out huge amounts of money for you. That feels like ownership to me."

"I have no idea what you're talking about," she protested in frustration, and he laughed softly.

"And you're still singing the same tired old tune," he mocked. "This is beside the point. I have no wish to rehash these details, it achieves nothing. Come on, we're going to bed!" He grabbed her hand and tugged her back toward their bedroom a few doors down the hall. She was so shocked by the abrupt gesture that she stumbled along behind him, before instinct kicked in and she dug in her heels, leaving him to practically drag her the last few feet.

Theresa was out of breath and furious when he finally released her hand. They were in the master bedroom, facing each other, and she glared at him . . . refusing to be intimidated by his scowl.

"When did you become the Neanderthal Man, Sandro? I never thought you would resort to caveman tactics." He didn't like being called a barbarian, not her suave, sophisticated, and rigid husband. She could see it in the way his mouth thinned and his eyes blazed. He grabbed her wrist and dragged her up against him.

"You haven't seen the Neanderthal in me yet, *cara*. I advise you *not* to push me on this, not unless you want things to get really ugly between us." He used his whole body to intimidate her, leaning over and into her, nose to nose.

"I don't see how things can get any uglier," she whispered.

"You really don't want to find out how much worse it can get, trust me on that." His eyes bored into hers, and her breath came in small, shallow gasps. She was suddenly aware of how closely she was pressed against him and felt a betraying flash of heat uncoiling in the pit of her stomach and radiating outward. Even though Sandro never really let himself go in bed, he was still an incredible lover, and despite, or maybe *because* of, the clinical precision with which he conducted the act, he *always* made sure she climaxed. She would have traded any number of those orgasms for a kiss of course, or even a show of affection afterward, but she couldn't help her reaction to him. He could always make her melt. Chemistry was a terrible thing; sometimes it simply sparked between the wrong people.

His eyes were still locked with hers, and she felt the sudden change in his breathing and his heart rate. He leaned even closer, his mouth nearly touching hers; their breath mingled and came in jagged gasps. If she moved her head, just a fraction of an inch, their lips would touch. She couldn't resist and she tensed herself to do just that, when he swore and stepped away from her. Theresa blinked and felt like someone coming out of a trance.

"Just go to bed." He put his hand in the small of her back and gave her a gentle push toward the bed.

"I'm not going to have . . ." she began to protest.

"I know. I'm not exactly in the right frame of mind for it either." He prodded her again.

"You won't touch me?"

"Not unless you want me to." He shrugged as if he didn't care either way.

"I don't want you to," she asserted firmly.

"Then you have nothing to worry about." He turned away from her and stripped off his casual shirt, leaving him abruptly naked from the chest up. As always, he stole her breath away, and she had to force herself to turn away from the seductive sight of her half-naked husband and head to bed. She crept beneath the covers and kept her back to him, but she was achingly aware of every sound he made as he headed toward the en suite, discarding even more clothes along the way. For such a precise and controlled man in every other aspect of his life, Alessandro tended to be a bit messy in his own space: he would casually drop a shirt here, a sock there . . . obviously expecting the magical cleaning fairies to pick up after him. That "magical cleaning fairy" was usually Theresa; she was a bit of a neat freak and would quite compulsively pick up and fold everything he dropped. Well, not anymore; he could damned well pick up his own shirts.

She wryly acknowledged to herself that this resolution would last only as long as it took for the maid to come in and clean it up. The one thing about being fabulously wealthy was that you didn't *have* to think about mundane things like picking up after yourself. And Alessandro had been spoiled since birth into believing the universe revolved around him. While Theresa's family had been wealthy too, she had never taken anything for granted, not when she had an emotionally detached father, who relentlessly pointed out her every flaw, and a depressed mother, who had exited Theresa's life via a bottle of sleeping pills. Theresa had been a scared and confused eleven-year-old at the time.

She sighed softly and turned over to watch the door of the en suite. He hadn't shut it completely, and a narrow sliver of light streamed into the darkened bedroom. Steam was creeping out along the edges of the door and she could smell the spicy scent of his soap. The shower stopped abruptly and she heard the rustling sounds of him towel drying. She smiled softly to herself as she heard the towel drop to the floor after he finished. She was achingly familiar with every detail of his nightly ablutions; he usually brushed his teeth and shaved while showering. Five minutes later, the light in the en suite went out and he stepped out into the dark bedroom. She could just make out his silhouette enough to see that he was naked, and she panicked slightly when she recognized that he had absolutely every intention of getting into bed that way.

He usually slept naked but she had honestly believed that he would drag on a shorts or something after the events of that evening. No such luck. She felt him lifting the covers and sliding beneath them. He smelled divine and she had to fight the impulse to turn toward him. He didn't say a word and made no move toward her, staying on his side of the bed. No surprise there. He usually stayed on his side of the bed anyway unless he felt the need to work on his long-term project to sire a son. Only then would he move toward her to touch her, caress her, and do everything but *love* her.

Theresa never instigated their intimate encounters. She had learned early on that any move toward such intimacy was usually rebuffed, and her fragile self-esteem didn't deal well with rejection, so she had stopped trying. Ironically enough, tonight, after her decree that he not touch her, was the first time in a long time that she was actually tempted to move toward him. She clenched her fists and curled into a ball, trying not to think of all that tantalizing naked male flesh lying next to her. She knew he was awake, she could tell from the rhythm of his breathing, and obviously he knew she was awake, she was way too tense to be asleep.

"Just go to sleep for God's sake." His impatient voice suddenly rang out in the darkness. "I said I wouldn't touch you and I won't . . . so you can relax!"

She tensed even more at the sound of his voice, and he swore softly.

"If you can't sleep, I have the perfect solution for your insomnia," he murmured suggestively, leaving her in no doubt as to his "solution."

"You're not helping matters," she gritted through clenched teeth and he laughed quietly.

"Well, if neither of us can sleep . . ."

"We haven't been in bed long enough to fall asleep . . . just *hush*!" she hissed.

"You know you're being ridiculous, right?" he murmured in his most patronizingly logical voice, which he knew would drive her absolutely crazy.

"I don't care *how* ridiculous you think I'm being." She flipped over to face him and could barely make out his profile in the dark. He was lying on his back, with one arm tucked beneath his head. When he felt her turn over, he turned his head to look at her. She could see only the whites of his eyes in the dark. "This is what I want, Sandro."

"I don't believe that for a second," he maintained, reaching out to touch her face with one gentle hand. "The sex has always been good between us, Theresa. That's one thing that's never been in doubt. It's the one damned thing that's working in this marriage."

"It wasn't working for me," she muttered defiantly. That bruised his masculine ego; she sensed it in the way he tensed.

"You weren't faking those responses," he negated stiffly.

"No, I wasn't. You're really *very* good," she agreed, realizing too late that she didn't sound very convincing at all. "It just isn't enough for me anymore."

"I'm not enough for you anymore?" he asked flatly, and she knew she had to tread carefully here, he was in an unpredictable mood, and she feared even more excoriating comments from him. It was in her nature to pacify rather than provoke, so she made one last attempt to explain herself.

"That's not *quite* what I meant . . ."

"Oh?"

"Sandro, you're being deliberately obtuse." Okay that wasn't quite the right thing to say either. She could practically *feel* him bristling next to her.

"It'll probably be best if you didn't say anything else, Theresa."

"Look, you're intentionally misunderstanding me here . . ." she began.

"*Not* another word," he warned.

"But . . ." Suddenly she was flat on her back with him straddling her hips. She gasped and writhed as she tried to dislodge him.

"I warned you," he growled.

"Get *off* me," she hissed angrily, pushing futilely at his hot, naked chest.

"No." He settled himself more firmly against her, moving his hips until her thighs reluctantly parted and he was lodged between them. Her T-shirt had ridden up to her waist, leaving only her tiny bikini panties as a barrier between them. She was achingly aware of his bare flesh rubbing against the tender skin of her inner thighs and felt herself responding. She helplessly moved with him, wanting more contact. He groaned and buried his face in her neck, his lips nuzzling her neck, moving up over her jaw line, then her chin, skirting past her mouth before brushing over her cheek and capturing one sensitive earlobe between his teeth. It was the blatant avoidance of her mouth that quite effectively doused the flame that had started a slow burn in her gut.

"This is not what I want," she said firmly, using all her strength to try and push him away, but he wouldn't budge.

"Yes it is," he whispered into her ear.

"If you do this, it'll be against my will," she asserted desperately. "And you *know* what that's called!" He froze abruptly before moving off her and back to his side of the bed.

"You would accuse me of something so despicable?" He sounded mortally offended, but Theresa wasn't about to allow herself to be swayed.

"If the shoe fits . . ."

"What does *that* mean?" he growled. "Some damned ambiguous idiom that doesn't apply to this situation at all! There was no force involved in what just happened."

"You pinned me down and refused to get off me when I asked you to. That's a pretty clear example of force." He didn't respond and lay there seething in outraged silence. She had once again succeeded in bruising his masculine pride, and Theresa was human and petty enough to give herself a mental high five. They didn't speak at all after that, and Theresa eventually fell into a restless sleep.

CHAPTER TWO

The air at breakfast the following morning was still thick with tension. The unobtrusive staff had set out the usual Sunday morning breakfast buffet on the sunny patio next to the pool before disappearing into the woodwork. Sandro didn't like distractions on Sunday mornings, so he preferred not to see the staff, and usually, even though he insisted Theresa have all meals with him for appearances' sake, he ignored her in favor of his Sunday *Times*. That morning, despite his usual barrier of the newspaper up between him and the rest of the world—meaning her—she could all but *feel* his fury. After an unbearably tense half hour, he balled the paper up between his fists and tossed it aside before glaring at her across the glass table.

"I want to know exactly where you were yesterday, Theresa," he demanded.

"Why do you even care?" she asked tiredly. "You've certainly disappeared without explanation enough times for the both of us."

"We're not talking about me here," he pointed out.

"No, but I think it's time we do talk about you, about your outrageous behavior, about the other women and your blatant disregard for the fact that you're married!"

"I don't *feel* married!" He sounded almost defensive.

"No?" she retorted recklessly. "Well, maybe I don't feel married either! Maybe I'm ready to be outrageous. Maybe I'm ready for other men and extramarital affairs too!"

"This had better not be your way of telling me that you were with another man last night, Theresa," he said ominously, his voice eerily calm. Theresa ignored the warning in his voice and plunged on.

"So what if that's exactly what I'm telling you?" she asked. "What will you do about it? Make my life hell? Well, surprise, surprise . . . it's already hell! Do your worst!"

"What's his name?" he demanded in a lethally controlled voice that sent an involuntary shudder down her spine. She recognized that she had pushed him too far, but she knew that even if she backed down now, it wouldn't assuage his anger. "Theresa, who the *hell* is he?"

Theresa couldn't help but feel an instinctive frisson of fear. She knew that he had a tight leash on his temper, but right now that leash seemed strained to the breaking point.

"I-I was speaking hypothetically," she stuttered, abandoning all pretense of bravado.

"I don't believe you," he bit out furiously.

"I wasn't with anybody, I just needed a break!"

"A break," he repeated with flat contempt.

"Yes a *break*! A break from you and a break from this life. I don't want to be in this marriage anymore. I want out and I want away from you! Please, I just want a divorce, Sandro. Please."

"You'll get your divorce when I get my son," he reminded ruthlessly.

"That's so sick," she protested. "Why would you even *want* a child with a woman you despise?" He didn't respond, and instead he gave her a searching look.

"You honestly don't know, do you?" he breathed in disbelief, and she blinked in confusion.

"Know what?" she asked blankly, distracted by the look on his face. Again he didn't reply. "Know what?"

"Why did you marry me?" he asked.

"You *know* why." She was outraged by the way he was rubbing salt in the wound, unable to believe, even after a year and a half of similar treatment, that he could be so cruel.

"Humor me," he prompted, and she exhaled shakily, before getting up with as much dignity as she could muster. She felt shaky and nauseous and couldn't stomach being around him anymore. She took an unsteady step away from the table, swaying so badly that he jumped up and clasped one large hand around her slender arm to steady her.

"Theresa?" He sounded almost shaken.

"I'm fine." She shrugged off his hand. "I just got up too quickly. Now, please excuse me, I have things to do!"

"Wait . . ." he said urgently. "I asked you a question."

"A stupid question that you already know the answer to," she retorted.

"Maybe I'd like to hear the answer again." He was being a total ass about this, and not for the first time in her life, Theresa felt like hitting him.

"Oh God, why do you insist on doing this to me?" she groaned.

"You really *loved* me, didn't you?" He breathed in amazement, and she shot him a haunted look before turning away.

"You may rest assured that whatever I felt for you when we married is no longer an issue. I want a divorce, and nothing you do or say can induce me to stay with you," she insisted, and he surprised her by nodding thoughtfully.

"Yes. I'm beginning to discern that," he acknowledged softly. There was nothing more to be said, and she left the room with her head held high and her dignity intact.

~

She was a mass of nerves when she got to the bedroom and sank down on the bed, feeling quivery and still vaguely nauseous. She felt like she had just gone ten rounds with a heavyweight boxer, but she also thought that he had actually listened to her and that she had made some headway. Feeling like she needed to speak to someone about what had just happened, she picked up the telephone receiver from its cradle on the nightstand, but she was taken aback to hear ringing on the other end. Realizing that Sandro was on the extension downstairs, she was about to put the phone down when the ringing stopped abruptly.

"Jackson Noble." Her father's voice snapped into her ear, and her eyes widened in shock. Sandro and her father did *not* get along, and she was surprised that Sandro had willingly called the older man. More than a little curious, she hesitated before replacing the receiver, but that brief hesitation proved to be enough to keep her riveted to the phone.

"Your daughter wants a divorce," was Sandro's opening sally, and Theresa's fingers tightened around the phone.

"What are you talking about? Divorce is not an option and you *know* that!" her father astounded her by responding.

"Yes," Sandro's voice was drier than the desert in summer. "*I* know that, but it appears that *she* does not. You didn't tell her about our agreement?" *What agreement?*

"Of course not," Jackson Noble scoffed contemptuously. "She would never have married you if I had. The little twit fancied herself in love with you!" Her father laughed nastily and Theresa winced. Her free arm wrapped around her midriff as she tried to keep her nausea at bay. Sandro did not react to her father's last statement.

"I thought she'd gone into this marriage consenting to sell herself for the sake of your sadistic little contract. Daddy's good little girl to the very end!" he said after a long pause.

"Would it have changed your mind if you'd known you were marrying a naïve little fool who thought you epitomized her every dream come true?"

"And she has no idea about the terms of our agreement?" Sandro asked slowly.

"Well, I assumed she would discover them from you eventually . . ."

"Are you telling me that she married me believing that I was *in love with her*?" He sounded incredulous that Theresa would ever have believed him in love with her.

"Of course." Her father snorted.

"And you just went ahead and let her believe that?"

"I know it was a ridiculous assumption on her part but it played right into our hands. It was like watching a sleepy kitten fall in love with a roaring lion," her father laughed, he actually *laughed*, after saying that. "But I doubt she would have married you otherwise."

"'Played into *our* hands? There is no *us* here, Jackson. I had nothing to do with your obscene little scheme."

"Oh, spare me your sanctimonious drivel, Sandro," her father scoffed. "It smacks of hypocrisy when you gained a hell of a lot out of this deal. And even if you'd known about Theresa's expectations, it would have made no difference to the eventual outcome. You know that as well as I do."

"She's your *daughter*!" Sandro suddenly roared. "That should have meant something to you."

"Of course it meant something to me. It meant that she could at last be of some use to me! Her role in my life is now quite vital. So you'd better keep her happy, get her pregnant, and stop her prattling on about divorce. You know what you stand to lose if your marriage dissolves before I get what I want."

"I had a life before we made this ridiculous arrangement and I would like to get back to it at some point," Sandro said. Theresa bit her lip hard to stop herself from crying out at the knowledge that her husband had always considered their marriage to be something outside of his real life. She had never met his family, all of whom lived in Italy. He visited them every other month for at least two weeks and never bothered asking her to join him. Of course he had never wanted them to meet her, not when she was just his "temporary" and unwanted wife.

"Well, you know what it would take to get out and I'm amazed that it's taken you so long to accomplish that task."

Sandro remained silent for a moment.

"You know we had a setback, it's been difficult to recover from that!" he responded. Theresa's brow furrowed, and her sweaty hand tightened around the receiver, which was practically welded to her ear. She tried to figure out what they were talking about. What was this goal that would set her free? It had something to do with a mutual business interest if the conversation was anything to go by. She would do *anything* to help Sandro accomplish whatever he needed to if it meant she could get out sooner. And once she was free, she would walk away from them both and never look back.

"Yes . . . that damned girl can't do anything right, can she?" her father suddenly grated, and Theresa's head came up when she realized that they were talking about her. What on earth did . . . ? "The one thing you'd expect the woman to be able to do and she botched even that." *Oh God!* Theresa finally understood what they had been referring to in such dry terms and she nearly doubled over in pain.

"No one was to blame for what happened," Sandro shocked her by saying. "It was just one of those things."

"Regardless," her father dismissed. "Sire a boy on the brat and be done with it. Surely the task shouldn't be too difficult for a strapping young man like you? After that, you're most welcome to obtain your divorce and live happily ever after with that Francesca woman of yours. 'The love of your life'—that's what the press once called her, right?"

Francesca? Theresa didn't know what to process first, the fact that this whole marriage had been about her being a broodmare for whatever sick goal they had in mind, or the fact that Sandro was in love with another woman. Both bits of information hurt so much that Theresa felt like she had been physically assaulted. She'd always assumed that Sandro's desire for a son was fueled by his Italian male ego; the need to propagate his line and all that. The thought that it was part of some kind of bargain that he had made with her father had never even crossed her mind! Even though she had hated the way he could never touch her without that ultimate goal in mind, she had always believed that it was something *he* wanted, a son to carry on his name and an heir to inherit his fortune. Instead the baby would only ever have been a way for him to gain his freedom and carry on his life with *Francesca.*

But what was supposed to happen to her and the baby once Sandro had fulfilled his end of the bargain? Would he leave and forget about them? The one thing she had never doubted was that if Sandro wanted a son, he would *love* the child. Now she wasn't even sure of that! Sandro seemed to despise her so much she now knew that even though any baby they had would carry his name, it would ultimately be neglected and unloved by its father just like she had been by hers. She couldn't allow that to happen and this made her even more determined not to have a child.

As for her father's role in all this, she certainly knew why he wanted a grandson. He had always bemoaned his lack of male progeny to carry on his line and his business. Theresa had never been good enough to inherit, which he had always made quite clear, but she had never grasped how far he would go to ensure a male heir. It was all so archaic.

Theresa was so wrapped up in her painful thoughts that it took her a while to register the low buzzing in her ear and realize that the two men had disconnected their call. She very carefully, as if it were the most fragile thing in the world, replaced the receiver in its cradle and sat quite still for a long time before suddenly exploding into action and dashing to the en-suite bathroom, where she violently threw up the meager portion that she had had for breakfast.

After she was done she rinsed her mouth, headed back to the bedroom, and crawled to the center of the huge bed. She sat there with her knees drawn up to her chest and her face buried in her hands, too hurt to even cry. She was shaking so badly that her teeth were chattering. She didn't know what to do or where to turn. She needed to get out of this situation, as far away from both men as she possibly could. Possible solutions and scenarios kept marching their way through her traumatized mind, but nothing viable presented itself. There was still Sandro's threat against Lisa's business to consider; she also had no real money of her own and she knew that with their considerable resources, her father and husband would find her before she could get very far.

She was still mulling it over when a soft knock sounded on the bedroom door. It swung open before she could respond, and her big, dark, *beautiful* husband stood framed in the doorway. His eyes swept over her small and disheveled form as she sat in the middle of the bed with her arms wrapped around her knees.

"You've been in here for nearly three hours, Theresa," he said in a quiet voice. It was the kind of voice one would use when talking to an unbroken, high-strung horse. *Three hours?* Theresa hadn't known that it had been that long, and when she moved, her muscles screamed in protest. She gingerly and with visible effort stretched her arms and legs, trying not to wince in agony as her blood started circulating more freely.

"I lost track of time," she murmured, padding over to the mirror to check her appearance. She sighed when she saw her reflection. She looked terrible. She had never considered herself more than average-looking, and she looked far below average today. There were shadows under her green eyes, her skin was unnaturally pale and gave her a washed-out appearance that made her red hair and green eyes look garish in comparison.

She wondered how she could ever have believed a man like Sandro De Lucci would want her in the first place. She tried to view her features objectively, but all she could see were too-large eyes framed by long, *red* eyelashes; a straight nose that wasn't too big or too small; high cheekbones that sometimes made her face look gaunt when she was tired; and lips that looked too big for her narrow oval face. Nothing impressive—just an ordinary face that looked tired and strained at the moment. She pushed her long hair out of her eyes and was startled when Sandro's reflection appeared in the mirror behind her.

"I'm going to visit Lisa," she told him.

"Why?" he asked sharply, and she shrugged.

"Something to do," was her casual response.

"I thought . . ." He hesitated and Theresa's eyes snapped up to his face in surprise. The hesitation was so unusual in her supremely confident husband. "I thought that we could go out somewhere and have lunch together. We haven't done that in a while."

"Try never," She half laughed incredulously, and his brows beetled slightly.

"Of course we have . . ." he began.

"Once." She nodded. "About a month *before* we were married. I remember that once quite vividly because I felt like a heroine in my own personal fairy tale. The giddy, foolish, and not-quite-so-fair maiden having a meal with her dark, brooding, and oh-so-handsome prince. Some prince! You couldn't be bothered to string together two sentences the entire time and checked your watch every five minutes like you had someplace much more important to be. But of course, I didn't care, that was just the way you were and I 'loved'"—she said the word with a sneer—"you anyway. We never went out again after that."

"Of course we did." Despite his assertion, he looked remarkably uncomfortable. He shifted his shoulders restlessly and shoved his hands into his jean pockets.

"Those other times were work-related dinners, the ones that you *have* to take your wife to." He frowned even more but chose not to respond to her statement.

"Well, then, I'd say it's about time we went out together, don't you?" he asked in an artificially cheerful voice, and Theresa slanted her head as she tried to read his expression. As usual he was giving nothing away. Her lips tilted slightly in a cynical and unamused smile.

"I don't think so, Sandro." She shook her head. "I think I'll go to my cousin's place like I'd originally planned." He nodded thoughtfully, swaying back and forth on his heels in an uncharacteristically restless manner.

"Suit yourself." He shrugged. "What time were you planning to leave?"

"Soon."

"Right." He shrugged again, looking strangely awkward. "See you later then." She nodded and he turned away and left without saying another word.

Rick and Lisa were doing nothing more productive than watching DVDs when Theresa came around. Lisa, in her advanced state of pregnancy, couldn't do much else. They were both lounging in the den, Rick looking devastatingly handsome in a snug, well-worn pair of jeans and a gray T-shirt that had definitely seen better days. Lisa, in the meantime, looked miserable in a huge blue-and-white-striped football jersey that Theresa knew had once belonged to Rick, who was a capable Sunday-afternoon player, and a pair of blue leggings. She was about the size of a baby whale. Theresa simply melted when she caught sight of her cranky younger cousin and once again resolved not to do anything to jeopardize her happiness and health. She dropped a kiss on Lisa's cheek and one on the top of Rick's head as she passed behind the sofa on which they were sitting. Rick grinned up at her.

"Nothing exciting planned for today, sweetie," he informed cheerfully as Theresa sank down onto the other sofa. "I'm afraid we're feeling a bit out of sorts today, a touch grumpy, if you will. So we're staying in, in the hopes that it will improve our temper . . . *Ouch!*" The last uttered as Lisa swatted him on the back of his head.

"Stop talking like that, you know it drives me crazy! I'm not a two-year-old throwing a tantrum, I'm the hormonal woman that *you* knocked up! So don't push me, buster."

Rick slanted a rueful gaze at his amused friend and mouthed a wisely silent *"See?"* Theresa grinned before kicking off her shoes and dragging her feet up under her. She was dressed casually too, wearing an old pair of jeans and a bright-blue T-shirt with a large, stylized butterfly printed on the front of it.

"What are we watching?" Theresa asked, leaning forward to help herself to a handful of the popcorn from a glass bowl on the coffee table.

"Some romantic thing that has Lisa dissolving into tears every two minutes or so." Rick shrugged dismissively, ignoring the way his wife was glaring at him over the top of her round little glasses. "God, the sacrifices I make to keep this woman happy," he said with a groan, and Lisa gasped in outrage.

"Well, if *you* had your way, we'd be watching some macho jerk swear and punch his way through two hours of relentless explosions, car chases, and gunfire," she retorted, and he grinned at her.

"Your point being?"

"Aaargh!"

For the first time in a long time, Theresa felt a giggle bubbling up in her throat. Rick suddenly grinned before dropping one arm around his wife's narrow shoulders to drag her closer. He placed his other hand protectively over her stomach, and Lisa put up a token struggle before sighing contentedly and dropping her head onto his broad shoulder. Theresa watched them enviously for a few moments before trying to focus on the movie. She had thought Rick was exaggerating about her cousin's response to the overly soppy film, but it was true; Lisa sniffled on an average of every two minutes. Theresa was just managing to get somewhat absorbed in the plot when the doorbell rang. Rick excused himself and jumped up to answer it.

Lisa watched him go with a slight smile on her face. She was quiet for a while before shaking her head in exasperation.

"You know, if I didn't love him so darned much, I would probably have killed him by now," she admitted sourly, and Theresa surprised herself by laughing out loud in response to her cousin's disgruntled confession. She couldn't believe that her sense of humor was still intact after the events of the last forty-eight hours. Rick made his way back into the room, looking uncharacteristically grim, and all the laughter and light drained from Theresa's face when she saw who was standing behind the tall, blond man.

"What are *you* doing here?" she managed to choke out after a moment of shocked silence.

"I thought I'd join you all for lunch." He shrugged, nodding apologetically to a still-gaping Lisa. "May I sit down?" He indicated the sofa Theresa was occupying.

"Yes, of course." Lisa nodded graciously.

"No!" Both Rick and Theresa yelled at the same time Lisa agreed. Sandro smiled humorlessly before choosing to ignore their vehement rejection and sitting down beside Theresa. She shied as far away from him as she could, but Sandro chose to ignore that too. He leaned forward and placed his elbows on his spread thighs, with his large, masculine hands dangling down between his legs. He focused intently on Lisa.

"How have you been, Elisa?" he asked gently. He was the only one who ever called Lisa by her full name, and Theresa could sense Rick bristling. Rick couldn't stand Sandro at all; he hated Sandro's coldness toward Theresa. Only Theresa's edict that Rick and Lisa not interfere in her marriage kept Rick civil around Sandro. Lisa had known almost since the beginning that Sandro and Theresa's marriage was troubled, and while she wasn't happy about Sandro's treatment of her cousin, she offered her support by being there when Theresa needed a sympathetic ear.

"Fine, thanks," Lisa murmured, rubbing her hands over her stomach in an instinctively maternal gesture. "A little tired, but I suppose that it's to be expected when you're lugging another human being around." Sandro grinned, he actually *grinned*, at that and nodded.

"Indeed."

"Rick, for God's sake, stop hovering and sit down," Lisa snapped at her still-glowering husband. "I would like to finish watching this movie sometime in this year! We're having lunch afterward, Alessandro, I hope you don't mind?"

"Of course not," he said smoothly, leaning back and making Theresa feel incredibly claustrophobic as he crowded her with his large body. "What are we watching?"

Lisa told him, and Sandro did an admirable job of concealing his grimace. Lisa barely contained her own grin before hitting the Play button. Rick rejoined her on the sofa, sending periodic glares over at Sandro, who kept his eyes glued on the screen and looked unfairly relaxed.

Lisa dropped her head onto her husband's broad shoulder and resumed her occasional sniffling, and Rick, unable to remain furious for long with his wife draped across him, dragged Lisa close again and snuggled her up against him. His fingers interlaced with the hand she had resting on her stomach, and Theresa felt like she was the only sane person in the room. Sandro was sprawled out beside her, his shoulders and thighs brushed against her every time he breathed; the other couple was snuggled together like a couple of lovebirds; and she, Theresa, felt like she was losing her mind!

She got up abruptly and left the room, stumbling toward the kitchen, where she stood in the middle of the room taking in great gasps of air. She should have known that he would follow her even there. When she turned back toward the kitchen door, there he was. He was watching her and looking splendid in his own version of casual wear—a pair of faded blue jeans and a black dress shirt with the top button open to reveal the strong, masculine column of his neck.

"*Why* did you come here?" she whispered.

"I thought that we should spend some time together," he said in a gentle tone that Theresa instinctively mistrusted.

"But I told you, I don't want to spend time with you," she said in a soft, bewildered voice. "I don't want to be anywhere near you!"

"Theresa . . ." he said, still gently, taking a cautious step into the room. Theresa backed up until she hit the fridge.

"The one place I had . . . the one place I could come and be myself . . ." She shook her head, her eyes were wide and shimmering with tears. "And you had to take that from me too." The tears overflowed and she desperately tried to blot them from her cheeks with the hem of her T-shirt. He made a soft almost dismayed sound in his throat before moving so quickly that she barely had time to register it. One second he was still close to the kitchen entrance, and the next he was right in front of her, sandwiching her between his body and the fridge. His large hands reached up to cup her face, and his thumbs brushed roughly at the tears on her cheeks.

"Don't." His voice was low and gravelly and so thick that she could barely understand that one word. She raised her much smaller hands to his and tugged futilely at his hold, trying to get him to release her.

"I want to make things less difficult for us, Theresa," he muttered awkwardly, his face so close to hers that his breath washed over her skin and raised goose pimples all over her body.

"Why *now*?" She challenged the ludicrous statement angrily, trying to ignore the effect his closeness was having on her very receptive body. Her soft green eyes snapped up to his through her tears. "Is it because I'm threatening to leave this marriage without giving you your precious son? Is that it?" She dropped her hands down to his hard, broad chest and tried to push him away. He wouldn't budge.

"No," was all he said. "That's not it . . . because I *know* you won't leave."

"What makes you so sure of that?" she hissed, and he was silent for a while before responding.

"The discussion we had yesterday," he admitted. She went limp against him, all the fight leaving her abruptly.

"Well, if you're so sure that I won't leave, what's this sudden need you have to spend your every waking moment with me?" she asked hollowly.

"We're *married* for God's sake . . . and we're like strangers! I know nothing about you!"

"Of course you know nothing about me." Her voice was hoarse with the effort it took not to scream at him. "You're the one who decided, even before we got married, that there was nothing *worth* knowing about me."

"Well, I've changed my mind." He didn't bother to deny her accusation, probably because it was true. Instead he dropped his hands down to her narrow shoulders and gave her a little shake.

"Which once again begs the question of *why,* after eighteen months of marriage, why now?"

His hands fell from her shoulders before he shrugged with an air of disinterest, which belied his urgency of just seconds ago.

"Why *not* now? Now's as good a time as any." He was back to being remote and icy and Theresa shuddered involuntarily.

"It's much too late, Sandro," she whispered, wrapping her arms around her slender frame. "I may be trapped in this marriage, but I want nothing to do with you! The very sight of you makes me sick to my stomach."

"There's a way out of this you know," he murmured.

"I know," she said, and his hooded eyes snapped back up to her face. "Have a baby, right? You want a son and I'm the chosen incubator." She watched his face carefully, but he betrayed not one iota of emotion other than a slight tightening of his jaw. "So what happens after I have this precious baby of yours? Who gets him after the divorce? You expect me to be nothing but a surrogate mother. I'm to bear him and you'll then take him away from me, right?"

She was aching to hear an affirmative from him, anything that would prove to her that *he* was the one who wanted the child and that she had misunderstood the conversation she had overheard between her husband and her father that morning.

"Of course I wouldn't take him from you." He shook his head, sending her heart plummeting. "I wouldn't be that cruel. Naturally you'd maintain custody." Theresa shut her eyes to shield her agony from him, and she felt her scalding tears seep down her cheeks.

"How very . . . magnanimous of you," she whispered. "To be so desperate for something only to give it up in the end. You're so much more generous than I gave you credit for. How often would you want to see him?"

"I would naturally move back to Italy, so I would probably see him two or three times a year. It is what you want, no? Less contact with me?"

She inhaled deeply and her brow furrowed. Two or three times a year? That was all the time he was prepared to spend with a child who was half hers? She opened her eyes and met his gaze squarely.

"Like I said before, you're being quite generous, but it's all moot anyway because I have no intention of having a baby with you!"

"You're being very childish, Theresa," he admonished quietly.

"No, I'm finally making my own decisions. Up to this point in my life, everything has been decided for me . . . this marriage would never have happened if my father hadn't decided that you would make the perfect son-in-law. After that, the wedding date, the venue, the cake, where we would live . . . it was all you or my father. I couldn't even choose my own *wedding dress*." The last emerged in a small, broken voice that quavered with remembered disbelief and outrage. Her father had simply had the dress delivered to her room with the direction that it was to be worn on her wedding day, no discussion and no choice.

"The only reason I got Lisa as a bridesmaid was because my father deemed it appropriate for my first cousin to be in the wedding party. If she'd been just a friend, I doubt she'd have fit the bill!"

"It turns my stomach to hear someone who has led such a privileged life whine on about how terrible her life is. You've been spoiled and you've had everything money could buy . . ."

"Except *love*, specifically my husband's love and my father's love. Apparently I'm not quite worthy of that."

"You're feeling sorry for yourself and I'm getting sick of it."

"*Yes*, I'm feeling sorry for myself," she acknowledged bitterly. "And it's very liberating. In the past all I've done is accept everything you and my father dished out . . . thinking it was my lot in life, even thinking I deserved it. After all, if two such powerful men as you thought that I wasn't worthy of love and respect, then who was I to differ? But I'm starting to recognize that *I'm* not the one at fault here. I'm not the one with the personality defect . . . at least my motives for marrying you were honest; I stupidly believed that I loved you. Yours were less than stellar, weren't they? They certainly had nothing to do with love."

"They had everything to do with love," he suddenly thundered, silencing her abruptly as she stared up at him in wide-eyed shock. "Just not love for *you*." She blinked up at him, her green eyes the only color in her deathly pale face.

"What does that mean?" she asked through barely moving lips. "Love for *whom*?" Was he referring to Francesca? If he really loved the other woman so much, why on earth marry Theresa? It made no sense.

"None of your damned business," he grated furiously, a muscle working frantically in his jaw.

"It never *is*." She nodded bitterly. "It has nothing to do with me, yet it affects every aspect of my life. You want something from me but you're unable to give me anything in return. Well, I've had enough of that, Sandro. You want a baby but this is *my* body and so it's my decision to make."

"I'm your husband . . ."

"No. You are *not* my husband," she interrupted in a voice thickened with hatred and tears. "You have *never* been my husband. A husband loves, honors, and cherishes. A husband is a lover and a champion. Look into the next room if you want to see what a real husband is, because you are *no* such thing!" He reeled away from her, looking like a man who'd just been bitten by his favorite pet, and she pushed herself away from the fridge to brush past him.

"Theresa, wait . . ." He grabbed one of her arms to prevent her from running off.

"I have to go, please tell Rick and Lisa that . . ."

"No," he interrupted gently. "You stay. This is your family. You are right, this is your place and I should not have intruded. I'm sorry." His eyes skirted away from hers as he apologized and Theresa's jaw dropped at his second apology in twenty-four hours. She felt certain that the world would grind to a halt at any moment. "I will leave now . . . it is how it should be." With that he dropped her arm and walked out, leaving her to stare after him in confusion.

CHAPTER THREE

The house was dark and quiet when she got home, with no seething Sandro waiting at the front door this time, just echoing silence as she made her way upstairs and back into the spare bedroom. After a hot shower, she collapsed into bed and didn't stir until the following morning, when she woke to bright sunlight. She sat up in confusion as she tried to get her bearings and saw that she wasn't in the spare bedroom anymore. She was back in the master suite and a glance down at the empty space next to her confirmed that Sandro had indeed slept beside her. She peeked down at herself and was relieved to note that she still had on the T-shirt she had worn to bed.

She checked the clock and groaned when she discovered that she had slept till nearly ten in the morning. Pushing the tumbled mass of her hair out of her face, she got up and was alarmed when the room started spinning wildly. She stumbled forward before reaching for the headboard of the bed and steadying herself. She frowned slightly as she tried to recall the last time she had had a decent meal . . . definitely *not* the previous day's breakfast, which had come back up after that overheard phone call, or lunch, which had been spoiled by Sandro's appearance at Rick and Lisa's place, and dinner had been a nonevent. Even though Rick and Lisa had urged her to eat the night before, Theresa just could not stomach the thought of food after the day she'd had! Saturday had been much of the same; all she'd had to eat was popcorn at the movies.

Now she was paying the price for all those missed meals. Heading for the shower, she decided to treat herself to a decent brunch. Monday was Phumsile's day off, and they had no other live-in staff, so Theresa had the house to herself. She was looking forward to spending the day on her own, trying to figure out what her next move would be. She couldn't leave him and it seemed that he couldn't leave her. So what now? Sighing she decided to switch off her brain until after she'd eaten lest she lose her appetite again.

Less than an hour later she was dry-heaving over the commode in the downstairs guest bathroom. Just the smell of frying bacon and eggs had been enough to set her off. After her stomach stopped revolting, she stumbled out onto the patio, as far away from the nauseating smell of cooked food as she could possibly get, and sank down onto a chaise longue overlooking the huge infinity swimming pool.

"No . . ." she whispered, staring blindly at the edge of the pool, where the aquamarine water of the pool seemed to merge with the darker blue of the ocean and the cobalt blue of sky. "No, no, no, no . . . *no* . . . please, God! No . . ."

She buried her face in her hands and rocked back and forth slightly. Her system was just off-kilter because of the gut-wrenching events of the last forty-eight hours. Naturally she'd feel nauseous after not eating in so long. It was all perfectly logical . . . she was simply overreacting.

She couldn't *be* this unlucky, not after actually making some kind of progress in achieving independence from this marriage. She tried to remember when her last period had been, but she had been under a lot of stress lately, and her period had been affected, so that was not the most reliable way to gauge anything. She got up gingerly and was relieved when the movement didn't upset her equilibrium.

Heading toward the kitchen, she braced herself for a fresh onslaught of nausea, but thankfully her stomach stayed as steady as a rock. Breathing a sigh of relief, she headed toward the stove and picked up the pan, averting her eyes as she deposited the congealed mess that would have been her meal into the waste disposal unit. She settled on black tea and dry toast instead, determinedly putting her irrational fear of pregnancy out of her head.

After finishing the unappetizing meal, she headed for the bright, sunny attic, which she had transformed into a workroom, and put on some music while she immersed herself in her work. She so often lost herself up here, loving the serenity that usually came over her when she was working, but today she just couldn't concentrate. She had an image in her mind, knew what she wanted, but it wouldn't translate to paper. She sat in front of her drawing board, staring at the fifth blank sheet of paper in half an hour, resting her elbow on the tilted board with her delicate chin in one hand as she stared at the paper and willed the image into existence. She raised her pencil, resting the nib on the paper, before sighing resignedly and shaking her head in frustration. She dropped the pencil and pressed the heels of her hands to her eyes.

"Theresa." The quiet voice coming from behind her sent her flying out of her seat in alarm; she half turned, half crouched in a defensive position before she realized that it was Sandro's voice. Of course that didn't make her feel any safer than an unknown intruder would have done. He had both hands up, palms facing her, to keep her calm.

"Relax . . . I'm sorry, I didn't mean to startle you," he soothed.

"Well, you *did*," she retorted. "Why on earth are you skulking around at home this time of day anyway? Usually you don't get home until seven or eight." He always left for work before seven in the morning and usually returned well after the time most "normal" husbands would come home.

"I thought that we could spend the afternoon together," he muttered distractedly while his keen eyes absorbed every aspect of the room. He walked around, barely paying her any attention, lifting things, fiddling with her tools, until Theresa couldn't take it anymore.

"Don't *touch* that!" she snapped impatiently when he lifted a pair of cutters that had cost the earth to import.

"You design jewelry," he whispered in astonishment, his eyes lifting to meet hers, and Theresa's own gaze fluttered away, while her cheeks fired with embarrassment.

"I know they're no good," she ventured nervously, waving at the large portfolio he had lifted from one of her other workstations. She had the drawing board for designing, a work table for actually making the jewelry, a small cutting table for cutting wire and shaping semi-precious stones, and her desk, which housed her laptop, for paperwork and correspondence. "And I know that I should not be wasting my time with it. It's just a hobby . . . so . . ." Her voice petered off as he continued to flip through her portfolio with an absorbed frown, occasionally lingering on a page before moving on. She stood in front of him, fidgeting, waiting for the scathing put down that would undoubtedly follow. He suddenly turned the open book toward her.

"This is your cousin's engagement set," he observed, tapping at the picture of the diamond and white gold earring, pendant, and ring set that she had made for Rick a few years before.

"Yes, but they're Rick's design. I just made them."

"I can tell they're not your design. Your things are more . . ." He paused and Theresa braced herself. "Raw and elemental. Why don't you work with real gemstones, instead of semiprecious stones?"

"Uncut precious stones are insanely expensive. Semiprecious stones are cheap and easy to find, and if they're damaged in any way while I'm setting them, it's no big deal." He grunted again, barely listening to her as he went back to flipping through her portfolio.

"And this is what you do all day?" He looked back up at her for confirmation.

"Well, I can hardly sit around and twiddle my thumbs, can I?" she challenged, and his eyes flickered slightly. She snorted disdainfully. He probably thought she spent her days shopping and lounging around in beauty salons.

"Why did I not know this about you?" he asked quietly, and she shrugged.

"Just one more thing you never bothered to learn about me," she said dismissively.

"Just one more detail *you* didn't offer about yourself," he responded fiercely, and her eyes snared his in challenge.

"Would you have been interested if I'd told you?" He was honest enough to avert his eyes at the question and remained silent in response to it.

"How many of these have you sold?" He changed the subject, indicating her portfolio.

"None." She shrugged. "The only jewelry in that portfolio that I don't still have is the set I made for Rick, and even those were just a favor."

"But why keep them hidden?"

"They're not good enough. Just a silly hobby, a complete waste of my time, really. I couldn't compete with the real designers out there anyway."

"It's uncanny, I hear *your* voice, but it's like listening to your father speak. He told you that you weren't good enough, didn't he?

And you believed him?" He seemed uncharacteristically furious about that.

"No . . . yes . . . *no*. Look, I know that I'm not good enough. I have received no formal training. I printed stuff off the Internet, did a bit of reading, and started experimenting. I'm the only one who ever wears these, and then only around the house!"

"I think that you should have Rick's brother, Bryce, or his partner Pierre de Coursey have a look at these." She fidgeted slightly, not entirely sure what to make of his sudden interest and praise.

"I wouldn't want to waste their time; they're busy men." Palmer and de Coursey co-owned one of the most exclusive jewelry companies in the world.

"I hardly think you'd be wasting their—"

"Look, Sandro, just drop it, please," she interrupted harshly, and his eyes snapped up to her strained face. His own expression remained impassive, and he shrugged before slowly closing the portfolio and placing it back on her desk.

"Suit yourself," he muttered before continuing his amble around the room. She watched as he picked things up, inspected, and replaced them. She remained seated, swiveling her desk chair ever so often to keep him within sight. He eventually stopped his restless pacing to come to a standstill directly in front of her. She lowered her eyes to his expensive size 11 Italian loafers and fidgeted with the pencil that she had picked up again.

She nearly leaped out of her skin and dropped the pencil with a muffled yelp when he captured her chin between his thumb and forefinger to gently tilt her face up until she raised her vulnerable gaze to his unfathomable chocolate brown eyes. He let go of her chin to stroke the back of his hand down her soft cheek, and she tried her best not to cringe from his touch. She wasn't quite successful in masking her reaction, because his eyes iced over and his hand dropped heavily back to his side.

"What other secrets are you keeping from me, I wonder?" he mused beneath his breath.

"I have no secrets," she responded.

"What would you call this?" He indicated the room with a sweeping gesture, and she laughed but there was absolutely no humor in the harsh and abrasive sound.

"This was hardly a secret." She shook her head bitterly. "If you'd come up here at any time over the past year and a half, you would have known about this. I never lock the door, so you were free to enter at any time."

"Why would I have had any reason to come up here?" he asked in his most maddeningly pragmatic voice. "It's hardly the most logical place for a workshop."

"It's also the one place I spend most of my time, so *of course* you've never bothered to come up here," she responded sarcastically. "You've never willingly sought me out before, Sandro, and I believe that the only reason you're doing so now is because things aren't going according to whatever master plan you have devised for this so-called marriage of ours. Pretending an interest in me is your latest way of trying to keep me compliant, isn't it?"

"Stop trying to second-guess me, *cara*," he reproved gently. "You have no idea what makes me tick or what's going on in my head."

"Oh, I think I could definitely say the same about you. In fact I think *I* know *you* a lot better than you do me!"

"I doubt that," he dismissed, dropping his hands into the trouser pockets of his expensive tailor-made suit and half reclining against her work table. He crossed one long leg over the other in a pose of sartorial, casual elegance.

"Fine." She tilted her head as she ran a contemptuous look over him. "How do I take my coffee?" He frowned at the question before shrugging.

"Black," he stated with the utmost authority.

"No, you take *yours* black, *I* don't drink coffee."

"This is pointless," he dismissed. "And juvenile."

"Everything about me, or to do with me, is pointless to you," she observed bitterly.

"That's hardly—" he began, but she interrupted him again, barely able to credit her own daring. She had never *once* stood up to him this way, but she was done being a doormat. Just because she was temporarily trapped in this marriage did not mean that she would allow him to walk all over her anymore.

"Everything except my womb of course." She laughed half-hysterically. "You have a lot of use for that! That's all I am to you, a womb on legs!"

"You're being *ridiculous* and completely melodramatic," he derided.

"What about my birthday?" she asked suddenly, still ignoring him. "When's my birthday?" His jaw clenched and he remained mute, keeping his eyes glued to hers.

"I see no need to prove myself in this way."

"You can't answer it, can you?" she challenged. "Yours is on the third of January. You have four older sisters—Gabriella, Sofia, Isabella, and Rosalie—and a large extended family. You dislike spinach and are allergic to bee stings. You like—"

"Enough!" He sliced an impatient hand through the air in front of his face, cutting her off abruptly. "This is bordering on stalkerish and it proves nothing other than you possess a creepy excess of information about me, which I must admit, I am more than a little uncomfortable with."

"Hardly stalkerish." She shook her head. "I have been living with you for more than eighteen months, and I *loved* you when I married you. I was interested in knowing you. These are the kinds of mundane facts married couples know about each other. Everything I know about you, I had to learn for myself, none of it was ever volunteered. You didn't know about my hobby, or how I take my coffee, or when my birthday is because you were not interested enough in getting to know me, not because I've been keeping secrets. That's how it's been for the last year and a half, and that's how it still *is*, despite your sudden feigned interest in me." He started to say something, but she raised her hand to quiet him. She was amazed when he actually shut his mouth.

"I know now that I wasn't the bride that you would have chosen for yourself," she managed to say despite the huge lump in her throat. She couldn't meet his eyes as she acknowledged that painful fact. "You made *that* pretty clear on our wedding night and every day since then. But I think that at the very least, I deserve to be treated with some show of respect . . ." She bit her lower lip to stop its trembling and wrapped her arms around herself. He said nothing in response, just kept staring at her thoughtfully.

"I don't really know what you want me to say," he eventually admitted, and she smiled sadly.

"I know," she acknowledged with a dip of her head. "That's a major part of the problem."

He unexpectedly shoved himself away from the table and took the couple of steps it required to bring him directly in front of her. He hovered threateningly above where she sat, and Theresa tried her best not to cower beneath his brooding regard. He then surprised her even further by dropping to his haunches in front of her, placing his hands on the arms of her chair, and trapping her in her seat.

"I may not know these things you asked of me, Theresa," his sexy accent thickened as his voice dropped a few notches, "but I do know *you*." She shook her head mutely, disconcerted by both his proximity and his direct stare. He was definitely not avoiding her eyes this time. She felt like a deer trapped in the headlights, and she wanted to look away, she wanted to escape but she could barely breathe, much less avert her gaze.

He raised one hand and Theresa braced herself for his unwanted touch, desperate not to flinch. In the end, she still jumped slightly when his fingertips brushed across her lips.

"I know what makes you tremble with desire." His voice had lowered even further, nothing more than a seductive rumble now, and her lips parted slightly. "I know where to touch, where to kiss, where to suck . . . I know how to make you moan, scream, and cry out in ecstasy."

"That's just sex." She found her voice but hardly sounded convincing. He merely smiled, lifting his other hand until he had her face framed, with his thumbs stroking across her cheekbones and his fingertips burrowing into the soft hair at her temples.

"It doesn't solve anything," she continued to protest, with the same lack of conviction as before.

"Maybe not"—he shrugged without concern—"but it *feels* fantastic."

"But we don't do it right," she murmured, thinking about the fact that he'd never kissed her, not on the lips, not once. His fingers stilled and she realized, rather belatedly, that he may have misconstrued her comment. That was fine with her, if it meant that he would stop this blatant seduction of her senses.

"What do you mean?" She could tell how much it cost him to keep the affronted heat out of his voice. He started up the lazy stroking again.

"I always thought that one day I would make love with my husband," she whispered. "But we don't do that, do we? We just have sex. We . . ." She used a word that she had *never* in her life uttered before. Sandro recoiled slightly in response, and the soothing stroke of his fingertips stopped abruptly.

"Don't use language like that," he rebuked. "It doesn't suit you!"

"Well, it's what you once called it," she defended herself hotly.

"I would *never*—"

"You did." She interrupted the imminent denial calmly. "On our wedding night, after the first time, I tried to . . . to . . ." She blushed as she remembered her naïveté back then. She had reached over to snuggle with him, and he had moved to the edge of the bed in an effort to get away from her. "Well, anyway, you told me not to mistake what we did with any act of love. That it was much more basic than that. Just sex, you said, just . . . well . . . you know . . ."

His hands had dropped from her face to her shoulders, and his eyes narrowed on her painfully humiliated face. His grip tightened on her shoulders, and she squirmed slightly before it let up and he kneaded her shoulders.

"Theresa, I was pretty hammered on our wedding night."

She nodded, her eyes bright with tears as she remembered how long he had made her wait for him. Her innocent, eager anticipation had been dashed when the dignified, distant husband who had left her all alone in their hotel suite had returned three hours later, so drunk that he could barely hold himself upright. He had fallen onto the bed and immediately passed out, leaving Theresa shattered. Two hours later, his skillful hands on her body had brought her out of a restless doze, and he had strummed at and played with her body like it was a finely tuned musical instrument, making her a willing slave to his every command.

Such had been her response that it had barely registered that his lips hadn't once touched hers. He had kissed just about every other part of her body, and afterward, while she strove to maintain the closeness between them, he had all but destroyed her fragile spirit by denigrating the act. She could tell that Sandro was recalling the events of that night too, and his eyes dropped to where her hands were still restlessly fidgeting with the pencil that had fallen into her lap. He dropped one huge hand over hers to stop the movement.

"I resented you very much," he admitted. "Because I felt trapped."

"Wrong tense, Sandro," she whispered. "Your resentment is still very current."

"Things change, Theresa."

"Some things are inexcusable, Sandro," she whispered painfully. "And unforgivable."

"We're not getting anywhere with this," he growled in frustration, and she dragged her hands out from under his.

"That's what I've been telling you for the last three days," she pointed out, and he bit off a curse before getting up abruptly. Theresa jumped up too, to avoid being intimidated by his height. But she had miscalculated; he was still standing too close to her, and when she got up, her breasts brushed up the length of his body from groin to torso. They both immediately went still as awareness simmered between them. Theresa made a soft sound and attempted to put some distance between them, but Sandro's arms came up to circle her loosely, his hands meeting in the small of her back and the tips of his fingers just brushing against the slight swell of her backside. Her own hands came up to firmly brace against his chest. She wanted to push him away but somehow her hands were idly stroking him instead of exerting any force.

His large hands moved down to fully cup her backside, and he lifted her slightly until she could feel his sudden arousal. He pushed himself against her, dipping his head until his mouth was next to her ear.

"Despite everything, *cara*, you want me," he whispered, his breath hot and moist against her ear. "And *God* knows I want you too . . ."

"Just sex," she protested weakly.

"Maybe." He nibbled her earlobe gently before moving down to nuzzle the sensitive spot just below her ear, something he knew made her crazy. It didn't fail this time, as she gasped and wound her arms around his neck to push herself closer to his hard body. His tongue gently circled the highly sensitive erogenous zone, and Theresa moaned, wanting more. His wickedly hot mouth moved down to her throat, licking, sucking, and nibbling the exposed skin along the way. Theresa buried her face in his short, soft hair and muffled a moan of pure sizzling lust.

His hands were busily yanking her blouse out of the waistband of her skirt and they both groaned when his hands finally made contact with the naked skin of her back. He muttered something in Italian before he swept his hands up to the clasp of her bra, unhooked it expertly, and brought his hands around and under the lacy little B-cups. She cried out and arched violently against him when his thumbs found her sensitive nipples. Sandro half laughed and half groaned in response to her wild reaction to his touch.

"I *want* you," he whispered, his breath feathering against the skin of her neck, where he was nibbling gently. "How I want you!"

She sobbed, wishing she was more adept at resisting him but desperately wanting him too, despite her bitterness, her anger, and her frustration. She nodded slowly, tears seeping from between her closed eyes and trickling down her cheeks.

"Please . . ." She didn't know if she was begging him to stop or to continue, but Sandro took it as assent. One of his hands dropped from her breasts and tugged at her skirt until it was bunched up around her hips. Her brief, lacy panties were swiftly dealt with, and his hot, urgent fingers found her melting core with unerring accuracy, stroking, plunging, and preparing her. Her hands dropped to his belt buckle and she fumbled with the opening of his trousers until she held him captive in her hands. She did her own stroking and caressing, loving the familiar satiny feel of him, loving the heat, the hardness, the substantial size.

He made an animalistic sound, swinging her around and backing her up until she was leaning against the workstation that he had so casually been half sitting on earlier. He lifted her up until her backside was firmly planted on the desk and moved between her spread thighs. Tilting her pelvis slightly until he had the angle just right, he at last, with a groan of pure satisfaction, sank into her soft and welcoming heat. Theresa's breath hitched as she was, once again, caught by surprise by his length, girth, and incredible hardness.

She lifted her slender legs and clasped them around his hips as, after the first gently thorough thrust, he simply rested against her. With his hands braced on the desk on either side of her hips, he lifted his head to look down into her eyes. Theresa was undone by that, as he had *never* just looked at her before, not in bed or out of it. His dark eyes continued to search hers, and she wondered what it was he was looking for. She licked her lips nervously and his scrutiny dropped to her mouth, and his pupils dilated until his eyes were virtually black.

Theresa's breath was starting to come in little gasps as she tried to control her own need to move against him. Her hips gave the slightest twitch, and she felt herself spasm around him. He hissed at the movement, his face clenching as he withdrew slightly, only to plunge back into her as if he couldn't bear to leave. That was all it took for Theresa's head to fall back limply and her mouth to open on a soundless scream of ecstasy. The record speed of her orgasm seemed to take Sandro by surprise, as well as trigger his own. With a shocked sound and another half thrust, he buried himself as deep as he could go, arching backward in the process and coming violently. It seemed to last forever, but eventually his entire body went limp and he half collapsed against her, burying his face in her damp neck.

So stunned was Theresa by the unprecedented swiftness of the act, it couldn't have lasted more than three minutes, that she nearly missed the words. In fact, she might have missed them entirely if she hadn't felt his telltale breath on the sensitive skin of her neck. But he said them. The words were muffled but she knew *exactly* what he was saying. His mantra, his prayer . . .

"Give me a son, Theresa . . ." and just like that, it was over for her. Her legs fell away from his waist, and she pushed at his chest until he levered himself up to look down at her curiously. He made a soft sound of protest when he saw the tears on her cheeks and attempted to fold his arms around her. Yet *another* unprecedented move, but she shoved him again until he stepped away from her.

"Why are you crying?" he asked hoarsely as he readjusted his clothing.

"I hate you," she said, dashing at the tears, despair weighting her voice.

"What we just did didn't feel like hatred to me," he pointed out.

"Just another . . ." Her mouth started to form the ugly word but he cut her off.

"Don't say it," he snapped. "Don't you *dare* say it!"

"Why not?" she protested. "It's the truth, and don't you try to pretend otherwise at this stage of our so-called marriage, Sandro. Do you think sex makes things better? It makes everything worse, like adding gasoline to an already raging fire. All you've proved is that I am unable to resist you!"

"*That* is entirely mutual," he responded dryly, and she went still.

"Oh, please . . ." she choked out. "Of course you can resist me. I'm just another woman to you. I'm of no particular consequence, so don't try to play yet another game with me, Sandro! I'm sick of your lies and deceit."

"Dio," he hissed furiously. "You're not just another woman, you're my *wife*! You hold a position of great consequence in my life."

"A wife you're ashamed of? I don't think so!"

"Whoever told you that I was ashamed of you?" He seemed outraged by the very notion.

"*You* did."

"Theresa, everything else that you've accused me of so far has had some element of truth to it. But this is just plain ludicrous! I have *never*, not once, told you that I am ashamed of you."

"You never *said* it; you didn't have to." She slid off the desk, making sure that her skirt was straight before looking up at him again. "You show me every day."

"What?"

"I've never met your family, the large and extensive family that means the world to you. I know that you have two close friends, Rafael Dante and Gabriel Braddock, they're university buddies if I'm not mistaken, and you play football with them every week. You didn't think I knew that, did you? I haven't met any of those people of *consequence* in your life." And there was Francesca, of course, but Theresa wasn't ready to confront him with that bit of knowledge. "They are the people who matter to you, and if I'd been the wife you wanted, a wife you were not ashamed of, I would undoubtedly have met them by now!"

"It's not like that," he denied, almost stumbling in his haste to reach for her, but she stepped away before he could touch her.

"Yes it is. Please don't insult my intelligence by denying it." She desperately looked around for her panties and saw them lying beside her drawing board. She very quickly swooped them up before turning back to face him.

"I need a shower," she whispered bitterly. "*You* know what it's like when you have an overwhelming urge to scrape the touch, the smell, the very *essence* of someone off your skin, don't you? After all, that's what *you* usually do thirty seconds after your orgasm, and I can finally relate to that." She turned and left the room before he had the opportunity to respond.

CHAPTER FOUR

They barely spoke over the next week or so, merely coexisting in the same house. Sandro insisted that they take breakfast and dinner together still and that they sleep in the same bed, but he never touched her, maintaining the distance that *she* had insisted on. Some part of Theresa was relieved while another bemoaned the loss of the one bond they had shared. She kept telling herself that it was just sex and it had never meant anything.

Besides, she had other, more immediate, concerns. Like the fact that she had thrown up every day for the last week and she was still stricken by dizzy spells at the most unexpected times and that her period was now later than it had ever been before. She was relieved that the intimacies between her and Sandro had ceased, because he was as familiar with her cycle as she was and she would really prefer absolute certainty before telling him anything. She also wanted time to figure out what her next move would be.

Yet *another* decision taken from her, she reflected bitterly, but at least she could decide the time and place to tell him—if indeed she *was* pregnant, which she desperately hoped was not the case. She worried at her lower lip with her teeth, staring blindly at the design she had been working on for most of the week. It was supposed to be a necklace, but it looked like no necklace she had ever seen before. She shook her head in disgust; she could not seem to get anything done. She seemed to be experiencing the equivalent of writer's block, and it was extremely frustrating. Her cell phone buzzed and she snatched it up, welcoming the distraction. She had been exchanging text messages with Lisa all day. Her cousin was feeling under the weather and Theresa had been trying to cheer her up with silly little jokes—a difficult feat when Theresa herself wasn't feeling all that great. She was expecting her cousin's response to her latest message but was rather unpleasantly surprised to see Sandro's name in her inbox. He usually refrained from contacting her during the day. She frowned down at his name, not all that keen on reading the text. Finally she exhaled gustily and clicked on the message.

"Eating out tonight. Dress: casual. 'Business thing.' Home by 6. Dinner @ 7:30"

She groaned. Sandro and his damned "appearances"! She was tempted to refuse but didn't have the energy for the argument that would ensue. At least he'd forewarned her this time. There had been a few incidences in the past where he had come home and told her that they were going out in an hour. A couple of times the events had been formal, leaving Theresa to scramble for appropriate dresses and silently cursing the fact that she hadn't even had the opportunity to have her hair professionally done. Sighing softly, she gave up on work for the rest of the afternoon and headed for the kitchen for some company. Phumsile was bustling around efficiently, but when she turned and saw Theresa she grinned.

"Teatime?" she asked, and Theresa nodded, settling onto a kitchen stool while Phumsile gathered a couple of teacups and set the kettle to boil.

"You finished with your work already? It's a little early," the older woman asked, while she prepared the teapot. Theresa's relationship with Phumsile was warm and friendly. Theresa knew that Phumsile had long ago discerned the unusual nature of her marriage and while the woman remained discreet and never brought it up, she tended to mother Theresa as a result.

"I couldn't concentrate, and Sandro and I are going out tonight, so I should probably think about getting ready for that." Phumsile made a noncommittal sound as she poured the hot water into the teapot and set it onto the counter between them to steep before putting a plate of freshly baked gingerbread biscuits next to it.

"Is it going to be another fancy night?"

Theresa smiled at the terminology and shrugged.

"He said casual. Not sure what that means." She picked up a biscuit and took a tentative bite.

"The ginger is very mild, it won't upset your stomach," the woman said quietly, and Theresa raised her startled eyes to Phumsile's wise ones. She should have known that Phumsile would notice her nausea over the last few days. The woman rarely missed much.

"Does Mr. De Lucci know?" Phumsile asked.

"*I* don't even know," Theresa admitted.

"A baby is a blessing. Mr. De Lucci will be very happy."

"He will," Theresa acknowledged bitterly.

"You're not happy?" Phumsile seemed confused, and Theresa forced a smile.

"I'm not sure there *is* a baby, Phumsile, it could just be a stomach bug." She took a sip of the chamomile tea Phumsile always prepared to perfection and another nibble of the biscuit.

"So what do you want to wear tonight?" Phumsile tactfully changed the subject and Theresa shrugged again.

"I don't know exactly how casual he means. Jeans maybe. What do you think I should do with my hair? Up or down?" Phumsile tilted her head as she considered Theresa's long fall of hair.

"Why don't you go to the hairdresser?" Phumsile asked. "It will cheer you up."

Theresa smiled at Phumsile as she considered the thought. Looking good tonight would give her ego a boost if nothing else.

"You know, I haven't had it styled in some time," she admitted, and rounded the counter to give Phumsile a quick squeeze. "That's a brilliant idea. Thank you. What would I do without you, Phumsile?"

"Starve," the woman joked. "You don't eat enough when I'm not here and you know it."

Theresa laughed, feeling immeasurably better after her exchange with the housekeeper. Nothing had been resolved, but she felt less alone now that Phumsile was aware of her possible pregnancy.

Sandro was home promptly at six. Theresa was curled up on the sofa, flipping through a coffee table book by an extremely popular photographer, which she had just purchased on her afternoon excursion. He was a wildlife photographer, but his subject matter this time around was a lot closer to home. His latest anthology, entitled *Man's Best Friend*, was all about dogs. Theresa, being a huge sucker for dogs, hadn't thought twice before buying the book. Sandro paused in the doorway, and she looked up to see his arrested eyes on her hair. She lifted a self-conscious hand to her newly cut hair, knowing that it was a big change. She had had her waist-length fall of Titian hair cut to just below her jaw. The style was straight and sleek, with a feathery fringe, and Theresa loved the way it made her look and feel like a new woman. Something she was so desperately striving to be.

Her hair had *always* been long; her father had absolutely forbade her to cut it, and Theresa knew that the one thing Sandro absolutely adored about her, aside from her rather small breasts, was her hair. When he was having sex with her, he was always touching, stroking, or tugging at her hair. Now she waited with bated breath for his inevitable negative reaction to the cut, which framed her face and emphasized her large gray-green eyes and high, delicate cheekbones. His hands clenched and he seemed to swallow with visible effort.

"You look . . ." His voice was hoarse and he cleared his throat before starting again. "You look *bellissima, cara*." His quiet voice seemed to ring with sincerity and something that, in any other man, would be akin to reverence. "Absolutely stunning."

She blinked.

"Oh," was all she could think of to say, and he came farther into the room, still so riveted on her hair and face that he very nearly tripped over a small footstool placed beside an easy chair. He frowned at the offending piece of furniture before sinking into the leather easy chair opposite the matching sofa Theresa was curled up on.

"Uh . . ." He dragged his focus down to the book in her lap and seemed strangely desperate to make conversation. "What are you reading?" His sharp eyes honed in on the title before he raised his gaze to hers in consternation. *"Dogs?"* He sounded so nonplussed that she hugged the book defensively to her chest.

"I happen to *like* dogs," she said fiercely, and his strangely gentle eyes swept over her tight features before coming to rest on the book. He leaned forward and extended his right hand.

"May I?" He watched her steadily until she reluctantly let up on the death grip she had on the book and handed it over to him. "Thank you." He leaned back and flipped through the glossy pages, pausing here and there before grinning almost boyishly at her. He looked so breathtakingly handsome that for a long moment she didn't know that he was talking to her.

"Sorry, I didn't quite catch that," she whispered, and his smile widened as he flipped the book toward her, tapping his long index finger on a picture of a grinning black Labrador retriever.

"I had one just like this," he informed her, and she frowned.

"One what?" she asked blankly, mesmerized by his devastating smile.

"Dog," he told her patiently before turning the book back toward himself. His expression was gently reminiscent. "I like dogs too. The way I see it, anyone who *doesn't* like dogs is not to be trusted. My retriever was called Rocco. He died just before I started university. I'd had him for sixteen years. I suppose you could say that I grew up with him." She smiled at his obvious affection for what must have been a well-loved pet.

"You must have had a dog too, growing up?" he prompted, and she nodded slowly. "What breed?"

"She was a bit of a mutt," Theresa whispered, more than a little reluctant to continue.

"What was her name?" *Why* was he being so damned persistent?

"Sheba," she supplied, her voice going even quieter, and his smile faded as he leaned forward intently, his eyes fixed on her downcast face.

"Tell me more," he invited quietly.

"Nothing much to tell," she shrugged, clearing her throat. "My mother took me to the SPCA for my eleventh birthday and told me to choose any dog I wanted. I'd been going on and on about getting a dog for months before that, promising that I would take good care of it. It was getting to the point where, I guess, she would have done *anything* to shut me up. So I chose Sheba, with her soulful brown eyes, her scruffy black-and-white coat, and her happy, wagging tail." He smiled at that and so did she. "She wasn't much to look at but I adored her." She sighed heavily before stopping and shrugging, ultimately lifting her eyes to meet his. "Time to get ready for that dinner now, isn't it?" He frowned before shaking his head.

"How long did you have your dog?" he asked softly in a tone that said he wouldn't rest until he knew everything, and Theresa tugged at her full lower lip with her teeth.

"About three weeks."

He smothered a soft curse at the whispered confession.

"What happened?"

"Mom and Daddy didn't agree on most things, and apparently my getting a dog was yet another excuse to fight. Getting Sheba was Mom's way of scoring points against Daddy and getting *rid* of Sheba was Daddy's way of scoring points against Mom." Her parents had been deeply unhappy together, and it really shouldn't have surprised anyone when her mother swallowed a handful of sleeping pills mere weeks later. Theresa had blamed herself for a long time, thinking that if she had been less insistent about the dog, her parents wouldn't have fought and her mother wouldn't have abandoned her. She had been petrified for many years that her father would desert her too if she wasn't the perfect daughter, but by the time she had finished high school, she had understood that Jackson Noble was too selfish to harm himself in any way. By then, being the perfect daughter had become an unbreakable habit.

Now she strove to sound flippant about the dog, but the tremor in her voice made a liar out of her. Sandro said nothing but he seemed to be struggling with something, his jaw so tightly clenched that she could see the little muscles knotting just below his ears, and his knuckles showed white where his grip had tightened on the book.

"What did he do to the dog?" he gritted out, sounding like he was chewing nails.

"I never knew for sure," she confessed. "Mom said Sheba went to a new family and was happy with them. But I don't know . . . I always feared that he took her back to the pound." Despite her best intentions, tears of long-remembered pain flooded her eyes, and she tilted her chin in an effort to appear casual. "I couldn't sleep for the longest time afterward, imagining how confused Sheba must have been, and on the really bad nights I pictured them taking her into the vet's operating room to be put down, because even though *I* loved her, she really wasn't cute or clever or all that special. If she went back to the pound, I don't think she would have gone to another home."

"You mustn't think like that," he admonished.

"I *know*. Never mind, it's so far in the past that the wound healed long ago. Not even a scar." The way he looked at her told her that he didn't believe a word of it.

"You were eleven?"

She nodded and dropped her eyes, uncomfortable beneath his burning regard. "Didn't your mother die when you were eleven?" Everybody knew that her mother had committed suicide. She had been found by a servant, and the news had been leaked to the press within the hour. One of the unfortunate by-products of coming from a family such as hers was the complete lack of privacy and respect from the press. Her mother's suicide had become fodder for the masses and her funeral a three-ring circus. It had made Theresa very cagey around the media and she tended to stay as far removed from the limelight as possible.

Her marriage to Sandro hadn't made that easy—not when his family history was almost identical to hers and his glamorous sisters were always being hounded by the paparazzi.

"About two weeks after I lost Sheba," she admitted, and he inhaled sharply, a muffled curse word dropping from his lips. "So, you see, I soon had bigger things to worry about than poor little Sheba's fate."

"I think I see a lot more than you want me to, Theresa," he stated cryptically, and she raised her eyes back up to his only to be confounded by the tenderness and understanding she saw there. He handed the book back to her, and she took it with a nod, making sure to avoid all contact with his large hands. He noticed the evasion and, while his eyes narrowed, he chose not to say anything about it.

"So how casual *is* this business thing?" she asked, changing the subject abruptly, getting up carefully, not wanting another revealing wave of dizziness in front of him.

"Extremely casual," he responded quietly, choosing not to challenge the blatant subject change. "Jeans, T-shirt, and a jacket will do."

"You mean I had my hair done for nothing?" She frowned, rather disgruntled that she wouldn't be showing off her new look in the best possible setting.

"I hardly think it was for nothing," he protested with another one of those rare, breathtaking smiles of his. "I think the result was well worth the effort. I loved your long hair, *cara,* but this new chic, sleek little cut . . . Words fail me. You look . . ." He shook his head and in a quintessentially Italian gesture, raised his fingertips to his lips and kissed them to signify his approval. For some reason that struck Theresa as funny, and she stifled a giggle with her hand. Her eyes were iridescent with laughter, and he stood for a long moment, staring at her, before he cleared his throat.

"Go on, Theresa," he prompted gently. "Meet me down here in half an hour?" She nodded at the question in his voice.

~

Sandro remained closemouthed about where they were going, ignoring Theresa's increasingly desperate pleas for information. It was highly unusual for him not to tell her what to expect. He usually drilled information into her, what their hosts liked and what he wanted her to talk about. He always seemed afraid that she would mess up somehow, but he was markedly different this time. He was relaxed, and every time Theresa asked about their eventual destination, he told her not to worry about it. She peeked at his handsome profile, hating his nonchalance in the face of her edginess. He was dressed even more casually than she was, wearing name-brand sweatpants that had definitely seen better days, battered sneakers of the same brand, and a jacket to match the pants.

"Stop staring," he growled, keeping his eyes glued to the road ahead. "You're making me nervous."

Yeah right! Mr. Nerves of Steel, who handled the powerful Ferrari with grace and confidence, was nervous. She didn't believe that for a second. She pursed her lips and diverted her eyes to the rapidly darkening horizon beyond her window. They had been driving for nearly forty minutes, and Theresa had no clue where they were. She tilted her head back and closed her eyes for a few moments, feeling like the past few weeks of uncertainty were catching up with her.

"We're here." Sandro's voice jerked her out of her doze sometime later, and she stretched before sitting up to take stock of their surroundings. The car was already parked in the driveway of a huge house. The place made their, not immodest, house seem like a garden cottage. There were five other sleek and expensive sports cars parked in the driveway, and every light, both inside and out of the house, seemed to be on.

Theresa unbuckled her belt and was out of the car before Sandro could even move. She stood with her hands braced on the roof of the Ferrari and stared up the immense house in unabashed curiosity. She was aware of Sandro, rummaging about in the space behind the front seats before climbing out of the low-slung car with feral grace and rounding the bonnet to join her on the passenger side of the car.

"Theresa, I don't want you to think that—" Whatever he had been about to say was cut off when another car, this one an expensive metallic-blue Lamborghini, slid to a stop behind theirs. Sandro glanced over and swore when he seemed to recognize the car.

The sole occupant emerged from the car and Theresa could see him quite clearly beneath the bright lights flooding the driveway. He was a tall, dark-haired, *gorgeous* man about Sandro's age, and he had a huge, friendly grin on his face as he strode over to them. Theresa found herself admiring his sexy, loose-limbed gait. He was dressed in similar fashion to her husband, just sporting a different name brand on his sweat suit.

"De Lucci!" He greeted her austere husband with a hearty slap on the back.

"Max." Sandro nodded in return, not seeming to share the man's exuberance. He turned to fully face the man and placed a peremptory hand in the small of Theresa's back to turn her as well. He kept his hand there even after they were both facing the other man.

"Who's this gorgeous babe?" Max turned that killer smile on her, and Theresa found herself unable to resist returning it. Sandro leveled a fulminating glare at the other man, who seemed to take his ill-humor in stride and grinned even wider.

"My *wife*, Theresa," Sandro snapped curtly, the warning in his voice more than a little obvious.

"You're married to this goddess?" Max kept his very appreciative focus on Theresa's blushing face, and his grin became a smile of genuine warmth. "I always *knew* you were a man of impeccable taste, De Lucci, but I have to admit, my opinion of you has just skyrocketed!" He held out a hand toward Theresa, who took it after only the slightest hesitation.

"Charmed, I'm sure." His smile gentled and he lifted her hand to his mouth, dropping a reverent kiss on the back of it. "I'm Max Kinsley."

"Uh . . . T-Theresa," she stammered, choking back a giggle at the man's theatrics. She suspected that he was just trying to wind Sandro up, and it seemed to be working because her husband's hand had curled into a fist in the small of her back. "I'm very pleased to meet you, Mr. Kinsley."

"There will be *none* of this formality between us," he admonished. "I'm Max and *you* are Terri! Or Tessa if you'd prefer. Now, please . . . allow me to escort you inside." His grip on her hand tightened slightly as he tugged her toward him, but Sandro's hand shot up to the elbow of her free arm.

"Her name is *Theresa,* and I will be escorting my own wife inside!" Sandro gritted out through his teeth, obviously holding on to his temper by the barest of threads.

"How remiss of me," Max said with feigned regret, releasing her slender hand with exaggerated reluctance. "I'd completely forgotten that you were there, De Lucci!" Sandro made a slight growling sound in the back of his throat, and Theresa couldn't stifle her giggle this time. Max looked delighted by the sound and stepped back with a jaunty little salute.

"We will continue our acquaintance inside, *Tessa* my darling," he promised before turning away and bounding up the stairs leading toward the front door of the house. He had a tog bag, which she hadn't previously noticed, slung over one broad shoulder.

"I like him." She smiled up at Sandro, who was glowering at the front door through which Max had just disappeared.

"Don't mistake his flirtation for anything more than it is, Theresa," he muttered in warning. "He's got a girlfriend."

"I'm not a complete idiot, Sandro. He was needling *you* . . . quite successfully too, I might add."

"*Dio*, this is not the best time to be arguing, Theresa." He sounded weary. "Let's try—"

"Are you coming in or what?" A voice interrupted whatever Sandro had been about to say and they looked up toward the house, where another tall, broad-shouldered man was silhouetted in the doorway.

"Come on," Sandro muttered, taking her hand and picking up a tog bag similar to the one Max had been carrying. He led her to the front door, where the rugged man stepped aside to let them in.

"Hey, Sandro . . ." His casual greeting was followed by some more masculine back-thumping, and this time the friendly overture was returned by Sandro.

"Gabe." Sandro nodded before tugging Theresa forward. "This is Theresa."

"Theresa?" The man did a double take as he took a closer look at her, before he recovered from his astonishment with a warm smile. "I'm very happy to meet you. I'm Gabe Braddock."

. . . And the penny *finally* dropped. Theresa stared up at the warmly smiling man and felt like a complete idiot for not connecting the dots sooner. It was Friday night, Sandro was dressed in his sports gear, and he had brought her to his regular bloody football game! How *typical.* The man certainly pulled out all the stops when faced with an obstacle, but this was just despicable and so unbelievably obvious. He had given her no warning whatsoever. No wonder he was such a successful businessman; he was a master at manipulating a situation to his advantage, and *this* was a classic example. Give the woman what she wants and maybe her rebellion will subside and she will get down to the business of being a human incubator.

"I'm so happy to meet you, Mr. Braddock," she said softly, taking the man's proffered hand and disguising her anger behind a sweet smile. "Why, just *recently* I expressed a wish to meet you!" She refused to look at Sandro but she sensed him uncomfortably shifting from one foot to the other. "And *here* we are."

"Indeed." The other man smiled even though it was obvious, in the way he glanced at Sandro, that he knew something was amiss. "I'm glad you overcame your aversion to football and decided to join us tonight. The guys will be delighted to meet Alessandro's beautiful wife." Her aversion to football? So that was how he'd explained away her conspicuous absences.

"And I'm looking forward to meeting them," she said warmly. She was annoyed with Sandro and hurt by his transparent ploys to keep her appeased, but this tall, broad-shouldered man with the warm smile seemed lovely, and Theresa could not help but instinctively like him.

"Everybody's around back, Sandro," Gabe informed the silent man who stood at her back. "I'll join you soon, I'm waiting for Bobbi." He relinquished Theresa's hand and grinned down at her. "Don't let the guys flirt with you too much, Theresa. They're an incorrigible lot and they're suckers for a pretty girl!" He seemed to mean it, if his lingering glance over her blushing face was any indication.

"Enough with the flirting, Braddock," Sandro suddenly growled, stepping forward to place a possessive hand on her elbow, and Gabe's grin took on a decidedly wicked slant.

"I can't believe it," Gabe hooted, his voice alive with discovery. "You're *jealous* . . . of *me*!" The very idea was so ludicrous that Theresa laughed along with him, but Sandro's grip tightened on her elbow.

"I'm not jealous," he retorted scathingly once their laughter had died down. "Just trying to protect my wife from your smarmy attentions, you smart-ass."

"No, I'm beginning to believe you kept her away from all of us for so long because you can't handle the competition," the other man ribbed with the nerve that only a long-standing friend would possess.

"I am confident of my wife's excellent taste," Sandro dismissed before trying to steer Theresa away, but she resisted.

"Now hold on a second, Sandro. I haven't exactly been spoiled for choice, you know! I may find that my taste has changed." Oh, he did *not* like that, not one bit! He slanted a hard, narrow-eyed glare at her that the other man, who was laughing in delight at her pithy comeback, did not see, and Theresa tilted her chin stubbornly and met his glare with a defiant glare of her own.

"Ooh, I like her, Sandro," Gabe laughed, wiping at his eyes. "She's a feisty one."

"Yes . . ." Sandro's eyes warmed with reluctant amusement. "This I am beginning to see for myself." He tugged at her arm again, and before Theresa could say or do anything more, he was leading her away. She followed docilely until she was certain that they were out of sight and earshot of the other man before she yanked her elbow from his grasp and turned on him furiously.

"You despicable, manipulative bastard!" she seethed, venting her frustration by punching him in the chest for good measure. He grimaced and rubbed at the spot she had hit before stepping out of the range of her swing.

"What the *hell* is your problem?" he growled angrily.

"My problem?" She managed to keep voice just under a screech. "My problem is *you*! You lied to me . . . again. You said that this was a business thing."

"Technically, it is. I am in business with at least five of the men here tonight!" he responded defensively.

"But this isn't really business is it? This is your precious little football game, the one I wasn't good enough to be invited to until after I threatened to leave you!"

"You said that you wanted to meet my friends." He seemed genuinely baffled. "Now when I give you that opportunity, you go crazy! I don't understand you at all."

"The only reason you brought me here tonight was because you thought it would appease me. Throw the vicious dog a bone, and it'll soon be eating out of your hand!"

"More like vicious *bitch*," he muttered beneath his breath, and when he realized that she had heard him, he shrugged unrepentantly. "If you're going to be using animal metaphors, you might as well get it right."

"Fine, I'm a bitch . . . whatever!" She knew her response was childish, but she was feeling more than a little put out by the situation.

"Look, I don't understand why you're so angry when you said you wanted to meet them."

"A year ago, sure. But not *now*! Don't you understand that this is too little too late?" She shook her head in frustration. "It's like putting a Band-Aid on an amputation!"

"You're being overdramatic, as usual," he said dismissively.

"Oh, you *knew* what my reaction would be, and the only reason you knew that was because you recognized how inadequate and pathetic this gesture really is."

"And how do you figure that?" he asked defensively, crossing his arms over his broad chest and glaring down his beautiful nose at her.

"Why else would you be *so* sneaky about bringing me here?"

"Maybe because you've been so ridiculous about going *anywhere* with me lately!" he snapped angrily. "I knew you'd refuse if I asked you to come here tonight, so I had to fabricate a business dinner. Recently you've done nothing but overreact to everything I say and do, as well as completely misread my intentions, so I couldn't take the chance. I was hoping that for once I'd be wrong about you . . . but sure enough you had to go and be unreasonable about this too. You're so determined to put a negative slant on everything I do these days, that you're not willing to accept anything at face value. There are no ulterior motives here. I merely recognized that you had a point about never meeting my friends. I have been unfair, and I wanted a chance to make it right." She bit her lip, unwilling to trust him but unable to resist the sincerity in his eyes. He looked like he actually *meant* his words.

"Don't you know how foolish I feel?" she whispered, looking down. "Meeting them now . . . What must they think of me? I feel like I'm on display, your mystery wife who has shunned them for more than a year." He took a hesitant step toward her before wrapping his arms around her and dropping his forehead to hers. He brought his hands up to cup her face.

"They'll know whose fault it was, Theresa. I'll make sure of that," he promised huskily.

"How?"

"I'll get them to believe that I really *was* too possessive to share you with them. They'll think that I wanted you all to myself."

"But that would make you look . . ." She struggled to find the correct word. "Insecure."

"Maybe." He shrugged. "Or maybe they'll take one look at you and understand why I'd react like that."

"What do you . . . ?" His thumbs pressed to her soft lips, silencing the question.

"Silly little Theresa," he chided softly. "I may not have said it much, or at all for that matter, but you're so beautiful I ache just looking at you sometimes." She wasn't beautiful—she *knew* she wasn't—but just this once she wanted to believe him. She had never seen such stark honesty in his eyes before, and it warmed her down to her toes. He leaned even closer, his lips just millimeters away from hers when an amused voice had them leaping apart guiltily.

"Come on, guys, your honeymoon ended ages ago. Give it a rest!" It was Gabe, coming up behind them. Theresa went a fiery red, while Sandro frowned, hunching his shoulders and dropping his hands into his pockets. He slanted a quick and inscrutable look at

Theresa, who averted her eyes. She couldn't think about that achingly sweet moment and she certainly couldn't wonder about that near-kiss. Not right now.

~

She was quiet on the drive home and still confusing reality with fantasy. Sandro's friends had been lovely, and she'd enjoyed cheering them on from the sidelines. She had been uncomfortable around the other wives and girlfriends at first, but they'd been so genuinely welcoming that Theresa had relaxed almost immediately. Sandro's constant attention had helped a lot. He would often trot over to where she was sitting to ask if she was okay, if she needed anything, if she was warm enough, and it had become embarrassing after a while, especially when his friends started ribbing him about it. Theresa had known, of course, that it was all an act, but it had still been a heady sensation to have his entire focus on her like that. Theresa had found the actual football game surprisingly riveting, especially since she had been unable to tear her eyes away from her graceful and talented husband. Afterward they'd had a barbecue, and again, Sandro had been constantly attentive and almost affectionate, holding her hand or wrapping his arm around her shoulders. After the initial awkwardness, Theresa had found herself relaxing more and more.

Now in the confined space of the car, there was a shimmering tension between them, and Theresa leaned forward to fill the silence with music, but he caught her hand to prevent her from turning on the CD player.

"Don't . . ." She turned to look at the silhouette of his profile, but he kept his eyes glued to the road.

"But . . ."

"Did you have a good time tonight?" he asked gruffly.

"Yes . . . they're all lovely people."

"I'm glad." Silence again. He still hadn't released her hand, keeping it pinned between his hard thigh and his large hand.

"Everybody really liked you." She could hear the warmth in his voice but didn't know if it was directed at his friends or at her. "I was . . . *proud* . . . to have you there." She blinked, not at all sure how to take that. "And I felt guilty for leaving it for so long. I never meant to make you feel like I was ashamed of you, Theresa. I didn't want to marry you, it's true, but not at any point did I ever feel that you would shame me."

"Thank you for saying that," she whispered. "It means a lot."

His hand tightened on hers before he let her go, and she reluctantly lifted her hand from his thigh. There was silence again, but this time it didn't feel quite so unfriendly and unwelcome.

CHAPTER FIVE

They got home after midnight, and while Sandro proceeded to lock up, Theresa wearily headed for the shower in the upstairs guest bedroom that she was still determined to occupy, despite Sandro's forcibly moving her back to the master suite every night. She was standing beneath the hot, relaxing spray of the multiple shower heads in the luxurious guest bathroom, her forehead pressed to the cool tiles, when a rush of cold air alerted her to the fact that the frosted glass door to the cubicle had slid open. She turned around with a resigned sigh and watched as Sandro turned to close the shower door behind him, offering her a tantalizing glimpse of the beautiful bottom that she had so admired earlier in the evening, while he'd been chasing a ball up and down Gabe's lawn. He turned back to her and shook his head with a tired sigh.

"You are, without a doubt, turning into one of the most stubborn people I know, Red," he said with a groan. She was flustered by the unexpected pet name. He had never called her anything other than her given name since she had known him, and she wasn't quite sure what to make of it.

"I *want* that divorce, Sandro," she insisted, getting her thoughts back on track and trying not to drop her eyes to his eager erection. He smiled slightly, taking a step toward her.

"I know," he admitted tiredly, reaching around her to grab the body wash and sponge dangling from the ornate faucets. His arms brushed against her naked flesh with every move he made, and she tried desperately to shield her body's eager reaction from him and folded her arms over the burgeoning red tips of her breasts.

"A-and . . . I don't love you anymore," she continued desperately, watching as he applied the fragrant body wash to the soft sponge. He remained focused on the sponge in his hand.

"I know." His voice sounded a little strange and his expression was neutral. When he looked up again, he gently started running the sponge over her folded arms.

"And I don't want to stay in the same room with you anymore." Her voice quivered embarrassingly when he grasped one slender wrist with a big, gentle hand and lifted her arm away from her breasts to run the sponge down the underside of said arm and up toward her sensitive armpit. Her already hard nipples tightened to the point of pain. She swayed slightly, trying not to moan in pleasure when he lifted the other arm and subjected it to the same sensual treatment.

"You've made that abundantly clear," he whispered in response, his eyes fixed on her obviously aroused breasts. He stepped even closer, crowding her with his large body and backing her up against the smooth tiles. The sponge swept across first one tight bud, then the other, so lightly she wasn't sure if she'd imagined the touch or not.

This time, because he was so close, his every little move brought his hard, smooth chest in brushing contact with the painfully erect little tips, and it was all she could do to maintain her train of thought. The sponge swept down between her breasts and over her torso, her flat stomach, and farther down still, over her abdomen and between her . . .

She sucked in a harsh breath when he quite deliberately dropped the sponge to replace it with his fingers.

"And . . . I want a . . . a . . ." she said, panting, when his fingers continued to stroke insistently where she was most sensitive, and one of her hands latched onto his wrist to curb the movement. He remained undeterred, staring down into her upturned face raptly. "A divorce . . ."

"You said that already," he pointed out, his chest starting to heave as he sought to control his reaction to her obvious arousal. His hungry stare dropped from her face to her small breasts, where her hard, raspberry-pink nipples were starting to peek through the rapidly disintegrating suds. With a desperate groan he removed his hand from between her thighs, dropped to his knees and palmed the small mounds, taking one sudsy bud into his hungry, hot mouth. Theresa arched back at the electrifying touch, her back bowing and her head hitting the tiles with a thud.

Her beautiful husband, who knelt like a supplicant at the temple of her body, licked and kissed his way across the shallow valley between her breasts to find the other aching peak while his large hands swept down her body to her narrow hips, which he determinedly anchored to the tiled wall in an effort to keep her still. Theresa shuddered wildly and her hands buried themselves in his wet hair before restlessly moving to his shoulders, where her nails dug in.

He rose to his feet, pinning her to the wall with his entire body, his erection throbbing urgently where it was trapped between his hard, ridged stomach and her narrow torso. He had his hands braced against the wall on either side of her head, while he thrust himself gently against her torso. He kept his hot, narrowed stare on her nakedly vulnerable face, his own face a mask of tight control while his eyes were ablaze with an emotion she could not read.

His eyes darted from her own half-closed eyes to the full lower lip that she had caught between her teeth. With a slightly muffled curse, he groaned and lowered his head until his mouth touched hers. Theresa's entire body went rigid as his lips gently nuzzled against hers, demanding nothing, just exploring the unfamiliar contours of her generous mouth. His hands moved from where they were braced against the wall to tenderly cup her face, fingertips meeting in the middle of her brow and palms resting on either side of her jaw. His mouth gradually demanded more, moving insistently against hers until she sighed and melted against him as her own mouth explored his. His tongue, tasting of mint, ran over her lips seeking entry into her mouth, and she opened up for him, wanting this so much that she ached.

Her hands fluttered up wonderingly, cupping his jaw in an effort to bring him even closer, and he was happy to oblige, his kiss going even deeper than before. She felt as if she were being consumed by him, greedily eaten alive and absorbed into him. It was the most intense experience of her life, and from the way he throbbed against her torso, she guessed he felt pretty much the same. He reluctantly lifted his mouth from hers to look down into her face with a penetrating stare that seemed to see right into her soul, and then he smiled. A completely open, unguarded and boyish smile, the likes of which she had *never* seen from him before. She barely had time to catch her breath before his mouth was on hers again, thoroughly plundering it. She moaned hungrily and wrapped her arms around his neck. His hands were moving now, roaming all over her soft, naked flesh before gripping her tight backside and hoisting her up until her slender thighs wrapped around his waist.

He lifted his mouth from hers and dropped his face into her neck to lick the droplets of water that had pooled in the sensitive hollow there before moving back up to claim her lips, again devouring her with his lips, teeth, and tongue. Theresa was completely overwhelmed by his unexpected passion—he had never seemed this out of control before, and she was being swept along with the tide. He tightened his grip on her behind before, half stumbling, he carried her out of the shower, through the bathroom, and into the bedroom, where he barely managed to get them both onto the bed. Theresa's feet touched the carpeted floor and her backside was half off the bed, but she didn't care one whit for the discomfort when, with barely a pause from his ravaging mouth, he surged into her. She managed to tear her mouth away to cry out, the sound harsh and raw in the silence of the room.

Her back arched until only her head touched the bed, while she raised her legs to wrap them around his waist again, her ankles crossing over his taut, pistoning buttocks and her arms wrapped around his broad back, while her nails dug into his flesh so deeply she drew blood. Sandro was making sobbing, desperate sounds into her mouth but he still refused to relinquish her lips, coordinating the thrusts of his tongue with those of his driving hips, and Theresa's muffled moans took on the same frenzied rhythm.

His hands moved up to wrap themselves in her wet hair, tilting her head back almost violently to get better access to her mouth. His wet body slid and rubbed over hers, his muscles bunched beneath the taut satin of his skin, and Theresa's body burned at every point of contact. One of his hands swept back down to one of her thighs, lifting her hips even higher to allow him even deeper penetration.

More! More! More! She tried to say the words but she couldn't with his mouth on hers, so she moved her hands to his behind to pull him closer. She wanted him harder, deeper, and he knew it because he adjusted accordingly, and she sobbed into his mouth, feeling like she was dying an exquisite death. She spiraled higher and higher, and when she reached the pinnacle, she spun out of control, freefalling back down to earth with a scream that he swallowed. Her entire body clenched around him, and Sandro, feeling her climax, was unable to hold back. His breath labored in and out of his lungs as he fought for control, but he was as lost as she was and lifted his mouth from hers long enough to release a hoarse shout that she barely recognized as her name. His body arched violently, and he lifted her from the bed and into his lap as he held her as close as he could, his strong arms wrapped around her narrow back as he jerked within her. His lips fell back onto hers, gentler this time as his body continued to thrust lazily. He hugged her even closer, and while he knelt on the edge of the bed, her legs straddled his hard thighs, her chest pressed to his, and her arms wrapped tightly around his neck as she fought to keep her balance while he nuzzled her mouth with his. He finally went completely boneless and collapsed down onto the soft bed, taking her with him and keeping her wrapped up in his arms with one of his hard thighs still pressed between hers. He was still kissing her, lifting his mouth from hers to nuzzle her neck and kiss her shoulders before coming back to her mouth over and over again, as if he could not get enough of the taste of her. He was petting her all over, and gradually their breathing slowed down and their mutual trembling abated slightly. He was a gentler, softer presence inside her now, only occasionally twitching as if to remind her that he was still there.

"God," he whispered. "Oh my God, Theresa . . . that was *amazing*." Theresa, who was only now coming back to herself tensed at his words, but he seemed not to notice, still stroking her, kissing her, whispering little endearments and half-finished Italian sentences into her hair. In a year and a half, during which time they'd had sex on average four times a week and at least twice a night on each of those occasions, this was the *first* time . . . *ever* that Sandro hadn't recited his standard mantra.

He shifted slightly to arrange her more comfortably against him, one arm tucked beneath her head and the other resting heavily across her breasts. His fingers formed lazy circles on the overheated skin of her upper arm, and he had his head on the same pillow as hers, so close she could feel his still-unsteady breath feathering through her hair. He occasionally dropped soft kisses onto the sensitive skin beneath her ear and along her delicate jawline.

Theresa was tensing more and more in his arms, not sure how to react. First the kisses, then the shattering sex, then the absence of those five words, and now this unprecedented display of *affection.* It was as if, just when she'd found a way to protect her already battered, bruised, and fragile heart from him, he found some other way around her defenses, leaving her vulnerable to even more pain.

He was still whispering into her ear, half-broken Italian words that she didn't understand at all, trying to pull her closer, but Theresa resisted, snapping out of the trance that she had been in. She could not let him do this to her . . . not again! He had hurt her too many times in the past with his careless disregard, his other women, and his contempt. She would *not* allow him into her heart again. *Finally* clueing in to the fact that Theresa was not as into the cuddling as he was, Sandro lifted himself up onto his elbow, resting his head on his hand and looking absolutely gorgeous in all his naked splendor.

"*Cara*, what's wrong?"

She nearly laughed out loud at the ridiculous question before struggling in earnest to escape from beneath his heavy arm. For a few seconds his hold tightened, but he raised his arm and allowed her to scurry off the bed.

"The sheets are soaking wet," she said breathlessly, refusing to meet his eyes. "I need to change them."

"Leave it for the maid in the morning." He grinned lazily.

"The cleaning service doesn't come in on a Saturday, and besides, I can't sleep on a wet bed."

"Don't be silly, Red," he admonished gently, sitting up gracefully. "You're sleeping with *me* in our bed!"

"I'm not." She shook her head adamantly, and his grin widened indulgently.

"Stubborn cat." He swung his legs off the edge of the bed and stood up with the lethal grace of a predator, stalking her languidly. "Of course you are." Theresa backed away but he pounced before she could get very far, his hands on her shoulders, applying just enough pressure to keep her from fleeing.

"Look at me," he demanded softly when she kept her eyes glued to his chest. When she refused, he muttered something beneath his breath before lifting one hand from her shoulder to tilt up her jaw until her eyes met his. Whatever he saw on her defiant face made his eyebrows lower and his eyes darken.

"I'm trying to fix this, *cara*," he whispered, the words sounding almost ripped from his throat.

"You can't." She shook her head sadly. "This . . . whatever it is . . . it's irreparable."

"Why?" He shook his head slightly in confused frustration.

"Because *everything* you do now feels insincere and forced!" she hissed in sudden fury. "Every touch, every apology, every endearment . . . it's like you brushed up on the 'Theresa Noble User Manual' and learned what makes me tick!"

"First, it's Theresa *De Lucci,* and second, I don't know what the hell you're talking about!" he practically shouted, shaking her slightly.

"The *kisses* for one," she said, itemizing.

"What?"

"A year and a half of marriage, Alessandro, and tonight was the first time you've ever kissed me," she pointed out. "You must have known how much it hurt me to know that you despised me so much that you couldn't even bring yourself to kiss me."

"That's not—"

"So of course tonight," she interrupted him, not at all interested in whatever he had to say, "after making me feel so special by finally doing me the honor of introducing me to your friends, this is when you decide to sweeten the pot with a few of your kisses! It probably struck you as a pretty effective way to keep the bitch muzzled and content, right?"

"You're misreading the entire situation, *cara*."

"Don't call me that! I am not your darling. I've never been your darling and I'm not going to be naïve enough to fall for your so-called charms again!"

"What do you *want* from me?" He suddenly demanded desperately, releasing her shoulders so abruptly that she stumbled and fell. He froze in horror, staring down at her with a look of such abject misery, contrition and despair that she almost felt sorry for him. She sat up and stared into his distressed face.

"I want a divorce," she whispered and he sank down to his knees beside her, lifting a hand to caress the curve of her cheek.

"I'm sorry," he groaned. "I'm so sorry for more things than you could possibly imagine but that's the one thing I can't give you."

"Then we have nothing more to talk about," she pushed herself to her feet, ignoring the hand he offered to help her. She suddenly realized that they were both naked and sighed heavily.

"Please, just go back to your room, Alessandro," she pleaded, and he hesitated, his eyes lingering on her face for a few long moments, before he turned abruptly and left.

~

She woke up in the guest bedroom the following morning . . . alone. She was both saddened and relieved by that. A quick glance at the clock told her that it was well after ten in the morning, and the gloom told her that it was probably raining. Theresa was shocked that she had slept so late and rushed through her morning ablutions while trying to ignore the ever-present queasiness. She gingerly made her way downstairs, feeling like someone with a hangover as she headed for the kitchen.

Fortunately, no food smells were emanating from the room, but when she walked in, it was to find Sandro sitting at the breakfast bar and staring thoughtfully down at his full coffee mug. He looked up when she stepped into the room his eyes sweeping over her figure, taking in the worn old jeans, faded sweatshirt, and battered little sneakers.

"How are you feeling, *ca* . . . Theresa?"

"Fine," she mumbled, getting herself a glass of orange juice before turning toward the breakfast bar and taking the seat opposite his on one of the quaint wooden chairs.

"Aren't you going to eat anything?" he asked softly, and Theresa grimaced, the thought of food making her stomach churn queasily.

"I'm fine."

He swore softly.

"You're obviously *not* fine," he growled. "I don't know what you think starving yourself will achieve."

"Oh, for God's sake, I'm hardly starving myself, just skipping breakfast."

"You look like you've skipped entirely too many meals recently." He shook his head and sent a scathing glare up and down her thin frame.

"If it'll get you off my back, I'll have some toast," she said, bristling, before slamming her glass down. She used too much force and must have placed it right on the edge because the glass went tumbling down to the floor and shattered on impact, spilling the bright contents all over the pale blue tile of the floor. The jarring noise completely unraveled Theresa and frayed her nerves to the breaking point.

"Oh." Her eyes flooded with tears. "I'm sorry . . ."

"Theresa." Sandro was beside her in seconds, his hands on her shoulders and his face peering down into hers in concern. "Are you okay?"

"I'm fine," she whispered, shrugging out of his grip, and he dropped his hands abruptly.

"Are you sure?" he demanded. "You're as white as a sheet."

"Just a bit of a shock." She waved his concern aside. "It's raining," she observed inanely in a very weak attempt to change the subject, and her eyes fixed on the dull grayness of the world outside.

"Yes." He stepped farther away from her and knelt down to pick up the shards of glass from the floor. "It is." She started to get up, but he looked up at her from where he was squatting at her feet and dropped a large hand on her thigh to keep her from moving.

"The floor's slippery and covered in glass; let me clear it up before you get off the chair." She shrugged and silently watched as he efficiently went about cleaning up her mess.

"What are you doing today?" he asked casually, keeping his back to her as he discarded the glass and paper towels he had used to sop up the excess juice.

"I need to do some shopping," she answered distractedly. "I was thinking of heading to the city for some stuff." She intended to buy about a dozen different home pregnancy kits, a task which she had delayed for much too long.

"I'm running low on some things too," he responded casually, turning around to face her. "I'll drive you."

Theresa came out of her daze with a wry smile.

"Wow. That lie was so transparent that I'm almost embarrassed for you."

He chuckled wryly in response to her dry wit and shrugged slightly.

"I know it wasn't up to scratch, but give me a break, it's been an eventful twenty-four hours and I'm not in top form," he joked lightly, even though his eyes were still running over her face and body in concern. "I don't want you to drive, Theresa; you look a bit out of it. Do you think you're coming down with something?"

Yes. Pregnancy.

"I'm fine but I do feel a bit out of sorts this morning, probably the whiskey in that Irish coffee I had with the ladies last night." Right, she'd barely made her way through a quarter of one mug before realizing that, if she *was* pregnant, drinking would probably *not* be such a great idea. Still, Sandro didn't know how much she'd had, so it was a perfectly acceptable excuse. He seemed to fall for it and nodded his acceptance of her explanation.

"When would you like to leave?"

Theresa sighed softly; she really didn't want him trailing after her while she tried to figure out a way to buy home pregnancy tests without him noticing. Sandro would *never* miss that.

"I really do have some stuff to take care of, Theresa," he said seriously, seeming to read her mind. "I'll leave you in relative peace." She chewed on her lower lip thoughtfully, not missing how his eyes flared when her tongue darted out to soothe the sting of her teeth where she had accidentally bitten too hard.

"Okay . . . give me an hour to get ready." To shower, get dressed, throw up, and such. He nodded.

~

He was as good as his word and mostly left her alone to unenthusiastically browse around the upmarket boutiques in the very high-end shopping mall that he had driven her to. She used the first ten minutes away from him to buy the pregnancy kits, six of them, all different brands (who knew there were so many choices available?), just in case he changed his mind about leaving her alone. Surprisingly he did constantly call or text her to be sure she was okay and didn't need him, which got rather tedious after the tenth text message in forty minutes and the fifth call in an hour and a half. In the end, she simply told him she was done shopping, and he suggested they meet up and head to a restaurant for lunch.

The upscale restaurant was obviously one Sandro often patronized, so, even though it was lunchtime on a Saturday afternoon and the place was exceedingly popular, they were seated immediately. Theresa watched the staff fawn all over him and bitterly wondered if he had brought any other women here. The suspicion seemed to be confirmed when the waiter turned to her with something resembling a leer.

"And what will the lady be ordering today?" he asked in that supercilious manner that servers in upmarket restaurants often have.

"Your Caesar salad, no dressing, toast, and water," she ordered brusquely.

"And have you decided on a main course yet?" he asked with an annoying smirk.

"That would be it," she responded shortly. His smug attitude was *really* grating on her nerves.

"Theresa." Sandro leaned forward in concern. "You didn't have breakfast; you need to eat something more substantial than just salad."

"I'm really not that hungry." She shrugged dismissively, handing the thick leather-bound menu back to the waiter. "Please just let it go."

"If you're on some crazy diet . . ."

"I'm *not* on a diet!" she snapped. "Just, please, stop trying to manipulate every single aspect of my life!" His jaw clenched and his lips thinned in obvious anger, but surprisingly enough he let it go before proceeding to order a staggering amount of food from the waiter. Once they were alone, he leaned back in his chair and stared at her thoughtfully.

"Seriously," he began after a long silence, which she had stubbornly refused to break. "What's going on with you?" She gaped at him, unable to believe the stupidity of that question and he lowered his eyes, apparently realizing that himself.

"Aside from the obvious," he qualified. "And try to keep the sarcasm down to a minimum."

"Well, *aside* from the obvious fact that I'm unhappy with my life as it is right now"—she shrugged—"I can't say that there's much going on with me."

"You're lying to me." He sounded so incredulous at that fact that she actually laughed in genuine amusement. "Are you having an affair?"

"Back to that, are we?" She laughed incredulously, unable to believe that he could seriously harbor even the slightest suspicion about her fidelity. "Sandro, not everybody stoops to adultery when things aren't going right in their lives."

"What the hell is *that* supposed to mean?" He sounded outrageously offended and leaned toward her, all affronted, bristling male.

"Oh, come on, Sandro, you know what it means!"

"No, I don't, do enlighten me," he invited sarcastically.

"It means . . ." She spoke with exaggerated and offensive slowness. "That *I'm* not the one who has been having the affairs. It means that I had the misguided notion that the sacred marriage vows we took were just that, sacred vows. It means that I'm not the one who deliberately set out to hurt and humiliate my spouse as publicly and as painfully as possible."

"I admit that I did some things to deliberately hurt you in a misguided attempt to punish you for a situation that wasn't your fault," he began carefully.

"How magnanimous of you to admit that," she interrupted sarcastically.

"You were misled into believing that I loved you," he ignored her interruption. "I was misled into believing you were . . ."

"Your drinks." The waiter's smooth voice interrupted the first really productive exchange they'd had on the subject of the unusual circumstances of their marriage, and Sandro slanted him an annoyed look before gritting his teeth and waiting in fulminating silence for the man to finish. When the waiter left, Sandro turned his attention back on her.

"I thought you knew about your father's scheme. I thought you were fully on board with it," he admitted softly.

"What exactly *is* my father's 'scheme'?" She asked carefully, wary of being shot down again.

"He owned something that I desperately wanted, and the only way he would let me have it was if I paid a huge amount of money for it, married you, and moved here."

"I see." She studied the intricately folded napkin on the table in front of her and traced her fingers lightly over the folds. "So, in essence, you paid an exorbitant sum for this mysterious something that you so desperately wanted, with me tossed in as your unwanted free gift?"

"I had no choice. To get what I wanted, I had to accept you as part of the deal. I thought . . ." His voice tapered off and he shrugged miserably.

"You flattered yourself into thinking that I was fully cognizant of this scheme and that I was so desperate to have you, I would have my daddy blackmail you into marrying me?" He nodded reluctantly. "Well, you got what you wanted, and since it's obvious that we're both miserable in this sham of a marriage, why won't you give me that divorce?" She continued to probe, desperately hoping that he couldn't tell how much actually *hearing* this confession hurt her.

"It's a bit more complicated than that. I think your father knew that we would both eventually want out of this 'sham.' So he added a little clause to the contract."

This was it. Theresa braced herself for what she knew was coming.

"Clause?" She repeated the word faintly, and Sandro cleared his throat uncomfortably.

"Your father—"

The waiter swooped in with great flair and began to offload a tray of food onto their table. Sandro muffled a curse beneath his breath while he waited with barely concealed impatience for the younger man to finish.

"Will there be anything else?"

"No!" he barked, keeping his voice low and menacing. The poor man gulped and beat a hasty retreat. Theresa barely registered the interaction between the two men, her horrified eyes were focused on the gastronomic feast Sandro had ordered. Pastas, pies, fish, meat, and vegetables were laid out in front of her rebelling senses.

"Theresa?" Sandro's voice seemed to come from miles away. "What's wrong?"

"So much food," she said sickly, feeling in danger of losing the precious little she already had in her stomach.

"I thought we could share," he admitted.

"I *told* you I wasn't hungry," she said, her voice flaring weakly, angry that he expected her to fall victim to yet another one of his manipulations.

"It doesn't tempt you? Not even a little?" He lifted his fork and stuck it into the closest dish, some kind of cheese bake, and lifted it toward her lips. Theresa could feel her gorge rise and jerked her head back abruptly.

"No!"

He lowered the fork and glared at her in outraged bewilderment. "What the hell is going on with you? Are you on some insane hunger strike?"

She laughed unsteadily. "That's what prisoners do, isn't it? When they want to make a statement about the unjustness of their imprisonment, they go on a hunger strike." She laughed again, aware of the edge of hysteria in her voice.

"You're not serious?" He seemed to think she was though, and for some reason that both saddened and amused her.

"I'm not hungry," she maintained wearily. "It's really as simple as that. Please finish what you were saying about that clause." He looked frustrated but seemed to recognize that she would not budge on the issue.

"Basically, we have an out," he began slowly. "We give him a grandson and we can divorce without any repercussions." Hearing him put it so bluntly took the wind clear out of her sails, and she needed a couple of moments to recover from it.

"An out," she repeated hoarsely. "Every single time you touched me, *every time* that's all you ever thought about, wasn't it? Getting out?" She laughed bitterly. "And how diligently you've worked toward your goal. So often and so very thoroughly."

"Theresa," he whispered, his voice alive with misery. Nothing more, just that, just her name. It was as if he recognized that nothing he could possibly say at that moment would make any difference to the pain she was feeling.

"My God." She swiped at a few errant tears, furious with herself for allowing him to see them. "Every time you came you practically *prayed* for me to give you a son. That was the only thought in your mind, every single time . . . escape! At a time when most people can't even remember their own names, you were begging me to give you a son because life with me was so incredibly unbearable for you."

"It wasn't you," he interrupted lamely. "It was the situation."

"So this son you so desperately wanted." She tried to keep her voice level, even while it cracked with strain. "You don't *really* want him, I take it? He's just a means to an end?"

"I've never thought about it," he admitted uncomfortably.

"I mean, surely you wouldn't want anything to do with a child spawned with a woman you despise and carrying the blood of a man you consider your enemy?"

"The child has never seemed real to me," he murmured with brutal honesty. "I had some vague idea that you would have him and I'd move back to Italy afterward. I never thought beyond that."

"With a father who felt nothing for him, a mother who didn't want to get pregnant, and a megalomaniacal grandfather waiting in the wings, it's probably best that the last one didn't make it," she concluded heartbrokenly.

"Don't you *ever* say that," Sandro snapped, one of his hands reaching out to enfold her tightly furled fists on the tabletop. "He would have been loved."

"What makes you so sure of that? When you admit that you don't know how you would have felt about him?"

"I know you," he murmured huskily. "And you have a capacity

for love that boggles the mind. Of course you would have loved that baby; it's the only way you know how to be."

"How am I supposed to keep living with you now, Sandro?" she asked him helplessly. "It was bad enough before but the thought of going home with you now is almost completely unbearable." His hand loosened its grip around hers, and he reached up to stroke the side of her cheek tenderly.

"We'll get through this," he whispered, and she flinched away from his touch. His eyes flickered with some strange emotion before his hand dropped back down to the table.

"I'm tired," she said quietly. "Take me back to the house." He nodded and summoned the waiter over to ask for the check. Theresa's eyes dropped to the full table regretfully.

"Such a waste," she whispered half to herself, but she was surprised when Sandro overheard her and asked the waiter to multiply their order by fifty and deliver it to the nearest homeless shelter.

Nothing much else was said between them until they got home, where Theresa excused herself under the pretext of being tired and closeted herself in her room for the rest of the afternoon.

~

"Sandro." Theresa cautiously breached the sanctity of his study later that night. In all the time they had been living in the house, it was the first time Theresa had ever set foot in the study while he was in it. He looked up to see her hovering uncertainly in the doorway and stood up abruptly, nearly sending his chair toppling. She jumped backward at the sudden violent movement, but he was around his desk in an instant and approaching her with one hand outstretched.

"Theresa," he intoned huskily. "Please come in." He seemed almost eager to have her there. Not exactly the reception she was expecting. He steered her toward the huge leather easy chair in one corner of the large study, seating her before taking the chair opposite hers. He leaned toward her, with his hands loosely clasped together and hanging down between his thighs.

"I want to know why," she whispered, after a lengthy silence. "I want to know what commodity you so casually traded my happiness for. What meant so *much* to you that you were willing to give up your precious freedom for it?"

He was quiet for so long that she wondered if he would bother to respond.

"Not many people know this, but my father has been extremely ill. We've tried to keep it out of the news," he said in a low voice, keeping his head down and his eyes fixed on his hands. "He grew up on a wine farm. Not a very profitable vineyard, but it had been in our family for generations and it meant a lot to him. It was the land he was born on, the land he imagined retiring to and eventually dying on.

"Unfortunately the bank ran into some financial straits after my grandfather died and my father exacerbated the situation by making some terrible financial decisions. The vineyard was one of many unavoidable casualties while my father tried to recoup his losses. He soon found his footing and got stinking rich, but by then the vineyard had been purchased by your father, who quite stubbornly, despite anything my father offered him, refused to sell. There's some bad history between them. Apparently they met at Oxford and formed their ridiculous business rivalry there. So while the vineyard was pretty worthless to a man as wealthy as your father, I can only conclude that he enjoyed having that kind of leverage over my father." He shrugged helplessly.

"All of my life I remember my father waxing lyrical about that place. He always regretted the fact that none of his children had been born on that land and the guilt of losing a huge chunk of family

history ate at him. Over the last few years, his quest to get it back became an obsession. In the meantime, his health started to deteriorate badly. He was diagnosed with cancer three years ago, and the doctors weren't optimistic. Medical science has managed to keep him with us this long, but it's an uphill battle. Naturally his impending death made the loss of that land even more unbearable for him, and it was killing us to watch him suffer emotionally, physically, and mentally. I wanted to give him his pride and dignity back. I wanted him to find peace and die happy. So I approached your father, who, having seen your reaction to me after our first meeting, finally relented and came up with the terms of sale as you now know them."
Theresa flushed miserably when she remembered how obviously infatuated she had been the first time she had seen Sandro and recognized her own, unwitting role in this façade.

"How's your father?" she asked tightly, and he nodded slightly, his face betraying the first hint of emotion since he had started telling the sorry tale.

"Content, now that he's home." His voice was absolutely racked with the pain he was trying so desperately to disguise.

"And your family knows about this 'deal' you made for the land?" she asked, her own voice high with tension.

"Yes."

"No wonder they never expressed any desire to meet me, or made any overtures of friendship toward me," she said, half to herself, and he made a muffled sound and moved a hand toward her face. She flinched away from his reach, and his hand dropped down into the no-man's land between them.

"I'm sorry about your father," she said tonelessly. "I see now how impossible your situation must have been."

"Even so, I could have treated you less . . ." he began, his voice bitter with something very close to self-loathing.

"Never mind," she cut him off, not really in the mood to hear his moans of regret and self-recrimination. "Thank you for telling me." She got up slowly, always mindful of the dizziness, and he jumped up along with her.

"Theresa, wait . . . please . . ." he began.

"I don't think there's much more to say." She turned toward the door.

"What about us? Our marriage?"

"I suppose we go on as we always have." She shrugged listlessly. "Only, without the intimacy, Sandro. I really couldn't handle that anymore. We lead separate lives."

"I don't want that," he said hoarsely, sounding almost horrified by the prospect.

"It won't have to be for too much longer," she murmured faintly, wondering why the door seemed to be getting farther away with every faltering step.

"What do you mean?" he asked in alarm. *"Theresa?"* This last when she swayed slightly. He put a steadying arm around her narrow shoulders and led her back to the chair she had just vacated.

"That's it," he snapped, crouching in front of her while his hands went up to frame her pale face. "I'm calling the doctor! This is—"

"I'm pregnant," she cut across his words in an appallingly weak voice. But quiet and shaky though her statement was, it was enough to stop him in his tracks. He went pale and sank back onto his heels as he absorbed the words.

"Are you sure?" he asked quietly, one trembling hand reaching up to brush her soft hair from her face.

"I just took four home pregnancy tests in the space of two hours," she confessed. "End result: three pink strips and one blue, all telling me that I'm going to be a mommy in a few months' time. I could take the remaining two tests that I have stashed away upstairs, but I couldn't force myself to drink any more water," she joked weakly. He didn't say anything, just kept his eyes glued to her face.

"So you see, Sandro? You're just a few short months away from getting rid of your unwanted wife, child, and life. No more need for pretense, no need to humor your sham-wife with Friday night football games or introductions to your friends." Her voice trembled with the effort it took to sound casual, while Sandro looked anything but fooled by her attempt to appear cavalier. His hands went to the arms of her chair and he seemed to be holding on for dear life, not touching her at all but still uncomfortably close.

"You still need to see a doctor," he said softly, sounding strained, and she nodded.

"I've already made an appointment with Lisa's doctor." He sighed softly before agilely getting up and moving away from her chair and back to his own.

"They would like you," he suddenly said, his eyes intent on her face.

"What?" she asked distractedly.

"My family," he elaborated, and she frowned, not sure why he'd felt the need to say that.

"I doubt that, Sandro. I don't think *I'd* feel any kind of charity toward someone who deliberately set out to trap my brother or son in a marriage he did not want, and I can't imagine your family doing so."

"But you didn't . . ."

"They *think* I did, and once you've made up your mind about someone, it's pretty hard to change it again."

"It's not as hard as you think," he said, half under his breath.

"I don't know why you think you have to say stuff like this." She shrugged dismissively. "Soon we'll both be getting what we want: freedom from this awful situation."

"What about the baby?"

"If I have a boy, you would have fulfilled the terms of your contract with my father. You'll be free. Of course, the baby won't be any of your concern, but you can be *quite* certain that my father won't be getting his paws on my child either. I ask only that you leave us this house and support us while I study jewelry designing. I don't think we'll need your support for much longer than two years. After that, I think I'll be able to manage on my own."

"You seem to have given this some thought," he said tonelessly, his face back to the familiar icy mask that she despised so much. She nodded nervously.

"I've been thinking about it all afternoon. Please, Sandro, after two years I'll be completely out of your life, and while you're supporting us, I won't bother you for anything. You won't have to talk to me or hear from us, and it doesn't have to be too much."

"You think I give a damn about the *money*?" He suddenly exploded, losing his icy reserve in spectacular fashion. "Do you think I would nitpick over pennies when it came to my wife and child's welfare?"

"Ex-wife," she reminded tentatively, fascinated by the incandescent fury she could see in his eyes. It flared even hotter after her timid correction.

"Nothing's set in stone," he gritted. "It could be a girl." She went dramatically pale at his words; oddly enough she hadn't even considered *that* possibility.

"No," she whispered. "It's a *boy*, it has to be."

He swore shakily beneath his breath.

"I'm sorry," he murmured quietly. "I know that this has to be stressful for you. Theresa . . . whatever the future holds, you can rest assured that I'll support you in every way possible for as long as you need me."

"It won't be for long," she assured earnestly. "I know you want to move on with your real life. Probably get married and have children."

"This *is* my life," he growled. "I *am* married and having a child."

"But it's not the life you wanted," she reminded. "Not the wife and child you wanted. This is certainly not the life *I* wanted."

"So, what the hell are you saying? That you're looking forward to getting married to someone else and having his kid?" he suddenly snapped, and she jumped, astonished by his unpredictable mood.

"Why are you being like this?" she asked in confusion. "I thought you'd be happy. It's what you've been asking me for since the day we married. Every time we had sex, without fail you'd ask me—"

"I *know*," he interrupted savagely. "You don't have to remind me of it again."

"Well." She got up yet again and he jumped to his feet, braced to catch her if she fell. She sent him an amused sidelong glance. "I'm off to bed."

"Have you eaten?" he asked in concern.

"Some toast." She shrugged.

"I don't like the way you're managing your meals, Theresa," he growled. "If you're serious about getting through this pregnancy healthy, you should eat better than you have been."

"I know that but I think my body might be adjusting to the pregnancy, so things are probably going to be a bit out of sync for a while. I'm sure my appetite will come back with a vengeance. Don't worry about it, Sandro. The baby will be fine."

"Yes, babies are resilient." He nodded. "I have no doubt he will be fine, but what about *you*? You won't be able to enjoy your newfound freedom if you damage yourself irreparably during this pregnancy."

"I'll be fine," she said dismissively, with a flick of the hand.

"How the hell can you be so goddamn cavalier about your health?" he snapped, and Theresa lost all patience with him.

"I really don't see how any of this is *your* business, Sandro. My pregnancy, my body, and the rest of my life are no longer issues you need to concern yourself with. For all intents and purposes, you're free to go off and have a blast. In fact, why don't you go out with a couple of the floozies you so enjoy dangling from your arm every time there's a photographer nearby? Go out, get wasted, and bang a bimbo. Celebrate your impending freedom in the time-honored tradition."

"What time is your doctor's appointment tomorrow?" he asked calmly, ignoring her rant as if it hadn't happened.

She glared at him before turning away and heading toward the door. She had her hand on the doorknob when he spoke again.

"I *never*, not once, was unfaithful to you during this marriage, Theresa."

She halted at the door, her back stiffening as his words sank in and she found herself caught between wanting to open the door and turning around to meet his eyes. In the end she just stood there with her hand on the doorknob and her head bowed. He came up behind her and she cringed when his hands dropped down onto her shoulders and his large body brushed against her narrow back.

"What makes you think I believe you or even care anymore?" she asked quietly, fighting to keep the anguish from her voice.

"I don't blame you for not caring." His lips were practically brushing against her ear as he whispered. "But I wanted you to know. I know how it looked, but I wasn't thinking about the consequences. I wanted to show your father how little his damned contract was affecting my life, and very selfishly didn't spare much thought to what it was doing to you. I want you to know that it wasn't *you* I was trying to hurt."

"So you keep saying." A betraying quaver crept into her voice. "But guess who always wound up getting hurt anyway?"

"I know . . ." His lips were doing more than just accidentally brushing up against her ear now, they seemed to be nuzzling the sensitive flesh beneath her ear, and they were *definitely* moving down her neck. "It was stupid and I know that it was a bad move from the first, but once the papers sank their teeth into the juicy story of the recently wed Alessandro De Lucci playing away from home, everything I did came under scrutiny, and any woman I had even a passing conversation with became my latest 'mistress.' It got completely out of control."

"Let me go," she demanded weakly when his lips trailed down to her collarbone.

"*Cara*," he groaned. "I honestly don't think that I can."

For a moment she was tempted to let him keep going, especially when one of his hands circled her waist to rest on her ribcage just below the upward curve of her breast. Her entire body tensed as her mind rebelled against what she was about to do, but she lifted her foot and deliberately trod down on his instep a little harder than she'd intended. He swore and leaped back, leaving her feeling momentarily bereft, before she came to her senses and fled.

CHAPTER SIX

"What are you doing here?" Theresa paused at the threshold to the kitchen and stared at the gorgeous man who stood in front of the open refrigerator wearing only baggy sweatpants. No shoes and no shirt. He turned around slowly to meet her eyes, and she swallowed past the huge lump in her suddenly dry throat; God, he was so much more beautiful than she remembered. Of course, she felt unattractive and sloppy in the Sylvester the Cat silk shortie pajamas that she was wearing. She knew that there was a sleep crease down the side of her face and that her hair closely resembled a bird's nest.

"I live here," he replied casually, one hand grasping a carton of orange juice and the other lazily rubbing back and forth over the rippled contours of his abdomen. Her fascinated eyes fell to that hand, and she imagined her own hand replacing his. She shook her head slightly to rid herself of the erotic image and focused on her outrage at seeing him so casually standing in the kitchen.

"You're usually at work by this time," she pointed out.

"Yes, I am," he agreed. "But since you go to great pains *not* to be around when I head out in the mornings or come home at night, I figured that the only way I'd know what the hell was going on with you was to stay at home today."

"You can't just stay at home." She was appalled by that notion. "You're the boss."

"Exactly, and if the *boss* can't take the occasional day off, then there's really no point in being the boss." His voice was casual, light even, but his eyes roamed over her small figure almost hungrily, taking in every single detail of her fuller face and rounder figure. They had been like ships passing in the night for nearly three months, with Theresa deliberately evading him when he was in the house. She tended to ignore his text messages and let the machine take his calls. He left little notes for her, sometimes asking her to dinner or asking after her health. He had recently stuck a Post-it on the refrigerator door reminding her to buy new prenatal vitamins because he'd noticed that she was running out. After she'd forgotten to buy the vitamins anyway, she'd found a new bottle on the kitchen table, and a Post-it with a half-dozen exclamation marks drawn on it stuck to the lid.

They still shared the bathroom that connected their bedrooms, which was how he had known that her vitamins were running low, but Theresa always took great care to shower after he left in the morning or before he returned at night. Now, after successfully avoiding him for nearly three months, finding him so casually standing in the kitchen, half-naked and gorgeous, was a bit distressing to say the least.

"Why are you even interested in what's going on with me?" she asked after a short pause.

"We live in the same house, you're pregnant with my baby, and I have no idea how you are. The situation is a bit abnormal to say the least, don't you think?"

"It works for me," she dismissed casually, turning away from him and toward a cabinet to fetch a cereal bowl.

"So it would seem."

She heard the fridge door closing and tensed as he padded toward her, coming to a standstill directly behind her and reaching up for another bowl. He was standing so close to her that she could feel the heat coming off his naked chest. His warm, musky scent enveloped her. Theresa shut her eyes and tried to regain her equilibrium in the face of such overwhelming sexuality. He lingered behind her for much longer than he should have before abruptly moving away and leaving her feeling bereft. When she turned back to face him, he was sitting at the wooden table in the sunny breakfast nook and shaking a huge amount of corn flakes into his bowl. When he noticed that she was watching him, he lifted the box inquiringly. She sighed before carrying her bowl to the table and sitting down opposite him. She watched as he sprinkled the flakes into her bowl and topped the dry cereal with strawberry halves and banana slices that he must have prepared earlier.

It was the housekeeper's day off, so Theresa hadn't planned on anything fancier than cereal anyway, but the company was unwelcome and unexpected. She watched as Sandro poured a generous amount of milk over her cereal and filled a glass with orange juice, which he nudged across the table toward her. She nodded her thanks before lifting her spoon and awkwardly beginning her meal. Sandro tucked in enthusiastically and was finished before she was halfway done. He leaped up and over to the fridge, digging around in there before triumphantly producing a grapefruit, which he halved, put into bowls, and carried back over to where Theresa was sitting. He placed one half in front of her before he sat down, grimaced to himself, and proceeded on his own half.

"I thought you didn't like grapefruit." She broke the silence between them and he grinned over at her while his hair, which was in serious need of cutting, flopped over his forehead endearingly.

"I don't," he admitted. "But I thought I'd give it a try anyway."

"Why?" she asked. He shrugged and she didn't push for a response.

"So, has the morning sickness completely passed?" he asked after another short silence, and she made a noncommittal sound that he could interpret any way he wanted. He lifted his eyes to hers and something in his expression made her sigh and shake her head.

"Not completely, no . . ." she admitted. "But it's a lot better than it was before."

"What are your plans for today?" he asked, keeping his eyes glued on hers.

"I was going to spend the morning with Lisa and the baby." Lisa had given birth to a beautiful son just a couple of days after Theresa had had her own pregnancy confirmed.

"Mind if I tag along?" he asked casually, and she frowned, disturbed by the notion of her husband "tagging along" with her all morning.

"Well . . ." she began reluctantly.

"I wanted to discuss some business with Elisa," he added.

"What business?" she asked flatly.

"It's about her loan," he elaborated.

"*What* about her loan?" Her voice rose in alarm, but his face remained impassive. "I won't have you upsetting her, Sandro."

"Well, I either tell her today, while you're there as moral support, or I tell her sometime when she's alone and vulnerable." He shrugged casually.

"What are you going to tell her?" she asked in a panic.

"I don't believe that's any of your business, Theresa," he dismissed. "Now why don't you hop into the shower while I clean up down here? I'll use one of the guest bathrooms this morning."

She shook her head desperately.

"Sandro, you can't do this . . ."

"Well, I have no aversion to doing a bit of housecleaning," he said, deliberately misunderstanding.

"You *know* that's not what I meant," she hissed, and he cultivated a baffled frown that completely infuriated her.

"Well, if you have a problem with me using a guest bathroom, then I have to tell you, I certainly don't mind sharing a shower with you." He grinned lasciviously, and she made an angry sound in the back of her throat before turning on her heel and stalking off with her head held high.

~

She refused to talk to him for the duration of the drive to Rick and Lisa's home. It was only as he slid the car through their security gates that she turned toward him.

"Sandro, please don't do this," she begged, her beautiful eyes pleading for mercy. The stony expression on his face went even grimmer, and he reached out a blunt forefinger to gently trace the delicate line of her jaw before turning away from her and getting out of the car. She was devastated by his lack of response and climbed out when he came around to open the door for her. He took her hand but she tensed and tried to drag her hand out of his grip. For a moment, when his hand tightened around hers, she didn't think he would allow it, but after a few moments he reluctantly released her. He placed a hand in the small of her rigid back and steered her toward the front steps, which led up to the house.

Lisa had been expecting her and was waiting in the doorway with a huge smile on her face. She still retained the few kilograms that she had picked up during her pregnancy, but she radiated happiness and good health. She greeted Theresa effusively, enveloping her in a warm hug, and spared a slight smile for Sandro, who loomed above both of them.

"Alessandro, what a surprise." She nodded politely. "I didn't expect to see you today."

"I took the day off," he responded. "And when I heard Theresa was coming for a visit, I thought I'd come along with her and see that baby of yours again." *Again?* Theresa wasn't aware that Sandro had troubled himself to see the baby before now, and she frowned in confusion, wondering why Lisa hadn't mentioned it to her. "Also, I had some business I needed to discuss with you." Theresa tensed at the last bit, but Lisa smiled and nodded, making Theresa wish that she had called ahead to warn her cousin of the impending disaster.

Why would Sandro do this now? When he was getting everything he could possibly want? What merit was there in destroying Lisa's business? She looked up into his relaxed face and wondered if she could have misread the situation. But what other business could he possibly have to discuss with her cousin?

Lisa led them into the house and Sandro immediately gravitated toward the three-month-old baby who was seated in a blue baby seat placed on the living room's coffee table. His entire face seemed to light up at the sight of the infant, and Theresa watched in fascination as he sank to his haunches until his face was level with the baby's.

"He's grown a fair bit since I saw him last," Sandro observed in delight, reaching out to grab one of the infant's flailing hands.

"Well, I should hope so since he never stops eating." Lisa grimaced and Sandro laughed. Theresa took a step back, feeling like she'd just stepped into some alternate universe. Sandro was crooning down at little Rhys in Italian, and the baby was staring up at him raptly, his green eyes unblinking. "Would either of you like something to drink?" Lisa asked politely, and Theresa shook her head numbly, watching while Sandro nimbly undid the straps of the baby seat and lifted the infant into his arms.

"Coffee would be nice." He nodded, rocking the baby soothingly. Rhys made an uncoordinated grab for Sandro's hair and managed to latch on to a tiny fistful of it. Sandro grimaced good-naturedly and said something admonishing to the baby in Italian as he reached up to loosen the baby's grip. Lisa excused herself to go to the kitchen, but Theresa barely heard her, she was too busy watching her husband with the baby.

"I didn't know you liked children," she whispered, one of her hands absently dropping to her still-flat belly in a protective gesture that he couldn't miss.

"I like babies well enough," he murmured casually. "I am quite fond of them actually." She tried to disguise the stab of pain at his words.

"Any baby except mine, of course," she murmured half under her breath, and he inhaled impatiently, his eyes flaring with fury that he kept contained because of the baby in his arms.

"If you're going to be making asinine comments like that, please make them when I have both hands free to throttle the life out of you," he said in the most personable, baby-friendly voice he could manage. He sat down on the sofa still holding Rhys in his arms. Feeling a flare of possessive resentment, Theresa made her way over to him and held out her arms for the baby.

"I would like to hold my cousin's baby, if you don't mind," she informed coldly, and he raised one arrogant brow before standing up and gently depositing the serene baby into her arms. She sat down gingerly in the chair farthest away from the sofa and cooed at the sweet baby she held. Sandro stood up and stretched.

"While you're busy in here, I think I'll go and have that chat with Elisa."

Theresa looked up in alarm, but he was smiling gently down at her, his eyes warm with some emotion she had a hard time defining. "Sandro," she began quietly.

"You stay in here with Rhys," he murmured softly. "I don't want you getting upset by anything Lisa and I may have to say to each other." Before she could utter another word of protest he was gone. Theresa got up nervously, holding the baby to her chest. Much as she tried to, she could not hear a single sound coming from the direction of the kitchen. She left the living room and slowly inched her way toward the kitchen. She was just outside the slightly ajar door when the sounds of their quiet voices finally reached her.

"But I don't understand why?" Lisa was asking, sounding baffled but not upset. "I still have at least a year within which to finish the loan. It's a substantial amount of money, Sandro, so I don't understand why you would do this." Theresa bit her lip, wanting to intervene but not sure how anything she could say or do would persuade Sandro to change his mind. She felt helpless and furious and strangely hurt that he would carry out his threat anyway.

"It's my only real option right now, Lisa." Sandro's deep voice rumbled quietly. "I gave you the loan for all the wrong reasons. Reasons which I now . . . regret. I can't in good conscience allow it to continue."

"So let me *pay* it, and we can put it behind us," Lisa implored, and Sandro said something that Theresa didn't quite catch.

"Sandro, this is crazy." Lisa was starting to sound upset, and Theresa braced herself, preparing to enter the fray come hell or high water. Sandro's next words cut her short, though.

"Elisa, please, you have to let me do this." He sounded desperate.

"It doesn't feel right," Lisa said, and Theresa frowned in confusion. What on earth was going on here?

"I've drawn up the papers, so it's practically a done deal." His voice rang with finality.

"I have to think about it and discuss it with Rick, of course," Lisa said softly.

"Of course," Sandro agreed amicably, and realizing that their conversation was at an end, Theresa very quickly made her way back to the living room. She was back in the chair and gently rocking a contentedly gurgling Rhys when the other two appeared. She sat up abruptly, her wide eyes flying from one face to the other. They both looked relaxed and neither face revealed much. Sandro placed the tray that he was holding onto the coffee table and sat down on the same sofa he'd occupied earlier. Lisa sat down next to him and busied herself with the tray, placing a tall glass of orange juice on the coffee table in front of Theresa.

"Don't argue," Sandro intervened when she opened her mouth to protest. "It's good for you." He helped himself to the coffee while he and Lisa proceeded to chat like old friends. Theresa sat there seething, hating to be so thoroughly excluded.

"I'm sorry I couldn't join you yesterday, Theresa," Lisa suddenly said. "How did your checkup go?" Theresa glared at her cousin for bringing up the topic in front of Sandro, who sat up and watched her like a hawk as he waited for her response.

"It was okay," she murmured awkwardly.

"What did he say about the dizzy spells?" Lisa asked, and Theresa was aware of Sandro tensing up like a coiled spring at the question.

"Nothing important," she responded evasively, keeping her eyes on the baby in her arms.

"*What* dizzy spells?" Sandro suddenly asked in a dangerous voice.

"She's been feeling faint for most of the last two months," Lisa helpfully informed, and Theresa gritted her teeth.

"And you didn't think to tell me?" Sandro snapped.

"I didn't think you'd care," Theresa muttered miserably, and Sandro swore beneath his breath.

"She didn't think I'd *care*," he repeated incredulously. "Oh my God, Theresa, you simply assumed that I would not care about something that directly impacts your health and the baby's well-being?"

"Of course, I *know* you'd care if anything happens to the baby, but I didn't want to worry you about something that I know is not a big deal."

"And how do you know that? Did you obtain a degree in medicine sometime over the last three months? Of course I've seen you so rarely lately that you could have gotten a degree in quantum physics and I wouldn't have known!"

Lisa choked back an irreverent giggle, and both Theresa and Sandro glared at her.

"Sandro, I can take care of the baby and myself. You needn't worry about it. Your responsibility toward me, *us*, is at an end," she reminded.

"We're still married," he pointed out. "And I think *I'll* decide when and where my responsibility toward you and the baby will end. From now on, you will keep me fully apprised of what's going on with your health."

"No," she maintained stubbornly. "It's none of your business. You made it clear that the only reason you ever wanted me to get pregnant was so you could escape from this marriage, so why don't you leave me alone while I attempt, *once again*, to do everything in my power to make you happy?"

"The only thing that would make me happy right now, you stubborn redheaded little cat, is if you would actually do as you're told for a change!"

"I'm *sick* of doing as I'm told, and I'm sick of being your obedient little lapdog. I was happy without your interference in my life these last few months, so I refuse to go back to the way it was before."

"I don't want to go back to that either," he unexpectedly conceded. "We didn't have a real marriage before."

"You can't possibly be telling me that you want a real marriage now?" she scoffed.

"What if I am?" he asked warily, and she laughed in his face.

"I'd think you were insane to believe that I'd want anything to do with it. How can a marriage with a life span of just six more months possibly be beneficial to either of us?"

"It wouldn't . . . but that's not what I want."

"Oh, it's always about what *you* want, isn't it? Well, I have news for you, Sandro . . ." She was still holding the now-sleeping baby to her chest and glowering furiously at the tall man seated opposite her, oblivious to her cousin, who sat watching the scene unfold in absolute fascination. "I don't give one damn about what you want. *I* don't want to stay married to you . . . *I* want my life back and *I* want you gone as soon as your contract with my father has been fulfilled."

The silence was absolutely deafening. Finally, after what seemed like ages, Sandro leaned back in his chair and shook his head slightly.

"We'll still be together until the baby is born," he acknowledged wearily. "Up until then, I want daily updates on your health. I don't want to be excluded from any bit of news no matter how trivial you may think it is."

"I don't understand what you'd hope to gain from such an arrangement," she said, confused and frustrated by how adamant he was being on this point.

"Absolutely nothing," he murmured. "But what do *you* stand to gain by keeping me out of the loop?"

Absolutely nothing, and he knew it; she had no reason other than pure bitchiness to refuse his request.

"Fine," she said begrudgingly. "I'll keep you updated but I want your word that you won't interfere in any part of my pregnancy and that you'll remain a casual observer."

"How can you expect me to make a promise like that?" he asked hoarsely. "I am *not* a casual observer, Theresa! I have a vested interest in both you and the baby."

"You signed away your rights to us before you ever had us," she reminded bitterly, and he flinched slightly at her words. "And you seem to expect me to not only forget that little fact but forgive it too? Sandro . . . I will *never* forgive you."

"I thought you understood what an untenable situation I was in." He shook his head angrily.

"I understand and I sympathize, but that does not change the fact that the person I thought I loved, the man I married in good faith, *never* existed. I just don't think I'll ever be able to get past that, Sandro."

He sighed heavily.

"Fair enough," he conceded. "But we need to make the best of this situation in the meantime and living like strangers in the same house isn't the best solution."

"Fine," she whispered reluctantly. "What do you suggest?"

"I would like to be present at your doctor's appointments," he said after a long pause, and she hesitated, slanting a helpless glance at her cousin, who shrugged slightly.

"Why?"

"Peace of mind," he responded succinctly, and she frowned, trying to think about it from all angles before sighing quietly.

"Fine, but your opinions and input are not encouraged or desired. So you'll be there as just an observer, a *silent* observer. I will manage my own health and pregnancy."

His jaw clenched in displeasure, but he kept his mouth shut and nodded reluctantly. "I also think . . ." His voice was slightly hoarse and he paused to clear his throat before continuing. "I also think that living in the same house and never seeing each other is, well . . .

ridiculous, actually. Please stop disappearing when you know I'm home. It makes me feel like a monster, knowing that you're cowering away in some corner of the house because you're afraid to face me." He couldn't have chosen better words to get her back up, and she bristled furiously.

"I do *not* cower," she seethed, barely aware of the amused look he exchanged with her cousin.

"It certainly feels that way to me," he responded. "I know that you find it difficult to be around me because of the *feelings* you once had for me . . ."

She gasped in outrage.

". . . And I also know that with the attraction between us, you're probably afraid the chemistry will flare up and we'll wind up in bed again. I mean it's fairly obvious how much you want me but . . ."

"I . . . you . . ." She was absolutely furious with him for bringing up their sex life in front of her cousin and appalled to discover that he thought she was hiding from him. Like some timid little rabbit. Okay, so maybe she *had* been hiding, but she had been doing it to keep both of them comfortable with the awkwardness of the situation. "Oh my God, the colossal ego on you! I'm not cowering or hiding or anything like that. I just can't stand to be around you."

"Of course you'd say that now." He shrugged dismissively and she gasped again, furiously rocking little Rhys back and forth as she desperately tried to find a suitably scathing response to his words.

"Anyway," Sandro murmured, "I was going to suggest we start having breakfast and dinner together again. No point in having separate meals."

"Fine," she snapped grudgingly.

"And can we try to be civil?" he asked pseudo-meekly. "Have a decent conversation while we're having our meals?"

Her eyes snapped but she merely nodded, silently telling herself that it would be for just six more months.

"Anything else?" she asked sarcastically, her tone of voice definitely not inviting any more of his "suggestions," but he chose to take her question at face value.

"Yes . . ." He nodded. "The Friday night gang was wondering where you'd disappeared to. The ladies were disappointed when you didn't come again." She said nothing, she couldn't do it . . . she quite simply *wouldn't* do it.

"I-I can't," she admitted softly. "They're *your* friends, and when we divorce . . . well, they'll still be *your* friends. I don't want to form ties with people when I know exactly how temporary the relationships will be. I can't keep saying good-bye to people I care about."

He swallowed before nodding slightly.

"Then one last request," he murmured, leaning toward her intently.

"What?"

"Two hours." His voice had dropped to a husky whisper.

"What does that . . . ?"

"In the evenings."

"Two hours for what?"

"Just to . . ." His face clenched in frustration and he shrugged helplessly. "Spend together. Talk, watch a movie, read, sit . . . anything, as long as we spend it together."

"But that's . . . I don't understand why you'd want that?"

"Please." The word, soft and pleading, stayed the rejection hovering on the tip of her tongue.

"Two hours, three times a week," she found herself stipulating against her better judgment. Still, enforcing some kind of restriction on his request made her feel like she had some measure of control over the way things were going. He nodded eagerly.

"Name the days," he invited, and she nibbled at the lower lip, giving it some serious thought.

"Mondays, Tuesdays, and Thursdays." She deliberately chose his busiest office days, the days he often trudged home much later than usual, hoping that it would force him to cancel a lot of the time. His sharp eyes told her he knew exactly why she had chosen those days, but he grinned and nodded.

"Fine with me," he acquiesced, and she sat back feeling like she'd been manipulated somehow. Lisa reached out to take Rhys from Theresa.

"I'll just put this little one to bed," the other woman said quietly, and Theresa nodded numbly. She felt completely drained and looked it too. Sandro sat down on the sofa and leaned toward her, very gently nudging the glass of orange juice in her direction again. She shot him a warning glance, and he grinned slightly.

"I'm not trying to bully you into drinking a glass of orange juice, Theresa," he said softly. "I just thought that you looked a bit parched." She gritted her teeth and sheer perversity kept her from picking up the glass and quenching her thirst. He said nothing further, merely leaned back in his chair with a soft sigh.

"So what did the doctor *really* say yesterday?" he asked after a pause.

"I'm slightly anemic and that's what's causing the dizziness. He adjusted my diet to include more iron," she responded quietly, and he nodded.

"Everything else is normal?" he asked after another short pause.

"Yes."

"You'd tell me if it wasn't?"

"Yes."

He seemed satisfied with her answer and smiled slightly. "Thank you."

She sighed and nodded an acknowledgment of his thanks. She leaned over to pick up the glass of orange juice, conceding that her childishness would achieve nothing, and took a thirsty sip. Fortunately he made no comment and his expression remained neutral. Again there was silence, and this time it lasted until Lisa returned. Things were surprisingly amicable after that, and Theresa and Sandro left about forty minutes later.

On the way home, she asked him about his private talk with Lisa, but he refused to be drawn into a conversation on the subject, and Theresa eventually gave up in frustration.

The following month sped by. Theresa and Sandro's new arrangement worked well, their meals together were civil, even pleasant, and her doctor's appointments were less of an ordeal with Sandro's silent support. He kept his end of the bargain, merely observing and never interfering. Still, just *having* him there made such a difference to Theresa's sense of well-being.

What surprised Theresa the most was how much she was enjoying the time together that he had requested. Contrary to her expectations, he hadn't cancelled once. Instead he came home earlier than usual on the designated nights. Sometimes they simply sat side by side in the den, sharing a bowl of popcorn and watching a movie, rarely saying much. Sometimes they would play Scrabble and Theresa usually enjoyed those nights very much. It wasn't often she got to beat Sandro at anything, and to his profound horror he was appalling at Scrabble. He blamed his lack of prowess on the fact that English wasn't his native language, but he approached every rematch with a never-say-die determination. Unfortunately said determination hadn't yet resulted in a victory for him, and Theresa was delighted by the fact that she was a better player than he was.

Despite his lack of skill, he played hard and often had her in stitches with his creative spelling and blatantly made-up words. They also had an ongoing chess rivalry and were a lot more evenly matched at that game. Theresa soon discovered that she was starting to look forward to those three nights a week and hated the fact that he was insidiously creeping beneath her defenses again. Unfortunately, much like a car accident, she could see it coming but couldn't seem to find a way to prevent the inevitable disaster from occurring. She was always very strict about the time, trying hard to maintain some kind of control over the situation and whatever they were doing, unfinished or not, had to stop exactly two hours after it had started. They usually picked up where they had left off the next time anyway.

"No," Theresa insisted adamantly one night, during one of their aggressive Scrabble games; they were sitting on the floor with the board placed on the low coffee table between them. "I totally challenge that word! *Lexiquon* is not a word, Sandro, and you know it."

"Of course it is." He nodded blithely. "You're challenging it because you don't want me to have the bonus points and the two triple word scores."

"Of course I don't," she agreed scathingly. "Two hundred and seventy-five points for a made-up word? *Never* going to happen! I'm not running a charity here." He grinned boyishly at that, and she averted her eyes, trying very hard not to be charmed by him. Finally he grumbled good-naturedly and removed his tiles from the board.

"Maybe it's a *French* word," he muttered defensively, and she rolled her eyes.

"Well, feel free to use it the next time you play a Frenchman!" He laughed outright at that, and she caught her breath at the carefree sound. Every day he relaxed more and more around her and she often sensed that he wanted to extend their time together. He contemplated the board again, muttering to himself in Italian and stroking his jaw thoughtfully as he considered his next move. Eventually he settled on "eel," which was so badly placed that it was worth only three points. She snorted disdainfully while taking down his meager points and then smiled sweetly up at him, while pointing out the free "t" that he could have used for the word "exit." She then went on to gleefully use that "t" for her own word, making use of the conveniently situated triple-word score in the process and amassing a handy thirty-nine points for "smithy."

"What *is* this word?" he growled. "Names aren't allowed!" She couldn't help but giggle at his outrage before whipping out a definition of the word for him. He glared down at the dictionary before grumbling to himself in Italian again and going back to studying the board. Theresa smiled slightly to herself, noting the way his hair slid forward over his forehead and just dying to brush it back; she hid her hands beneath the table and clenched her fists to quell the unreasonable impulse.

"I know that it's early days yet, but I've been thinking about decorating the nursery," she said just to get her mind off her crazy desire to touch him. Her words caught his attention and he looked up with an unguarded smile.

"That's a terrific idea." He nodded eagerly. "We could go shopping for furniture and toys, I saw this *huge* panda bear at a toy shop a week ago that would be perfect for a baby." His enthusiastic response completely threw her and she stared at him blankly for a few moments.

"A toy shop?" she asked, and he went slightly red.

"There's one close to the office and I've visited it a couple of times during my lunch hour," he admitted. "Just to see what kind of toys and things babies need these days."

Theresa had no clue how she was supposed to respond to that. Should she be concerned that he seemed to be taking more than a casual interest in the baby or should she be pleased? And how on earth was she supposed to react to his assumption that they would be decorating the nursery *together*? Her emotions were in such turmoil that in the end, she said nothing and shoved it aside to be processed later. Sandro, sensing the shift in her mood and seeming to recognize that he'd said too much, lapsed into an uncomfortable silence and toyed with one of his tiles.

"I'm feeling a little tired. I may just head up to bed," she suddenly said, and he looked up in resentment.

"I still have an hour left," he pointed out bitterly, and she bit her lip nervously.

"Yes, you do," she finally said, and gestured toward the board. "It's your move." His eyes glimmered with some indefinable emotion before he shook his head and got up.

"You're not my prisoner, Theresa. If you're tired go to bed," he said wearily, shoving his hands into the pockets of his tailored business suit trousers and totally ruining the cut of the expensive garment.

"Far be it from me to renege on a bargain," she maintained, remaining stubbornly seated, even though she would have liked nothing better than to flee.

"You're being so goddamned childish," he seethed, and turned to leave the room before she had a chance to retaliate. She sat there for a few minutes before she acknowledged that he really wasn't coming back. It was the first time in more than a month that they'd had any kind of serious dispute, and Theresa regretted that. She knew that she *had* been childish, because she hadn't known of any other way to deal with her emotions. She sighed, acknowledging that she needed to apologize to him, and pushed herself up from the plush heated carpet, thinking that it was best to get it over with as soon as possible.

She headed toward his study, and as she approached the slightly ajar door, she realized that he was speaking to someone in a low voice. Not wanting to intrude on his telephone call, her steps slowed slightly and she turned around to head toward the kitchen for a small snack. She was just about to walk away when she heard him groan huskily before saying, "Francesca . . ." in a quiet and intense voice. The single word was enough to freeze Theresa in her tracks. Sandro was still talking in that low voice, his words, which were in Italian, sounding more urgent. Theresa took a step toward the study's open door, and his voice became slightly clearer, even though he was murmuring intimately.

". . . Francesca, *cara* . . ." were two of the incriminating words she could understand amid the torrent of Italian, and she bit her lip uncertainly, not sure if he was talking *to* Francesca or about her. God, why hadn't she learned more Italian? Right now she understood just enough to make her miserable with jealousy and pain. After hearing the woman's name for the first time so many months ago, Theresa had tried to put her out of her mind. Knowing nothing about her, it had seemed wisest not to speculate for fear of having her imagination run wild. Now, she wished she had done some research on this Francesca, even though having only one name to go on would have made it difficult, and Theresa wasn't *about* to ask her father or Sandro for details about the mystery woman.

Sandro was oblivious to her presence outside his study door as he continued his low-voiced conversation, and Theresa understood only a few random words that meant little to her. He kept using endearments, though; *those* she knew very well because he'd frequently resorted to them while having sex with her. She had often wondered if that had been his way of depersonalizing the act even further since he had rarely used her name during their most intimate moments. She hovered outside her husband's study door, much like she had been hovering on the outskirts of his life for nearly two years, before turning away and heading back upstairs. She had showered, changed for bed, and had long since turned off her bedroom lights when she eventually heard his light tread on the staircase. She held her breath when he paused, as he *always* did, outside her door but instead of feeling the usual relief when he moved on a few moments later, this time Theresa turned her face into her pillow and cried herself to sleep.

CHAPTER SEVEN

I won't be able to go to the doctor with you today, Theresa," Sandro informed Theresa while they were breakfasting in the sunny conservatory the following morning. She would *never* have admitted it, but she had really been relying on having him there that day. She was in her sixteenth week of pregnancy and had been scheduled for a precautionary amniocentesis that day. She was a nervous wreck about the procedure and even though she knew the risk of complication was very low, it was still there. While her logical mind told her that her baby would be fine, she was still dreading the possible outcome of the test. Sandro had been a rock during her first ultrasound the month before, holding her hand while he listened to the whooshing sound of their baby's heartbeat for the first time and squeezing it tightly when they had seen of the fragile fluttering on the black-and-white monitor. The doctor hadn't been able to determine the baby's sex but Theresa was confident that it was a boy and had said so. Sandro had remained quiet during the entire procedure but he had been a comfort to her.

"Why not?" she asked casually.

"I have to go to Italy next week and I have a lot to finish at the office before I leave," he informed her tightly, and she lowered her eyes back to her plate.

"Is your father okay?" she asked softly, and he hesitated before responding.

"Yes. My visit is unrelated to any family business."

She shut her eyes in pain, suddenly *knowing* that he was going because of that phone call last night. "Okay." She nodded, battling to sound nonchalant. "It's just . . . I'm getting the amniocentesis today." He swore quietly beneath his breath.

"I'm sorry, Theresa," he murmured, seeming almost stricken by the news. "I completely forgot."

And *that*, of course, brought the major problem with their marriage into sharp relief. She had been worrying about the procedure, stressing about possible complications, and terrified of the slight risk of miscarriage it presented. She had suffered through sleepless nights thinking about the birth or genetic defects the results could reveal while her *husband* had simply forgotten about the test. Of course, she would never reveal just how much she had depended on having his solid and stoically silent presence there, so she shrugged carelessly.

"I'm sure Lisa will go with me." She nodded confidently, and his eyes shone with relief.

"That's a great idea," he enthused. "I'll be at your next appointment. I'll only be gone for a week or so. I'll be back before you know it."

"I'll be fine," she dismissed airily, digging into her scrambled eggs like someone who didn't have a care in the world. There was an awkward silence while he watched her eat, but Theresa very determinedly kept her head down while she scooped the eggs into her mouth with as much gusto as she could manage without choking.

"I don't want you to be alone while I'm gone." He breached the uncomfortable silence, and Theresa frowned at his words, looking up at him with her laden fork lifted halfway to her mouth.

"I won't be alone. Rick and Lisa are always around and the staff is ever-present." As if to prove her words, Phumsile entered the room carrying a plateful of pancakes, which she deposited in front of Theresa with a challenging look.

"Eat it all," the woman commanded.

"It's quite a lot of food, Phumsile." Theresa stared at the pile of pancakes in dismay, but Phumsile crossed her arms over her ample chest and glared at Theresa, looking for all the world like she was prepared to stand right there to ensure that Theresa ate every morsel. Phumsile made no secret of the fact that she thought Theresa was way too skinny for a pregnant woman and had taken it upon herself to ensure that Theresa ate healthily. Theresa secretly suspected the older woman of being in cahoots with Sandro—a suspicion that was now backed up by the approving little nod he gave Phumsile before he avoided Theresa's eyes.

"It's not all for you," Phumsile pointed out. "It's also for your baby. You don't eat enough. Stop wasting my food and eat everything on this plate." On that note of insubordination, she swept back out of the room.

"You'd better finish every scrap, *cara*. You don't want to get on Phumsile's bad side," he said with a little grin, putting their former discussion on hold for the moment.

"You're all ganging up on me," Theresa accused him, and he shook his head.

"We're taking care of you, we're concerned about you, and that's why I want you to stay with your cousin while I'm gone."

"No." She went back to her eggs but also helped herself to a pancake, really not wanting to incur Phumsile's wrath. The silence seethed from the other end of the table.

"I insist."

"No." She didn't even bother meeting his eyes this time.

"Theresa, you're being very difficult." He kept his voice level and patient.

"And you're being unreasonable," she snapped, glaring at him. "Rick and Lisa have a new baby. I will visit them regularly, and I have no doubt they will come around here, but for me to *stay* there? That's just ridiculous. I won't intrude and I don't need a minder; I'm perfectly capable of taking care of myself."

"What if something goes wrong? What if you need help in the middle of the night and no one's around?"

"Why don't you just *stay* home if you're so concerned?" she retorted furiously and immediately wished the words back when his scrutiny turned speculative.

"Would you like me to stay home?" he asked quietly.

"It makes no difference what I want," was her mutinous response.

"Of course it does," he placated gently. "I'd stay if you wanted me to."

"What about your *important* business?" she asked sarcastically.

"You're more important," he said softly.

"You mean the *baby* I'm carrying is more important?" she corrected, and his jaw clenched.

"No, that's not what I meant," he maintained patiently, and she blinked before shaking her head.

"You're trying to confuse me," she complained, frowning at him, and he grinned.

"Not at all, sweetheart," he murmured. "I'm just trying to be honest with you."

"Well, stop it, I don't believe anything you say anymore," she hissed, and pushed herself away from the table. He sighed before getting up as well.

"You didn't answer my question," he had the nerve to prompt, and her glare deepened until she looked like a bad-tempered child.

"No, I want you to go off and take care of whatever *business* you have in Italy. I would hate to keep you from something important, only to have it thrown back in my face at a later date." His jaw clenched at her vitriolic words, but he didn't respond. She got up abruptly, sick of the conversation and the company.

"Excuse me, I have to get ready for my appointment," she snapped, turning to leave the room.

"I still want you to stay with your cousin while I'm gone," he insisted, directing his words to her narrow back as she retreated from the room.

"And I still say no to that," she threw over her shoulder.

"This subject is far from closed, Theresa." He raised his voice slightly as she moved farther away from him, but she waved dismissively as she turned a corner that she knew would take her out of his sight. Once she got to her bedroom, she sank down onto the bed and inhaled shakily, feeling drained.

Lisa was unable to join her for the amniocentesis; Rhys had a medical checkup and naturally that took priority. So Theresa found herself waiting alone, a nervous wreck even though she knew that the odds of anything going wrong were slim. She fidgeted, flipped through magazines, and chatted with other women in various stages of pregnancy, but through it all she just wished that Sandro was there with her. The other women were all accompanied by their partners or friends, and Theresa had never felt so achingly alone before. She was so deeply buried in her thoughts that she didn't even notice the person sitting down next to her until her husband's deep voice rumbled in her ear.

"Why is your cell phone off? I've been trying to reach you all morning."

She jumped in fright before blinking up at him stupidly, not quite sure how he came to be there. He grinned down into her confused face and Theresa found herself responding helplessly to the open warmth of that smile, rewarding him with a blinding one of her own.

"What are you doing here?" she asked breathlessly, and he shrugged.

"When I couldn't reach you, I tried Lisa, and when she told me that she was at the clinic with Rhys, I knew that you were probably here all alone and thought you might need some moral support," he explained.

"B-but what about your work?"

"It'll keep."

"You didn't have to come, I was okay on my own," she felt obligated to protest.

"Theresa, you visibly paled every time the mention of this appointment came up. It's obvious that you find the thought of this procedure daunting. I couldn't let you face it on your own." So much for thinking that she had kept her fear and reservations well hidden from him. He seemed able to read her like an open book.

"I'm not *really* scared," she said with more bravado than conviction, and he determinedly bit back the smile that was curling up the sides of his mouth.

"*You* might not be but I am terrified, *cara*." He shuddered slightly. "Needles, *big* needles especially, are not my thing." She could tell by the way he whitened that he was sincere. She stared into his eyes for the longest time, getting lost in the melting chocolate depths before shaking herself slightly.

"Thank you for coming, Sandro," she whispered. "I *was* a bit intimidated at the thought of this procedure." The confession cost a lot but she was rewarded by the warm, intimate smile he directed at her.

"It'll be fine," he assured quietly, unexpectedly linking his fingers with hers. "You'll see." Even though there was no logical reason for it, her reservations melted like ice under the hot sun and she smiled gratefully.

In the end, Theresa sailed through the procedure. After some initial discomfort she was fine, but it was Sandro who had difficulty with the process. Apparently he hadn't been lying when he had said that he didn't like big needles. When he saw the needle, he swayed enough for an alarmed nurse to hurriedly bring a stool over for him to sit on. He thanked her but manfully chose to stand instead. That macho display of coolness lasted only long enough for them to insert the needle into her abdomen, at which point he paled dramatically and practically collapsed onto the provided stool. From that point onward he kept his eyes determinedly away from the needle and on Theresa's amused face.

"Once, when I was ten," she started talking to distract him, "I fell out of a tree." That certainly caught his attention.

"What were you doing in a tree?" He sounded skeptical. "You don't strike me as the tomboy type."

"I wasn't but there was this poor little kitten stuck up there and I was a complete sucker for animals." She shrugged and winced slightly when the needle pinched more. His hand tightened around hers, while the doctor cheerfully informed them that it was "nearly over."

"So what happened?" he asked softly.

"Well, Lisa was with me and she was desperately trying to reason with me but I wouldn't listen." She shook her head. "Sometimes I can be a bit stubborn."

He snorted. "*No!* Really?"

She tilted her chin up and chose to ignore his sarcasm. "Just as I was leaning out and reaching for that stupid cat, he hissed at me, scratched my hand, and climbed back down." She felt the pinching sensation gradually decrease as the needle was withdrawn from her abdomen. "But the cat had scared me and I lost my balance before tumbling out of the tree."

"What happened after that?" He seemed riveted even though the doctor was stepping away from the table.

"I broke my arm and I've disliked cats since that day," she confessed sheepishly. He chuckled before unexpectedly leaning over her and dropping a quick kiss on her forehead. "I don't know why I just told you that story. You just looked in desperate need of distraction."

"And how," he acknowledged shakily. "I'm still feeling a little queasy after seeing that needle." He swallowed and paled again. "I don't know how you could do that without anesthetic."

The doctor had offered her a shot to numb the area but one huge needle was bad enough, Theresa hadn't been enamored with the thought of having to deal with two.

"It was a little uncomfortable," she admitted as the nurse helped her sit up. "But not too bad."

After dressing, she and Sandro anxiously faced her obstetrician across the wide expanse of his desk.

"That went very well, Mr. and Mrs. De Lucci." Doctor Shelbourne beamed over his desk at them. "Both you and your baby came through it with flying colors. Right. So for the next two days, I want you to do no heavy lifting, no sex, and no flying. Try to relax and don't overtax yourself. You may experience some cramping for a day or two but that's normal. If you do have cramping and it carries on for too long or is too severe, come in immediately. Especially if it's accompanied by spotting or bleeding." Both Sandro and Theresa flinched at the dire warning. Theresa instinctively sought out his hand with hers.

"We should have your results in a couple of weeks," the older man continued cheerfully. "We'll contact you when they arrive."

"Do you think I'm at risk for another miscarriage?" Theresa suddenly asked, and the doctor looked surprised by her question.

"Not at all." He shook his head vehemently.

"But the last time . . ." she began shakily.

". . . was just one of those tragic things that sometimes happen in life. You're healthy and your baby looks healthy. There's absolutely no reason you shouldn't carry to term and deliver a perfect baby. Now onto happier topics; would you like to know the baby's sex?"

"You could tell?" Theresa asked with a smile.

"The image was as clear as a bell today." He nodded indulgently.

"No." Sandro shook his head. "I'd rather not know."

"But Sandro . . ." She turned to him in surprise but he refused to meet her eyes. "Why don't you want to know?"

"It makes no difference." *Nothing* he could have said would have hurt her more, and she immediately retreated back behind her shell, withdrawing her hand from his. Of course it didn't make a difference. If it was a boy, he would leave without getting to know the child, and if it was a girl, he would be stuck in his unwanted marriage for even longer. He groaned when he saw her expression and immediately grabbed her hand again. "I really didn't mean it the way you obviously think I did, Theresa."

"It's okay," she informed the doctor, who looked uncomfortable to be witnessing their dispute. "I don't have to know." Not when she was 100 percent certain that it was a boy anyway. The doctor nodded and cleared his throat.

"Very well then, my lips are sealed." He nodded, trying to maintain his jovial manner, even though it was evident he was still uncomfortable. Sandro said nothing, keeping his eyes on Theresa's determinedly averted face. The doctor added a few more of his usual cautions that she not overtax herself before he dismissed them with a hearty good-bye.

"Just let me explain," Sandro said the moment they were outside the clinic. It was raining and Theresa hurriedly raised the hood of her coat before scurrying for her car. He followed her even though she was still ignoring him and keeping her back to him. She fumbled for her car keys in her large bag and he groaned in frustration before dropping his hands onto her narrow shoulders to turn her around. Her face was wet, and he sighed deeply as he wiped at the moisture, not sure if it was tears or rain.

"I'm sorry," he whispered, lowering his head so that she could hear him over the clamor of cars driving by and the freezing rain. "Theresa, that didn't come out right. It didn't mean what you thought it did."

"What does it matter what I think?" she asked bitterly.

"It matters." His large hands cupped her face and he rested his forehead on hers. "It matters very much, Theresa."

"No." She shook her head slightly. "It doesn't." She put her hands to his broad chest, wanting to push him away, but the rain had soaked through his white shirt, plastering it to his skin and turning it so transparent that he may as well have been naked. So instead of pushing, her hands stroked and petted and he moaned hungrily before touching his lips to hers. Theresa didn't even pretend to fight. She melted into him and wrapped her arms around him. She dug her fingers into his back as she arched up against him and opened her mouth to his hot, demanding tongue. His hands were wrapped in her wet hair and he tugged her head back to gain better access to her mouth as his tongue hungrily probed at hers. He left not one inch of her mouth unexplored.

The sound of a car horn close by brought them to their senses, and they jumped apart guiltily, both flushed and breathing rapidly, both shaking uncontrollably. Theresa stared up into Sandro's dazed eyes and blinked at the vulnerability that she thought she saw there.

"I'm sorry that I hurt you," he murmured hoarsely, and she stared back at him uncomprehendingly.

"You were just being honest," she whispered, and his brows slammed together in a formidable frown.

"*No*! I mean . . . yes I was, but you misunderstood me." He sounded completely muddled, and Theresa stared up into him in wonder. She wasn't entirely sure what to make of this overly emotional man standing before her.

"So make me understand," she invited after a long and uncomfortable pause. He seemed shocked by the invitation and for a moment looked unable to respond.

"I meant that the baby's sex made no difference to me either way because I would love it regardless of what it was," he said in a rush, and she gaped up at him incredulously for a moment before placing both hands on his chest and pushing him away violently. He was taken by surprise and staggered back, nearly sprawling to the wet pavement before catching himself and finding his balance.

"*Why* would you say that? Why would you lie like that? I don't deserve it, Sandro. I haven't done anything to deserve any of this but you keep finding new and creative ways to hurt me." She went back to fumbling in her bag and finally found her keys.

"Don't try to pretend that you care," she hissed at him. "I know you don't. Five more months of this and you'll be free to go back to your *Francesca* and start your real life with a real wife and babies that you will *really* love!" He seemed stunned by her attack but her mention of Francesca brought his eyes sharply up to hers.

"What? You didn't think that I knew about your precious Francesca? The woman you love, the woman you wanted to marry before my father forced you into this sham? I know you see her every time you go back to Italy, just like I know you were speaking to her last night and will be going to her when you go back this week!" She was practically screaming now, frustrated by the way he just stood there. Like someone who'd been caught in a bomb blast, he looked dazed.

She was starting to feel strange, lightheaded and nauseous. She braced her hands on the roof of her car and tried to steady herself, aware that Sandro was moving toward her. His hands reached for her and she weakly tried to evade his grasp, but the movement made her even dizzier and she swayed slightly. Sandro's arms wrapped around her and she was too faint to really care.

"Theresa, *cara*. I'm here. You're okay . . ."

Those were the last desperate words she heard from her husband before everything went black.

"When I said she shouldn't overtax herself, I meant both physically and emotionally, Mr. De Lucci." Theresa heard the sharp admonishment in the slightly familiar voice and frowned as she tried to hear over the weird buzzing sound in her head. "What on earth were you thinking, upsetting her like this less than half an hour after the procedure she'd just been through?"

"Will she be okay?" Theresa heard Sandro's unusually subdued voice over the rapidly subsiding buzz and she wondered at the strange panicky edge in it.

"She bled a little, which is never a good sign. I'm not willing to take any chances, not after this. I want her to remain in bed for at *least* a week. Complete bed rest."

"I can't stay in bed all week," Theresa protested, opening her eyes. Sandro surged forward to grab one of her limp hands.

"*Theresa*, thank God! How are you feeling?"

"Like I was hit by a bus," she admitted shakily, lifting her eyes to the doctor, who stood on the other side of the cot. "My baby? Is he all right?"

"Your baby's just fine. In fact the baby is doing a hell of a lot better than you are right now, Mrs. De Lucci. I want you to stay in bed for a week; you are to do *nothing*, is that understood?"

"I take it that I am allowed bathroom breaks?" she asked sarcastically.

"You can get as snippy as you like with me, young lady, but if you want a healthy, full-term baby, you will do what I say! Or I will be forced to hospitalize you to ensure that you get the prescribed bed rest."

"She'll do what you've ordered, doctor," Sandro assured grimly, and Theresa bit her lip and nodded. She wouldn't risk her baby's life out of sheer perversity.

"Right," the doctor seemed satisfied. "I'd like to keep her here overnight. Tomorrow, you may take her home and try to get beyond the parking lot this time." With that final admonishment, he turned and left the room, grumbling under his breath as he did so. Theresa and Sandro watched as the door swung shut behind him before turning to face each other awkwardly.

"I'm sorry," they blurted simultaneously after a long pause.

"Why are *you* sorry?" Sandro asked in confusion, dragging up a chair and sitting down beside the bed, still clutching her hand like it was a life preserver and he a drowning man.

"I shouldn't have brought up your private life like that. What you do after we split up is none of my business and after . . . after everything my father has done to you, I honestly believe that you deserve the happiness you'll find with the woman you love. I didn't mean to eavesdrop on your conversation with her last night, either; it was an accident." He looked so confused by her words that she paused.

"What conversation?" he asked.

"With Francesca?" Theresa was no longer so sure of what she had heard and the words emerged on a questioning note. "Last night, after Scrabble, you were on the phone with her?"

"No, I was on the phone with my sister, Isabella, and Francesca's name came up in conversation. Isabella can be a little *insistent* on the topic of Francesca, and I was getting a bit frustrated with her. I've never called Francesca from our home, Theresa. In fact, I rarely speak to her when I'm not in Italy."

"Oh." She obviously needed to learn more Italian. She didn't doubt that he'd spoken to his sister—not when he was so determined to be apologetic. His words had an unmistakable ring of sincerity to them, yet she couldn't *quite* bring herself to believe that last statement about rarely speaking to Francesca. It just seemed too good to be true.

"Anyway," she continued, deciding to let the subject of Francesca go for now. "I'm sorry for overreacting like a hysterical fishwife earlier; I just I got so *angry* after what you said. I don't need empty platitudes, Sandro. You don't have to say anything to make me feel better about our situation. You really don't have to pretend to care about me or about the baby." He swore shakily before lifting her hand and resting his forehead on the back of it.

"What an unholy mess I've made of things," he said, half laughing, his voice sounding strained. "Nothing I say now will ever make a difference to how you feel, will it? Everything I try to say or do will come across as desperate and insincere."

"What I don't get is why you're still trying?" she whispered in confusion, watching his bowed head intently. "You've won. You have everything you want within your grasp, the vineyard and freedom. Yet you keep trying, coming to me with all of these demands to be involved in my life. Why?"

"Why don't we just let it go for now?" He lifted his head to meet her eyes, his own brown gaze liquid with regret. She nodded slightly and he smiled halfheartedly.

"I've called Elisa and asked her to bring you a change of clothes. Are you thirsty?" She nodded shyly and he smiled. "I'll go and find you something to drink, okay?" He stood up and brushed a gentle, slightly shaky hand over her hair. "You scared the hell out of me, Theresa. So from now on you are to remain calm and not let your idiot of a husband upset you again. Okay?"

"Okay." She smiled up into his gentle eyes.

"Good." He leaned over to brush his lips over her forehead. "That's good, Theresa." She watched him leave and sighed softly, wishing that her life could be different and that they were a normal couple, excited about having their first baby. She ran a hand over the slight bump of her stomach, gently communing with her baby, apologizing for the recklessness that could have cost his life. She was lost in thought, humming a gentle lullaby while she continued to stroke the small baby bump, when she gradually became aware of a presence in the open door. She gasped in surprise, not sure how long he'd been standing there. He stepped forward almost reluctantly, his handsome face more grim than usual. For a man who usually had his emotions sealed up tight, he looked like someone who was struggling mightily to keep his expression absolutely neutral. But the muscles bunching in his jaw, the cords tightening in his neck, and his thinned lips were strong indicators of how hard he was fighting to keep whatever he was feeling hidden. Fascinated by the incredibly *bad* job he was doing of pretending to appear completely detached, she was still absently running a hand over her stomach when she gasped and jumped for a completely different reason.

All pretense of detachment tossed aside, Sandro's face paled and his eyes darkened in alarm as he surged toward the cot in the luxurious private room and thumped the bottle of fresh juice down on the cabinet beside the bed.

"What's wrong, Theresa? Are you in pain?" She shook her head, before lifting her beaming face up to his. He stopped short, inhaling sharply at her radiant expression. Her eyes were alight with tears and absolute joy while her lips were parted in the most serene, stunning smile he had ever seen.

"He *moved*," she breathed in awe. "I just felt him move, Sandro! For the first time."

"You . . . he . . . The *baby*?" he asked incoherently, moving even closer to the bed and leaning over her small figure.

"*Yes*. Oh my God! There he goes again . . ." She laughed in delight and without thinking grabbed one of his hands and placed it over the gentle flutter, low in her abdomen. His hand was so big; it covered nearly the entire little mound of her stomach. He sucked in a ragged breath when the baby fluttered again as if on cue, and uttered an incredulous laugh.

"*Dio* . . ." he breathed, sounding as awed as she felt. He kept his eyes glued to their hands, his on her stomach and her smaller, paler hand resting over his. "Does that hurt, *bella mia*?"

"No," she giggled. "It kind of tickles."

"Yes, well, give it a couple of months and it's going to be hellishly uncomfortable," a dry voice interjected from the doorway. Theresa squeaked in surprise, lifting her hand from Sandro's while he, keeping his warm hand on her stomach, turned leisurely to face her cousin. Lisa stood framed in the doorway with Rick and Rhys, and they were the portrait of a perfect family.

"That was fast," he observed before, reluctantly, moving aside and removing his hand from her belly. Theresa felt the loss keenly and tried to hide it by smiling brightly at her cousin.

"Thank you for coming," Theresa murmured, her eyes filling up, and her cousin moved farther into the room, leaning over the bed to hug Theresa warmly.

"Oh, darling, I'm always here for you," Lisa whispered into her ear, and Theresa, without any warning whatsoever, surprising even herself, burst into tears. "No . . . oh no, sweetheart, don't . . ." her cousin was crooning. "Don't upset yourself like this; it's not good for you or the baby."

Theresa made a concerted effort to pull herself together, embarrassed by her mini breakdown. Rick was on the other side of the bed; he had Rhys cradled to his chest in a baby sling and was holding one of her hands with both of his, adding his silent support to her obvious distress.

"I'm sorry, I didn't mean to do that," she choked out slightly, and Rick grinned down into her distraught face.

"Hormones. You know what *you-know-who* was like. The cost of tissues was bankrupting me," he said in a stage whisper, jerking his jaw in Lisa's direction, and Theresa half giggled, half sobbed in reaction before looking around the room in confusion.

"Where's Sandro?" she asked warily.

"Never thought I'd ever feel sorry for the guy," Rick told her half-seriously. "But when you turned on the waterworks, the poor dude looked like someone who'd just been told that both his best friend and *dog* had died in the same freak accident. He hovered for a few seconds before hot-footing it out of here like the hounds of hell were on his tail."

"Well . . ." Theresa shrugged bravely. "This is more than he signed up for."

"Oh, please." Lisa rolled her eyes disdainfully. "This is *exactly* what he signed up for. He wanted you pregnant, remember?"

"I remember." Theresa nodded forlornly.

"Look, far be it from me to defend the guy," Rick intervened reasonably. "I mean you know I can't stand him after the way he treated you. I would have cleaned his clock ages ago if you hadn't called me off, Terri . . . but quite honestly the man looked downright pitiful just now. Not your typical ruthless Sandro."

"I've seen a change in him lately too, Theresa," Lisa said.

"Please." Theresa shook her head. "He's the same as he's always been. He wants out of this marriage and so do I."

"Theresa . . ." Lisa murmured in her most reasonable voice.

"Lisa, don't defend him. You don't know what he's done . . ." And suddenly it all came out: how he'd blackmailed her to prevent her from divorcing him, using Lisa's loan as his leverage. "He probably gave you that loan so that he would have some kind of future hold over me if I ever stepped out of line!" Rick and Lisa exchanged a meaningful look before Rick shrugged, seeming to answer some unspoken question from Lisa.

"Theresa." Her cousin still clasped one of her hands tightly. "I know about that."

"You do?" She was shocked. "*How*? How long have you known?"

"Sandro confessed all the last time you two came by. Remember? He wanted to talk to me alone?" Theresa nodded dazedly. "For whatever reason, he doesn't want or *need* that leverage anymore. He offered to write off my debt entirely. I refused but I get the feeling that he's going to do it anyway."

"*That*'s what he wanted to talk about that day?" Theresa gasped incredulously.

"Yes, and he made me swear not to tell you about it but I suppose these are extenuating circumstances." Lisa nodded and Theresa frowned in concentration.

"I don't understand any of this . . . why would he do that?" she asked in confusion before her face cleared up and she laughed at her own stupidity. "Well, he doesn't really need the leverage anymore, does he? Not when I'm doing exactly what he wants? But to clear the debt before the baby's born still doesn't make sense . . . unless . . ."

"Is this a private conversation or can anyone join in?" Rick interrupted her musing drily and she blinked up at him. "I think you're overanalyzing. From what Lisa tells me he was desperate to cancel that debt. She thinks, and I'm inclined to agree after what I just saw, that he wants a clean slate with you but doesn't really know how to go about it."

"Well, I live with him and I know you're both wrong," she maintained stubbornly, shoving all those Scrabble and chess nights to the back of her mind determinedly. She tried not to think about the companionable meals and the silent support that he had lent her at every doctor's appointment. "He's in love with someone else. I'd say *another* woman, only in this case, I think I'm probably the *other* woman."

"What the hell is that supposed to mean?" Rick asked furiously.

"He was in love with her before my father forced him into this marriage. She's the woman he wants to have a family with. I'm the one who screwed up his life, Rick, not vice versa. Once I have this baby we'll go our separate ways and both be happier for it."

"This is so messed up." Rick shook his head in disgust. "What about the baby and you? Don't you count for anything?"

"I would hate it if he stayed out of some outdated sense of duty. I think I deserve more than that, don't you?"

"Absolutely," Lisa whispered, squeezing Theresa's shoulders reassuringly before sitting down on the chair beside the bed and leaning toward Theresa. "So you felt the baby move?"

Theresa's eyes lit up with remembered joy.

"It was amazing." She nodded and both Rick and Lisa went misty as they verbally recalled Rhys's first movements. "After the fright I got, it was such a relief to feel him moving around in there."

"Is he doing any wriggling now? His auntie Lisa wants to meet him."

Theresa shook her head with a slight laugh.

"He's all quiet right now." She rested her hand on her stomach. "I can't believe I have to stay in *bed* for a week."

"Yeah, that's a bit crappy." Lisa nodded sympathetically. "So glad I wasn't confined to the bed at any time during my pregnancy."

"God, if only . . . she was like a little dynamo, I had to force her to slow down," Rick recalled with a shudder.

"Do you think I could stay with you for the next week or so?" Theresa asked hesitantly, and Rick and Lisa both frowned before nodding.

"Of course," Lisa said. "But *why*?"

"Sandro's going to Italy for a week and before this happened I had every intention of staying in my own home but—"

"If you think I'm going to Italy with you confined to a bed, you can damned well think again," Sandro's gruff voice suddenly interrupted from the doorway and three heads swiveled toward him. He looked . . . strange. His hair was disheveled, his suit wrinkled, and his tie loosened. He was also clutching a wilted bunch of flowers in one hand and a gaily wrapped square box in the other. Added to that he had an incongruous bunch of foil helium balloons trailing behind him. It was the latter that caught and held everybody's attention. They were colorful, some were downright garish, and most of them either read Happy Birthday or Happy Anniversary and one woefully out of place dolphin had the legend "Yippee for SUMMER" emblazoned across its side, a very optimistic sentiment considering that it was July and the middle of winter.

"Sandro, bro . . ." Rick managed in a voice that only *barely* trembled with laughter. "Did you go raiding all the wards in the hospital for those?"

"These were all the seriously understocked gift shop had," Sandro grumbled, obviously sensitive to Rick's mockery, which raised Theresa's brows because she had never heard her self-assured husband sound so defensive before.

"Thank you, Sandro," she said before Rick could come back with anything else. "I love helium balloons."

"I *know* you do," he said fiercely, surging forward until he elbowed Rick aside and stood staring down at her intently. "I know that you like helium balloons and pink gerbera daisies. I know that you like praline truffles." He shoved the gift-wrapped box, which probably contained praline truffles, and the wilted pink daisies into her arms. "I do *know* things about you, Theresa. I've been learning."

"Um . . ." *Okay*? Right, so he remembered the conversation they'd had months ago when she'd accused him of knowing nothing about her. He'd obviously been paying attention during their evenings together but what on earth was he trying to prove with this? "Thank you."

It was all she could think of to say, and she saw both Rick and Lisa wince and watched Sandro's shoulders droop slightly before he nodded.

"You're welcome," he muttered in a devastatingly unemotional voice as he took a step back from the bed. "I've postponed my trip to Italy. I want to make sure that you get the rest you're supposed to."

"Okay." She nodded.

"Good." He seemed to be at a loss for a moment, looking unsure of his next move, before he reached out to stroke one soft cheek. "Are you feeling better?"

"Fine," she whispered. "A little tired."

"Righty-o . . ." Rick sing-songed. "That's our cue to vamoose."

"Oh, but I didn't mean . . ." Theresa was appalled that they thought she was hinting for them to leave.

"No, you didn't." Lisa smiled down at her. "But you are tired and you do need your rest. I'll leave the clothes right here." She dropped a small canvas bag onto the visitor's chair. "Call if you need anything."

After a flurry of hugs and kisses they were gone, leaving her grim-faced, silent husband behind. Theresa sneaked a glance up at said grim-faced, silent husband and was suddenly attacked by a fit of irreverent giggles. Now that nobody was around to witness it, she felt free to laugh at the image he presented. He looked like an under-dressed, forlorn clown with those balloons clutched in his hand.

"What?" he asked, the grim façade melting away in the face of her amusement.

"It's just . . . those *balloons*, Sandro." She snorted, trying to control the giggles. His own devastating grin lit up his face.

"I know, right?" He shook his head sadly as he tied the balloons to her bedpost. "A hospital without a single 'get-well-soon' balloon in sight. Craziness."

"Thank you for them anyway. They always brighten up a room."

"I remember you saying that when you talked about a friend's tenth birthday party. You wanted some for your own . . ." But she hadn't even had a party that year, much less balloons. She didn't even *know* why she'd confessed that sorry tale to him. There was an awkward silence while he stood hovering by her bedside.

"You don't have to stay, Sandro . . ." she whispered. "Why don't you go into the office and get some work done? I am sure you have better things to do than hang around here."

"I'm exactly where I want to be," he gritted implacably. He reached over and took the truffles and flowers from her arms.

Dumping the box on her bedside table and sticking the flowers into the half full plastic water canister that a nurse had left on the over-bed table, he then dragged over the chair that Lisa had recently abandoned, moving the bag to the floor and sitting down almost defiantly.

"Okay." She was too tired to argue, and truth be told, rather relieved to have him there. For a long time neither of them said anything. He leaned back in the uncomfortable-looking chair and stared off into space. Theresa lowered her lashes and watched him surreptitiously, marveling at his absolute stillness. He was usually filled with so much restless energy, always on the move, typing away on his laptop or fiddling with his smartphone or barking orders into the telephone. When he wasn't doing anything work-related, he would swim endless laps or work out in their home gym. She had never seen him merely sit down and stare off into the distance, and it disturbed her in a way that she could not quite define.

"Do you think my father will come to see me?" Theresa broke the silence nearly half an hour later, having dozed off in the interim. Sandro's eyes met hers and he shook his head grimly.

"Highly unlikely, since he doesn't know that you're here." He shrugged and she gasped, struggling to sit up.

"But how could you not tell him?" she asked, rather offended on her father's behalf. The man was a bully and a tyrant but he *was* her father.

"The doctor said you shouldn't be upset and I can't *quite* envision a visit from your father being anything other than stressful for you," he said sarcastically. He was right, her father would antagonize Sandro, which would upset her and they would all wind up arguing. It was always the same. She sank back feeling depressed and sad and Sandro's expression gentled.

"I'll call him if you want me to, Theresa," he offered quietly, and she shook her head, suddenly feeling an overwhelming urge to burst into tears again.

"You're right, a visit from him wouldn't be very pleasant," she said in an alarmingly wobbly voice. "But I keep hoping . . ." She left the rest unspoken but he seemed to understand.

"I know." He hesitantly reached for one of the limp hands resting on her stomach, engulfing it in both of his.

"I don't know why he's like that." she kept her eyes averted. "All of my life, I tried so hard to make him love me, but he never could. For a short while I thought I found what I was looking for, someone who could love me . . ." She was barely aware of what she was saying while her blurred gaze remained fixed on their joined hands. There was a long silence while they both contemplated their entwined fingers and Sandro sighed heavily.

"Why don't you take a little nap?" he suggested gently. "I'll be here to keep an eye on things." What things he felt he had to keep an eye on, she had no idea but just having him there made her feel better and she lay back with a contented sigh and was asleep almost immediately.

CHAPTER EIGHT

"You are an extremely difficult patient, *cara*," Sandro gritted out from between his teeth three days later. It was midafternoon and he had walked into her workroom, only to find her guiltily standing in the middle of the room. She was clutching the sketchbook that she had crept upstairs to retrieve, to her chest.

"I was bored," she whined. "So I thought if I had my sketchbook handy, I could work on some designs."

"Why didn't you call me or Phumsile to get it for you?"

"You were catching up on some work," and he had missed enough of it already, taking the week off to stay with her. "And Phumsile has dashed out to do some shopping."

"This is ridiculous," he growled, reaching her in one stride and swinging her up into his strong arms as if she were a featherweight. "You're being impossible. Why didn't you watch some TV or read a book or take a nap or *anything* until Phumsile got back?"

"Because I'm bored *now*," she complained sulkily, and he muttered something in Italian beneath his breath.

"What does that mean?" she demanded to know, and he slanted a wry sidelong glance at her before snorting softly.

"I said, 'God save me from stubborn women,'" he obligingly translated, and she scowled.

"I am not stubborn," she insisted stubbornly, and his gorgeous lips twitched in amusement.

"Of course not." He shook his dark head in a most condescending manner, one that Theresa immediately took exception to.

"And you don't have to patronize me," she seethed. "I'm not made of glass."

"You're just *spoiling* for a fight aren't you?" he mused, his lips curling up slightly. She folded her arms over her chest and kept her eyes mutinously fixed on his strong jaw. He sighed dramatically and hoisted her farther up against his chest before making his way downstairs. When they got back to her room, he deposited her gently onto the side of her bed and stood staring down at her placidly with his hands shoved into the pockets of his navy blue cargo pants. She *loved* him in cargo pants; they rode low on his lean hips and certainly did wonderful things for his already gorgeous backside. Now, while he brooded above her, her mouth went dry at the picture of masculine perfection he presented in those pants and his favorite old T-shirt, a torn, stretched gray thing with a Batman emblem on the front. His hair was a mess and he was in serious need of a shave but he looked absolutely gorgeous and she was suddenly breathless with desire for him.

His eyes narrowed speculatively on her flushed face. The corners of his lips tugged upward as he stretched abruptly while adding a jaw-popping yawn to the movement. His T-shirt rode up over his toned, ridged abdomen and revealed his smooth bronze skin. Theresa nearly groaned out loud as she squelched the urge to reach out and stroke the satiny skin on display just inches from her face. The elaborate stretch finally ended and he groaned as he rolled his head on his shoulders, working the kinks out of his neck.

"I'm exhausted," he informed her huskily, sinking down beside her, and she hurriedly scooted closer to the headboard. He ignored the evasive movement and threw himself backward, lying down with his knees over the side of the bed and his feet braced on the floor. Once again his shirt had ridden up and Theresa stared at the tempting skin of his ripped torso mutely. He lifted his hands to cover his face, hitching the shirt up even further, and he sighed again. "Just let me rest here for a couple of minutes, *cara*. I need to recover my strength after hauling you down those stairs. You have put on a lot of weight over these last few months." She was so captivated by the delectable picture he made, laid out like a buffet in front of a starving woman, that it took a moment for the words to sink in. When they did, she yelped in outrage and thumped his hard bicep in response. His mouth, the only part of his face that she could see beneath his hands, shifted into a lazy smile.

"You hit like a girl." He smirked, keeping his eyes covered and she attempted to hit him again. He was ready for her this time and grabbed her clenched fist to tug her toward him until she was awkwardly sprawled on top of him. She tried to shift off him but his arm tightened like an iron band around her waist, keeping her in place with the barest of efforts.

"Let me go," she demanded between clenched teeth, wriggling urgently as she tried to get away from him. To her frustration she could barely move and eventually she wore herself out and stopped moving. Her hands were braced on his hard broad chest as she tried to keep her upper body away from his; one of her feet was dangling over the side of the bed and the other was trapped between his legs. She glared down into his face but his eyes were closed and he looked so relaxed that for an implausible moment she actually believed that he might have fallen asleep. His eyelids lazily drifted up when she stopped moving.

"Just *relax* will you?" he implored wearily.

"I can't relax like this," she whispered, and he groaned before, with seemingly *great* effort, he shifted until they were both lying in the middle of the large bed. He was on his back, his sock-clad feet, because he had somehow managed to kick off his sneakers in the process, crossed at the ankles. She was stretched out beside him and he had one hard arm wrapped around her waist and the other curled up beneath his head. How he had managed to change their positions without once releasing her remained a mystery to her.

"You're still not relaxed," he observed after a few minutes of silence, and she lifted her head from where it was resting just beneath his armpit and frowned grumpily up into his face.

"Of course I'm not," she snapped. "How am I supposed to relax when you're exactly where I don't want you to be?"

"You brought this upon yourself." He shrugged, unconcerned.

"How on earth did I do *that*?"

"By not following the doctor's orders," he mumbled, sounding half-asleep. "This is the only way I can be sure that you'll stay in bed."

"I'm not going to have sex with you," she said, and he sighed, the sound so long-suffering that Theresa's hackles rose.

"Of course not but you *are* going to sleep with me," he informed her, his voice filled with grim purpose. "So you might as well relax." She said nothing, merely remaining tensed up like a coiled spring beside him. The hand he had resting at her waist began sweeping lazily up and down her side, while he brought his other arm around to lay his large hand low on her abdomen, where the baby rested. She tensed even further but he did nothing more threatening than pet and stroke her gently. Gradually she began to relax, allowing her thoughts to drift slightly.

"Have you thought of names for the baby yet?" he asked after nearly half an hour of increasingly comfortable silence, and Theresa was so relaxed by that time that she couldn't even summon up any outrage at what she considered to be a forbidden topic.

"Hmmm . . ." she moaned, inhaling his warm, clean scent with visible pleasure. "I like the names Kieran and Ethan. Liam maybe, but I'm leaning toward Alex . . ." Her voice trailed off awkwardly as she realized what she had revealed and hoped that he wouldn't notice. But this was Sandro and he was sharper than the proverbial tack.

"Alex?" he observed casually. "Alexander?"

Stupid, stupid fool! She berated herself angrily. How could she have revealed that she was leaning toward naming her son after him? He said nothing further on the subject, and she relaxed after a few tense minutes.

"What about girl names?" he asked. "You haven't thought of any?" Of course she hadn't thought of any. She was having a *boy*. She refused to answer his question.

"I like the name Lily," he murmured, his voice almost dreamy as he continued to gently stroke the slight mound of her abdomen. "Or Sofia . . . Lily would have black hair like mine but beautiful green eyes like yours, but I think a Sofia should have red hair and brown eyes, don't you?" He didn't wait for her response, merely continued on in that same dreamy voice. "Lily would be a sweet child, but Sofia, she's temperamental. She likes to throw things . . ."

"Stop it," she hissed. "There will be *no* Lily or Sofia! There will be a Liam or an Ethan, maybe a Kieran or an Alex, and he will have red hair and green eyes. He will be a sweet and lovable child." He didn't comment, merely kept up the soothing, nonthreatening movements of his large, strong hands. A while afterward, the lazy stroking slowed down, before stopping completely and his hands became heavy on her body. He slumped heavily against her and a soft snore confirmed that he had fallen asleep. Theresa sighed quietly before allowing herself to drift off as well.

~

The natural light in the room had a warm orange glow to it when she woke up later and she saw it was just after dusk, meaning that she had slept for nearly five hours. She sighed lazily, feeling remarkably warm and comfortable with her head cushioned on Sandro's hard chest and her neck supported by his upper arm. That same arm was curled around her shoulders with his big hand snuggled just under her right breast. One of her hands was tucked under her cheek and the other was . . . she tensed abruptly when she discovered where her audacious hand had come to rest. It was cupped over the firm bulge of his crotch. A bulge that was rapidly swelling and hardening beneath her palm.

"Don't panic," Sandro's sleep-roughened voice growled. The deep tenor of his voice rumbled through the chest beneath her head. "*Don't* . . . it's nothing."

"It doesn't *feel* like nothing to me." Her own voice was husky with sleep, and she amazed herself when, instead of following her first instinct and snatching her hand away from his crotch, she gently and almost tentatively, curled her hand around the thickening shaft of flesh.

"*Madre de Dio, cara* . . ." he choked out on a strangled voice. "What the hell are you doing?"

"Nothing," she murmured, her small hand petting and stroking him in much the same way he had done to her earlier. Only this was a lot less innocent.

"Theresa." His voice was strained. "Sweetheart, please if you keep doing that I don't know . . . I don't think . . ."

"Don't think," she purred, lifting her head from his chest to meet his pleading brown eyes. "That's a good idea."

"What the hell has gotten into you?"

Theresa didn't really know the answer to that, only she had missed having him in her bed, in her arms, and in her body the last few months. Logically, she knew that her raging hormones had a great deal to do with her unwanted urges, but she also knew that a large part of it could be attributed to her annoyingly undying love and desire for him.

"Theresa, I don't think this is what the doctor had in mind when he recommended bed rest and you don't really want this . . ." he muttered, reaching down to drag her hand away from his straining, fully erect length.

"I *do*," she protested, trying to pull her hand free from his strong grip.

"No . . . you're . . . I don't know . . . your hormones are out of control because of the pregnancy, that's why you feel like this." His voice trailed off when one of her slender thighs moved up to where her hand had just been. He moaned helplessly when she applied slight pressure and relaxed his hold on her. That was all she needed, and she was straddling him before either of them realized her intention. Suddenly her warm feminine mound was grinding up against him and both of them were groaning. Theresa watched as his head tilted back on the pillow and smiled in catlike satisfaction when his hands dropped to her thighs to drag her even closer. She braced her hands on his broad chest in order to maintain her balance and continued to sensuously rub herself against him.

"I think you may be right," she eventually gasped. "About the hormones . . . I want you but I don't *want* to want you." Her frustration with herself and the situation were clouding her clear green eyes, and *his* eyes went stormy with some kind of ruthlessly repressed emotion.

"Sssh . . . sweetheart . . . I read that pregnant women sometimes, well, *most* times, get really . . ." His voice trailed off as he struggled to find the right word, his mind obviously not on what he was saying as sweat started to bead his brow and his eyes took on a glazed, faraway look.

"Horny?" she supplied, and she sensed the utter shock in his absolute stillness. She had never used the word before, even though he had on numerous occasions.

"Yes . . ." he said, after clearing his throat awkwardly.

"Because I *am*," she reiterated, enjoying his discomfiture immensely as she continued to move sensuously against him. His hips were starting to strain upward slightly with each lazy movement she made, and she relished the absolute power she had over him.

"You said that there would be no sex," he reminded her desperately, his breathing becoming more labored. "And I don't think we *can* have sex while you're on bed rest."

"But maybe we can fool around a bit?" She smiled down into her husband's shocked face, feeling like the cat that had stolen the cream. He lifted one of his arms and covered his eyes, biting back a cry of pleasured anguish as she exerted more pressure right where it counted. He lifted his arm from his face, and his fevered eyes bored into hers. His face was taut with the control he was exerting over himself, the harsh planes standing out in sharp relief beneath his tanned skin. He reached up and tangled his large hands in her tousled red hair, tugging her toward him until their lips were a breath apart, but Theresa smiled serenely down into his strained face and pushed her hands onto his heaving chest to force some distance between them. He reluctantly let her go, relinquishing the opportunity to use his larger size and superior strength against her, obviously content, for now, to let her control events.

"Theresa, *please*," he begged. "Give me your mouth. I need to taste you . . . *per favore*."

"No lips." She shook her head. "This isn't . . ." She hesitated, and his eyes flared and his body went still beneath her, taut with tension.

"Isn't what?" he demanded. "Isn't *what*, Theresa?"

"Personal . . ." she completed in a whisper, and was shocked and dismayed when she saw a flash of hurt in his usually unreadable eyes.

"This feels pretty damned personal to *me*, *cara*," he hissed.

"I just . . . *need* you," she half sobbed, and he shook his head, grabbing her narrow hips between his large hands.

"Not me." He shook his head, keeping her hips steady as he ground himself against her. She shuddered in involuntary pleasure. *"This!"*

"Yes," she cried out, pushing herself against him. "*Please* . . ."

"I won't let you use me like that, Theresa." His voice was so brittle it cracked.

"Why not?" she keened, tears of frustration, anger, and heart-break sliding down her cheeks. "You used me in exactly the same way, and you kept it impersonal too. No kissing, no cuddling, no intimacy, no talking, no warmth . . . *nothing*! You stripped the act of everything but the bare essentials, and right now, that's all I want from you."

"What is this? Some kind of payback? You want me to see what it feels like to be used? Well, you're doing a pretty damned good job of it, Theresa. Consider it a lesson well learned." He used his superior strength and lifted her off him as if she weighed nothing, and she curled up into a humiliated ball, tears slipping down her cheeks as her entire body clenched with sexual and emotional frustration.

"I wasn't trying to prove anything," she protested thickly. "I just didn't want to get emotionally involved again! I didn't want to start thinking that there was anything other than physical attraction between us. I can't afford to make that mistake again."

"*Mi dispiace, cara*," he said regretfully as he got up and shoved his hands into his pockets to stare down at her. "I can't give you what you want. Not the way you want it."

"You did it before," she pointed out, sitting up and swiping at her hot, wet cheeks. "We can just go back to that."

"There's no going back to that," he negated harshly. "Never again."

"I know I'm not your type." She strove to sound casual about that painful fact and ignored the slight sound of dismay that seemed to rumble out from deep within his broad chest. "Compared to all those supermodels and actresses, I know I've always been Miss Dull and Dowdy, but you overlooked that once. I thought maybe . . ."

"Are you fishing for compliments?" he asked, his face creased into an incredulous glare. "Because I know that you cannot be serious with this load of tripe!" She looked into his outraged face, and he barked out a disbelieving laugh at the confusion in her eyes.

"Well, how do you explain the fact that you can barely stand to *look* at me?" She found her voice a few moments later, and he winced at the painful embarrassment and anguish that she couldn't disguise. "I know how much you hated touching me. I may have been a virgin when we married, Alessandro, but I knew enough to understand that a man who has to drink himself into a stupor before touching a woman, a man who can barely exchange a civil word with her and has to scrub her scent and touch from his skin as soon as he's capable of getting up after sex . . . a man like that *has* to be repulsed by the woman in his bed." Another harsh sound was torn from his chest, and he lifted both hands to scrub over his face and eyes and up into his hair, leaving it in messy peaks. Finally he stood there, staring down at her with his fingers linked across the nape of his neck, seemingly unable to respond to her pained words.

He sat down next to her, dragged her back into his lap, and groaned helplessly. He turned her until she was straddling him again. This time he dragged his knees up to support her back and wrapped his arms around her slender frame, building a fortified human cage around her trembling body.

"Theresa . . ." he groaned, burying his face into her soft, fragrant hair. "I do want you, *cara*. I've *always* wanted you." He cupped the back of her head in the palms of his hands and stared intently down at her, trying to convey his earnestness through sheer force of will. Theresa's tear-drenched eyes swept over his deadly serious face and she found herself unable to read his expression. Once again he had his emotions under tight control and even though he was saying the words she couldn't tell if he was being sincere.

"You don't have to lie," she whispered, dropping her head to one of his broad shoulders and closing her arms around his broad back, feeling safe, warm, and protected. "I'm sorry I brought this up again, Sandro. I didn't mean to. I don't mean to keep throwing the past back into your face like this. I do recognize how difficult the situation must have been for you and—"

"Stop it." He finally interrupted the burble of words that she couldn't seem to control. "Just stop it. Yes the situation was beyond my control. It was, and still is, incredibly difficult but this does not mean you deserved the treatment you got from me and it certainly doesn't mean that I *never* wanted you. Theresa, most nights I could barely keep my greedy hands off you."

"You couldn't?" She lifted her head from his shoulder to stare up into his grim face.

"Why do you think I insisted that we share a bed?" he pointed out. "That way, I didn't have to go and find you when my need for you overrode all else."

"Oh . . ." she responded.

"Yes . . . 'oh.'" He nodded. "And despite all of my idiotic stratagems to keep intimacy between us to a minimum, remember I blamed you for this marriage as much as I did your father, I could never get enough of you."

"Oh . . ." she muttered redundantly, and his lips twitched into a little smile.

"That's why I never slept with those women the tabloids kept pairing me up with," he whispered, his long thumbs stroking back and forth across the satiny skin stretched over her high cheekbones.

"You really didn't sleep with any of them?" she asked in a small, uncertain voice, and he nodded, never shifting his eyes from hers.

"Why would I? When I had *you* waiting for me at home," he growled, and she blinked back her tears, which threatened to overflow.

"Why should I believe you?" she asked.

"Why would I lie to you? I have nothing to gain from it; we're getting divorced, going our separate ways in a few months' time . . . right?" The last emerged a bit uncertainly, and Theresa blinked at the unwelcome reminder.

"Right. Of course." She nodded.

"So lying about this now would achieve nothing." He shrugged.

"Thank you." She wasn't sure what she was thanking him for. Telling the truth? Not sleeping with those women? All she knew was that she felt incredibly relieved because the public humiliation hurt so much less now that she knew the rumors of his many infidelities had been unfounded. She shut out the painful, lingering memory of the omnipresent Francesca and dropped her head back onto his shoulder. He stroked her back gently. There was nothing sexual in their embrace anymore, just comfort and support, which Theresa needed more than the physical release she had been craving before.

"You must be starving," he murmured into her hair, lifting his head to smile down into her eyes. "I'll get us something to eat. We can have dinner and watch a movie in bed, okay?" She nodded and reluctantly allowed him to lift her from his lap. He dropped a sweet kiss on her head and left the bedroom with a smile.

CHAPTER NINE

That day signaled a turning point in their rocky relationship. The peace remained and along with it a mutual, ever-deepening respect blossomed between them. Sandro consulted her on some of his business decisions, seeming to value her opinions and take her advice. Taking her cue from him, Theresa started asking for his opinions on some of her designs and developed a keen admiration for the eye he seemed to have for quality jewelry. With his encouragement, she started attempting more difficult pieces using new mediums and was pleasantly surprised with the results.

Life was better but by no means perfect—they still slept apart at Theresa's insistence. While he accompanied her to all of her doctor's appointments and was even her coach at the natural childbirth classes she had started attending, Theresa hardly ever talked to him about the baby and did her utmost to discourage any discussion. Lisa was meant to be her coach but her cousin had her hands full with Rhys and promised to be there for the birth but could not put in the time commitment at the classes. That, of course, meant that Sandro was nothing more than a temporary replacement, which she knew grated on his ego. Francesca still loomed large between them, and even though Theresa was careful never to mention the other woman's name, she was never far from Theresa's mind.

Sandro had gone to Italy a couple of times during the past three months and after compulsively checking the Internet for any news about him while he was away, she had finally found pictures of the two of them together, attending some glamorous function in Milan. She couldn't read the Italian article, but it had been an extensive four-page spread on the event and Sandro and Francesca Delvecchio, as the captions had identified her, had been two of the most beautiful people there. So of course there were at least a dozen pictures of them smiling, dancing, and drinking. Sandro had looked so relaxed and happy with the statuesque, gorgeous brunette on his arm that Theresa had been unable to stop staring at the pictures. That was how he should have looked on their wedding day, carefree and in love. Instead his face had looked like it would crack wide open if he so much as tilted his lips at the corners. It had physically hurt her to see those pictures, but the one that had torn her apart had been of him bending down to drop a kiss onto Francesca's cheek. Never had she seen two more evenly matched people.

Theresa sighed and shook herself slightly, as she found herself thinking of that picture again. It had been more than a month since she'd seen it, and she hadn't mentioned it to Sandro, knowing that it would achieve little, especially with their separation looming less than three months away. She ran a gentle hand over the football-size mound of her stomach, trying to ease the restlessly moving baby beneath her touch. She had no right to be jealous, despite the fact that they had a much better relationship now than they'd had during the first year and a half of marriage. She couldn't lose sight of the fact that they were married in name only and would separate as soon as the baby was born.

She had started decorating the nursery, and Sandro, who had thrown a fit one day when he'd returned from the office early to find her perched on a ladder attempting to paint the walls, had done the painting. She spent a great deal of time in the nursery, adding little touches here and there, often going out and shopping for furniture and toys. There really was very little left to do but she still kept adding little stuffed toys and tiny infant-size clothes. The color scheme was cream and pale lilac. She had started out with blue but had come home from visiting Lisa one day to find that Sandro had changed the color to something more "gender neutral" as he'd put it. She hadn't protested too much because she had found the new color scheme soothing and prettier than the blue on white she'd planned.

She also found Sandro's touches elsewhere in the nursery. He bought toys—girls' toys. Stuffed dolls, teddy bears, toy ponies, anything a little girl's heart could possibly desire. Theresa chose not to acknowledge them in any way, and every time she came across one, usually sneakily hidden among the toys that she had bought, she would relegate it to the corner farthest from the beautiful crib that they had selected together. There was quite a collection forming in the area which she had dubbed Toy Siberia. She did not know *why* he kept buying those things, and she refused to ask. He never mentioned the heap of toys that she had stowed in the corner but just doggedly kept adding more and more to the nursery.

Their two hours three times a week had branched out into a few hours every day. There was no longer a time limit on the amount of time they spent together because Theresa had stopped enforcing it once it became clear that Sandro was going to sneak a little time every day. It just became easier to pretend not to notice it. Theresa's health continued to fluctuate, her pregnancy being a lot more difficult than she, Sandro, or the doctor had ever anticipated. She had been diagnosed with preeclampsia the month before, and Sandro had turned into a paranoid old woman about what she could and could not do. He had even stopped going into the office, working from home and hovering twenty-four seven. She didn't know how she would get through the final two months of her pregnancy without resorting to some form of violence because the man was driving her completely crazy.

Now she sat with her feet up, staring gloomily out at the rain pouring down outside. It was an unusually wet and miserable spring afternoon, and Theresa had long ago abandoned her book in favor of her roiling thoughts. So absorbed was she in those thoughts that she didn't hear Sandro come in, and nearly jumped out of her skin when she felt a large hand on her shoulder.

"I didn't mean to scare you," he murmured, bending down to drop a quick kiss onto the soft, exposed skin where her shoulder and neck met. "I called your name at least twice but you were totally wrapped up in your own little world."

"I was just thinking . . ." She shrugged, her voice trailing off.

"About?"

"Everything. Nothing." Another listless shrug.

"How are you feeling?" he asked, coming down on his haunches in front of her.

"I'm fine. A little tired . . ." He lifted a hand and gently traced one of her delicate cheekbones with his thumb before nimbly jumping to his feet and sitting down on the sofa next to her. Neither of them said anything for a while; they just listened to the rain and watched it cascading down the window like a waterfall.

"I want you to meet my father," he suddenly announced unexpectedly, and she froze before turning her head slowly to meet his brooding eyes.

"What?"

"My father," he repeated, and she bit her lip before clearing her throat uncertainly.

"I don't know if that's . . ." she began, but he interrupted her before she could finish.

"His condition is deteriorating rapidly," he said abruptly. His voice broke slightly as he said the words and his jaw clenched.

"Oh, Sandro, I'm so sorry," she whispered, her eyes going liquid with sympathy for him. "When's your flight?"

"I'm not leaving," he told her grimly, and her eyes shadowed in confusion, before flaring as she realized *why* he refused to go and be with his father.

"Sandro." Her voice was so low it barely carried to the man who sat inches away from her. "You can't stay because of me. You have to go and be with your family. Your place is with them right now."

"*You*'re my family too, Theresa," he snapped, a maelstrom of frustration and pain welling up in his eyes. "And I refuse to leave you here alone."

"Hardly alone, Sandro," she dismissed airily. "The staff, Lisa and Rick, and even my *father* are here for me. Go home to your family."

"This is where I have to be, this is where I'm staying. Stop arguing with me for God's sake!" he growled.

"You are *not* going to blame me for this too, Sandro," she fumed impotently. She recognized the stubborn tilt of his jaw and the steely resolution in his eyes and knew that his mind was made up. He wouldn't budge on the issue unless something drastic happened to change his mind. "The only reason you're here now is because of my father and his corrupt little blackmailing scheme! My father and I have messed up your life and your family enough; don't make it worse by staying here with me of all people, when the family you sacrificed your freedom for needs you the most."

"Don't you *ever*," he seethed, grabbing and gripping her hand so tightly that he nearly cut off the circulation, "lump yourself into the same category as your father again, Theresa. None of this is *your* fault and right now you need me too."

"I do not need you," she enunciated clearly. "I refuse to let you martyr yourself like this. Duty above all else. Is that right? Long-suffering Sandro, who's always doing the right thing and always putting everybody else's needs before his own. Sacrificing his happiness at the altar of familial obligation. I am not going to be your obligation, Sandro. I refuse to. Go and be with your family!"

"You are my family, damn it! You, you, *you*!" He shouted, and she jumped in fright, her jaw going slack as he leaped from the sofa to loom over her furiously. So rarely did Sandro lose his cool that Theresa stared up into his frustrated, wretched face in shocked silence. All the air seemed to leave his sails and his shoulders sagged as he dropped to his knees in front of her, bringing his eyes down to the same level as hers. "I want to be here with you. Why is that so hard for you to understand?" His voice had dropped to a whisper. His eyes suddenly, *shockingly*, filled with moisture, which he made no attempt to hide from her, and he muttered something in Italian, his voice thick with emotion. She bit her lip and shook her head.

"I don't understand," she whispered regretfully, and he reached out a hand to cup her cheek.

"My father is *dying*, *cara*," he repeated in English, his voice absolutely wracked with emotion. "Please, I need you not to fight with me right now." She nodded and reached out with both hands to stroke his hair back from his broad, proud forehead. The gesture seemed to undo him, and his face crumpled before he wrapped his strong arms around her thickened waist and buried his face in the mound of her stomach while Theresa curled her upper body protectively over his head as she whispered soothing little snippets into his hair.

"I'm sorry," she said softly. "I didn't mean to make this more difficult; I just thought that you were staying out of some misguided sense of honor and obligation. I would hate that, Sandro. I would hate for you to stay and then if the . . . if the worst happened, you would blame me because you couldn't be there at his side."

"I know," he murmured, lifting his head to look up at her, his face inscrutable, despite the roiling emotion she could see in his eyes. "And I can see why you would think that. I have blamed you for way too much in the past and treated you terribly, but you *have* to believe me when I tell you that the last thing in the world I want to do anymore is hurt you, Theresa." She said nothing, knowing that even though it would not be intentional, he would still hurt her when he eventually left. And then again when they divorced and he eventually married Francesca. All of those things were as inevitable as the sunset. They would happen and they would *devastate* her.

"So what did you want to ask me?" she asked, without acknowledging his fervent words. The omission did not go unnoticed and Sandro flinched slightly before taking a deep breath and levering himself up off his knees to sit down on the sofa beside her, angling his body so that he could face her.

"I want you to meet my father," he repeated, and her eyes showed her confusion.

"I'm not sure I understand. You know that Doctor Shelbourne has prohibited any flying during my third trimester."

He smiled slightly before shaking his head. "Theresa, *cara*, you really need to catch up to the twenty-first century," he teased half-heartedly. It had become a standing joke between him and *Rick*, of all people, that Theresa was so technologically backward. She could barely operate her mobile phone, so e-mailing, instant messaging, and every other form of electronic *–ing*ing left her completely baffled. She had wiped out the hard drives on three laptops in as many years and now kept her records strictly on paper in a filing cabinet in her office.

"So then, what do you have in mind?" she asked.

"Certainly nothing that involves either you or my father flying anywhere. Have you never heard of video-conferencing?" he asked, brushing back a strand of hair that had slipped from its anchor behind her ear, to swing into her face. He always did little things like that lately; he was always touching her, petting her, and after her initial discomfort with all the contact, Theresa now barely noticed it and just enjoyed the pampering.

"That thing where you have a meeting and you can see people on the other side of the world on a monitor in the room?" she asked vaguely, and he grinned.

"Yes . . . I often speak to my family in Italy by that means," he revealed.

"Okay." She nodded slowly. "So when do you want to do it?"

"I was thinking tonight?" he asked, and her stomach did a slow, nervous roll before she nodded again.

"Okay," she said again, actually physically incapable of saying much else.

"They're going to love you," he reassured, squeezing her hand.

"They?" she asked queasily, suddenly filled with doubts. "I thought it would be only your father."

"My mother and grandmother will probably be there and maybe a couple of my sisters too. With my father so sick, they're probably all there."

"Your father's at home?"

He nodded, his eyes darkening again.

"He refuses to be hospitalized. He says that if he's going to die, he wants to do it at home. He has the best medical care and facilities money has to offer to him at home."

"That's understandable." She nodded sympathetically. "He's waited so long to go back home." There was a moment of awkward silence.

"I'm really glad you could get it back for him, Sandro," she blurted impulsively. "Even if it cost you more than it should have." Again the silence, before he nodded tautly, his grim face looking hewn from rock.

"So do they know I'll be . . . are they expecting to meet me?" She broke the uncomfortable silence a few moments later and he cleared his throat.

"I've been making noises about wanting them to meet you for a while now," he informed. "So they won't be too surprised by it."

"Always thinking ahead aren't you?" she asked with a hint of resentment.

"If you mean that I'd anticipated having to introduce you to my dying father by these less than ideal means, then *no*, I wasn't really preparing for this eventuality!" he snapped irritably.

"I didn't mean it like that," she whispered defensively.

"Of course you didn't," he agreed sarcastically. Stung, she managed to lever her bulky form up from the sofa, ignoring him when he jumped up lithely to offer assistance.

"I'm tired, I think I'll take a nap before dinner," she said wearily. "I'll see you later." She left him behind without a single backward look, just plain sick and tired of the constant tension that they both had to live with.

~

"Are you ready?" he asked her quietly a few hours later. They were both in his huge study where he had set up the computer and camera for the video conference. No simple webcam and computer screen for Sandro, he had a proper video camera with a large television screen set up. He explained that it would enable his family to see both of them at the same time, further explaining that his parents had a similar setup at their home.

"As ready as I'll ever be, I suppose." She nodded nervously, and he led her to a large, comfortable sofa that was facing the camera. He made sure she was sitting comfortably before kneeling in front of her unexpectedly.

"I'm sorry about earlier," he said softly, his dark eyes piercing as they stared intently into hers. "Being around you is a curiously humbling experience. I do not believe I have ever apologized this much to one person in my entire life before. I always seem to be getting it wrong with you."

"You're under a lot of emotional strain at the moment, Sandro, and I know that I probably wasn't making it any easier on you. Please just forget about it." He sighed deeply before nodding and sitting down next to her. He picked up a small remote control from the coffee table in front of them and started up the camera, indicating toward the blinking red light that he had told her would mean that the camera was on. An image of an elderly couple suddenly filled the previously blank screen of the big television to the left of the camera. Broad smiles suddenly lit up their faces and they both started chattering at the same time. Theresa knew that they were his parents from the pictures she had seen in Sandro's study. His father looked a lot frailer and more tired than the robust man in the photographs, though, and Theresa could see from the sallow skin and sunken eyes how very ill the older man was.

Sandro was smiling warmly as his parents continued to chatter, before he finally raised a hand and they reluctantly fell silent. He said something to them in Italian, before indicating Theresa, who sat with a frozen smile on her face. She wasn't sure what to do or what to say; she wasn't even sure if they spoke English.

"Mama, papa . . . I know this has been a long time in coming," he said, in heavily accented English. "But this is Theresa . . . *mia moglie*, my wife."

"*Piacevole per incontrarli*," she murmured haltingly, not sure if she had said it right or if they even understood her, but the smile Sandro directed down at her was filled with so much overwhelming pride and tenderness that Theresa felt bathed in its warmth. He entwined the long, lean fingers of one hand with hers, but she didn't understand why he felt the need to make the gesture when their hands were out of the camera's sight.

"I'm pleased to meet you," she repeated in English, in case the couple hadn't understood her, which seemed likely if their baffled expressions were anything to go by. His mother's lips pursed in what looked like disapproval but his father's smile broadened and he said something in rapid-fire Italian that Theresa didn't stand a chance of understanding.

"My father says that you are truly beautiful," Sandro translated for her. "And that he is very happy to finally meet you." Her eyes flooded with tears and she nodded slightly.

"Thank you . . . *grazie*." She smiled warmly at the fragile-looking old man, and he looked delighted by it. He once again said something in high-speed Italian, and Sandro chuckled before responding in an amused voice. It was obvious that they were talking about her, and she turned to Sandro, waiting for the translation. When it didn't look like it was forthcoming, she prodded him with a nudge from her shoulder, and he grinned before saying something in a wry voice to his mother and father before turning to her with that same warm humor in his eyes.

"My father says that while you look as sweet and docile as an angel he does not imagine that a woman with your red hair can be easy to live with. He believes that the angelic exterior must hide a fiery temper."

"Oh?" she asked in a deceptively calm voice, even while she narrowed her eyes at him. "And what did *you* say?"

"I told him that he definitely knows women a lot better than I do because when I married you I thought that the angel was all there was, until I provoked the fiery demoness into showing herself, to my detriment."

"Demoness?" she asked in a highly offended voice and both his father and he chuckled simultaneously.

"Easy, *cara*." He lifted his free hand in a gesture of surrender, and his father burst into warm, genuine laughter, the sound so happy and carefree that for an instant everyone, including his wife, stared at him with huge smiles. The older man brought his laughter under control and said something in Italian, which seemed to be aimed at Theresa. She looked at Sandro for a translation, and he hesitated for a millisecond before clearing his throat and turning back toward Theresa.

"My father says that it's great to see me with a woman who isn't intimidated by me and who can give as good as she gets. He thinks we will have strong sons and daughters." He cleared his throat before continuing, even though the huskiness persisted. "He is honored to call you daughter and is proud that his son's children will come from a worthy woman like you."

"Oh . . ." Theresa whispered, her hand going up to cover her mouth, and her eyes flooding with tears. "Oh God."

"*Cara*." His soft voice in her ear pleaded with her to keep it together and she nodded, closing her eyes briefly to keep her surging emotions under control, before bracing herself and opening her eyes to meet the wise, old eyes of a man who was halfway across the world.

"Thank you," she told him again. "You are so very kind to say that. I am equally proud to know that my child comes from a strong family such as yours. I look forward to the day I can present my son to you, sir."

"Or daughter," Sandro inserted smoothly, before translating what she had said to the beaming older man.

"You are . . . lovely girl. I sorry for all trouble," the man suddenly said in broken but understandable English, and Theresa's lips trembled with emotion. "You make my boy happy. I see this . . . *grazie*. I so worry . . . but I see now, he very happy with you. Very much love here. I see."

She couldn't respond to that with much more than a nod and another emotional *grazie*, overwhelmed by the perception that had allowed the sick old man to see how much she loved his son. He and Sandro were now having a solemn conversation, and the older man started pausing more and more frequently, seeming to lose track of his thoughts more and more until his wife stepped in and called a halt to the conversation.

"Mama says he is tired and needs to take his medication and rest," he whispered to Theresa, as they watched the older man protest before allowing himself to be wheeled, for he was in a wheelchair, out of the room with a few last farewells to Sandro and Theresa. Sandro's hand was squeezing hers so hard that it stopped the blood flow into her fingers, but Theresa didn't protest, knowing that Sandro was probably wondering if it would be the last time he would ever see or speak to his father. They watched in silence as the door closed behind his mother's elegant form before they became aware of the fact that another person was in the room on screen. A wizened old woman suddenly plonked herself into the seat Sandro's mother had just vacated, and Sandro's entire face lit up.

"Nonna!" he greeted with warm enthusiasm and turned to Theresa, who had already gleaned who the little old lady was. She was tentatively starting to smile, when the woman launched into speech, her voice low and furious. Whatever she was saying wiped the smile off Sandro's face in seconds, and she watched as his eyes darkened in fury and his lips tightened in an expression she was more than a little familiar with. He released Theresa's hand and hissed something equally dire sounding back at his grandmother, who gasped in horror before launching into an even angrier-seeming tirade. By this time two younger women, whom she recognized as Sandro's sisters, had stepped into the room and upon hearing whatever it was their grandmother had said added their own two cents' worth until there was nothing but unintelligible squawks coming from the speakers. Suddenly the old woman's words turned to English, and her eyes were seemed trained on Theresa.

"*You* make my family miserable! You take my grandson and keep him away from his family, keep him away from his dying father. You nothing but selfish. Why you want a man who no love you? No pride . . . you no pride. He love a good woman, he no love *you*!"

Theresa gasped in horror and raised her hands to her mouth, defenseless against the hatred she saw burning in the old woman's eyes. Her eyes flooded with tears, and Sandro swore shakily before saying something soft and dangerous sounding to the three women on the other end of the camera, but Theresa had blocked them all out and was struggling to her feet, ignoring Sandro's desperate protest.

She was out the door and halfway up the stairs before he caught up with her.

"She's old, *cara*," he said desperately, holding on to her arm as she tried to wrest herself away from him. "She's old and stubborn. What she said was *not* true."

"I *didn't* make your family miserable?" she asked brokenly. "Of course I did, Sandro. You know that's true. I didn't keep you away from them? Or away from your dying father? I did that too. You don't love me? No news there. You're in love with someone else? Again: old news . . . and she was right. I have absolutely *no* pride. None whatsoever. If I did I would never have stood for this sham of a marriage. Everything she said was true. So she was just being honest . . . and that's *my* shame to deal with."

"Theresa, please . . ." She didn't know what he wanted from her. She yanked her arm from his grip and found herself teetering desperately on the edge of the step, nearly falling until he yanked her back toward his strong body and braced himself to absorb her weight.

"You foolish woman, stop fighting me and just *listen*, damn it!" he hissed into her ear. Shocked by her close call she could do nothing but stand trembling in his arms. "She didn't get it all right; you have more stubborn pride than any person I have ever met. You did not keep me away from my father, I chose to stay."

"Because of me," she inserted despondently.

"Because I chose to be with you," he emphasized but not really seeing the difference, Theresa remained quiet. "Don't you see, Theresa? I wanted to be with *you*!"

"I'm tired, Sandro," she whispered after a long pause, sending a pointed glance down at the restraining hand he had on her elbow. His grip tightened slightly before he reluctantly released her and stepped back to allow her to proceed up the stairs.

~

When Theresa woke from a restless sleep a few hours before dawn, it didn't take her long to discover that Sandro was lying in bed with her. His big, hard body was curved around hers, his knees spooning in behind hers. He had one arm curled under her neck and the other slung heavily across her waist, his hand cupped protectively over her swollen abdomen. She could feel his deep breath against the nape of her neck, indicating that he was asleep and it had been so long since she'd found herself in bed with him that she allowed herself to enjoy his relaxed warmth and closeness without the tension that was usually between them when he was awake.

Even before they'd started sleeping apart, he'd never held her in his sleep. So this was a novel and overwhelmingly enjoyable experience that she couldn't deprive herself of. She was just about to doze off again, when the telephone buzzed quietly from the nightstand beside her bed. She jerked slightly, and the movement woke Sandro, who was instantly on alert behind her.

"You okay?" he asked groggily, and she nodded just as the phone buzzed again.

"Hmmm. Who could be calling at"—she squinted at the digital clock beside the phone—"four in the morning?" She knew the answer the instant the question escaped her lips and from the sudden tension in Sandro's body, she knew that he realized it too. He sat up abruptly, and she immediately felt cold as he leaned over her to yank up the receiver.

"De Lucci," he barked once he had it up to his ear. "*Si . . . si . . .*" She sat up and pushed her hair out of her eyes as she tried see his expression in the dim light of the LCD display of the clock. His face closed up tighter than a fist and he bowed his head slightly. Biting her lip, as she fought back the tears, Theresa laid a comforting hand on one tense, naked shoulder.

"*Quando*?" he asked tersely, his voice hoarse. He said a few more things, but Theresa tuned his words out, hearing only the pain he kept at bay behind the rigidly controlled voice. She lowered her head to his broad shoulder, wanting only to comfort and kept stroking his back as he spoke. He was silent for a long time before she realized that he was done speaking and that he had lowered the receiver to the bed beside him. She turned her head to look up into his face and saw that he was staring off into the distance. It was still too dark to see much of his face but from the grim set of his jaw the news was obvious.

"When?" she asked gently, reaching for the receiver and placing it gently back into its cradle. A slight shudder rippled through his body before he turned his head to face her.

"About ten minutes ago," he whispered, and she nodded, lifting a small hand to cup his tense jaw.

"You go and grab a shower, I'll pack a bag for you." She clicked on the bedside lamp before awkwardly heaving herself up and off the bed. He remained where she had left him and she sighed softly, before leaning down to kiss the top of his head gently.

"Come on, Sandro," she murmured firmly. "You grab that shower and I'll take care of everything else." Something about the tone of her voice got through to him, and he nodded and got up like someone in a trance before heading to the bathroom. Theresa stood there for a while until she heard the shower going before she waddled out to his room down the hall and packed a bag for him.

Twenty minutes later, when she returned to her guest room, it was to find the shower still running. Concerned she stepped into the bathroom and could barely make out his shape behind the frosted glass of the shower door but she could see enough to tell that he was still in there and not really moving. She sighed and bit her lip before, decision made, she stripped down to her skin and stepped into the cubicle with him.

He was standing with his back to the cubicle door, his head bowed beneath the strong spray and his hands braced against the tiled wall, long arms outstretched in front of him and muscles tensed. He didn't seem to know that she was there until her hands touched the bunched muscles of his shoulders. She could feel his instinctive jerk of surprise beneath her touch and very gently moved her hands until they crept down under his arms and around to his broad chest. She could feel his bone-deep tremors and with gentle insistence tugged him back toward her until she was able to rest her cheek against the warm, wet skin of his back. Her hands were splayed across his chest, and she could feel the strong beat of his heart beneath her touch.

"I'm sorry," she whispered, dropping warm kisses across the skin of his back. "I'm so sorry, Sandro." He shuddered violently before turning with a groan and gathering her into his arms, hunching his body around hers and burying his face in her still-dry hair. They stood that way for a long time before he lifted his ravaged face and looked down at her. His eyes were wet with tears, and he reached up to cup her face before lowering his lips to hers and kissing her hungrily. He did nothing more than that just kiss her like he would never get the chance to do so again. He kissed like a man who knew that he would have to go without sustenance for an unknown amount of time. Finally, chest heaving, he lifted his head and stared intently down into her dazed face.

"You're so beautiful," he whispered gently. "The most beautiful thing in my life. I don't want to leave you here. Not now."

"I'll be fine," she reassured. This time she was the one to reach up and stroke his worried face. "The baby will be fine. I have Lisa and Rick. You have to take care of your family now, Sandro."

"You're my family too." He repeated his words of the previous afternoon. "I have to take care of you too."

"No." She reached around him to shut off the water and met his eyes squarely. "I can take care of myself. And to be honest, having you here when you should be with your family will just add to my stress." He said nothing for a few moments before shutting his eyes and nodding abruptly.

"Okay." He inhaled deeply. "Okay, I'll arrange my flight immediately." She opened the door and reached for a couple of the heated towels hanging from the railing beside the shower cubicle, handing one over to him before wrapping one around herself, happy to be covering up her huge frame again.

~

An hour later she and Sandro were standing on the doorstep. The chauffeur of the driving service they sometimes used stood waiting patiently beneath an umbrella next to the shiny black sedan.

"Promise me that you'll eat well," Sandro urged, and she nodded somberly, knowing that he would need to have his head clear for what was to come. "And you'll contact Elisa and Richard if you feel unwell." Another nod. "And you will remember to take your vitamins?"

His voice was starting to get hoarse with emotion, and she gave him a wavering smile before nodding again.

"I promise."

"You say this but you forget. I know you." He shook his head in frustration. "It is important for your health, *cara,* and you no remember to take. It drive me crazy. I worry . . ." It was a sign of his anxiety and stress that his normally impeccable, lightly accented English had failed him so completely, and she stepped toward him and went on tiptoe to drop a kiss onto one of his lean cheeks.

"Why don't you call Phumsile and Lisa once you land?" she suggested gently. "And if you're worried about me forgetting, you can have them remind me."

"Yes." He nodded, appeased. "I will. Please, Theresa, call me. Anytime if you need anything, if you want to talk . . . call me. I'll call *you* every day."

"That's good," she said quietly, not sure if he'd have the time to talk with her every day but knowing that he needed to make the promise. "Now you'd better go before you miss your flight." He nodded and dragged her into his arms for a passionate, desperate kiss before letting her go abruptly and striding down the steps toward the car. He paused when he reached the car and turned around for one last, lingering look at her before he climbed in and was gone.

Theresa turned blindly toward the house and once she was inside she felt completely lost. Not sure where to turn or who to turn to, she found herself walking toward Sandro's study. She'd been in the room very few times before, and those times had always been in Sandro's company. Now she felt like she was intruding into his domain, but it was the one place she felt closest to him. Everything bore his stamp. It was the only room he had insisted on decorating himself. He'd largely left the rest of the house up to Theresa, and she now knew it had been because he hadn't much cared what their home together would look like since he'd never had any intention of it being permanent.

As she looked at the masculine room with its dark, heavy furniture and minimalist, almost Asian decor, she grasped how completely different it was from the rest of the house and her heart broke at this additional sign of how doomed their relationship had been from the start. She sank down onto the plush, black leather sofa, curled up into a ball, and cried for the life she could have had if she'd just been the woman Sandro had wanted. Once the bout of self-pity had passed, she sat up and wiped at her eyes before gently running her hands over her distended abdomen.

"You and I will make our own lives, darling," she promised. "And we'll be so happy. Just you wait and see."

CHAPTER TEN

Sandro had made good on his promise and had enlisted both Lisa and Phumsile's aid in ensuring that Theresa took her vitamins and rested enough but that was the only promise he kept. A month passed with barely any word from him, and his phone calls, the few that came, were rushed and impersonal and barely lasted three minutes. When Theresa tried to contact him, he was never available, or so the cold female voices on the other end of the line told her. She had no choice but to take them at their word.

She kept track of Sandro's movements through the news—online, televised, and printed. His father's death and Sandro's subsequent taking over of the family's banking and investment empire were pretty hot news items and hardly a day went by that it wasn't mentioned in some form of news. There had been paparazzi coverage of the funeral; despite the media ban the family had put on proceedings, some intrepid photographer had managed to get a picture of Sandro standing over his father's open grave, his face closed up tighter than a fist, flanked by his mother and Francesca, who had stood beside him offering the support only a lover or a wife would offer. A lot had been written about that photograph, and a lot of cynical criticism had been aimed at his cold, absent wife, and a lot of praise given to the stoic Francesca who stood by him through thick and thin.

There was no mention about her difficult pregnancy that made travel nearly impossible for her. A few local reporters had contacted her, wanting her "side of the story" and her refusal to be interviewed or offer any comment had merely added fodder to fuel the rumor that she was unfeeling and cold. The media, when given free rein, were ruthless. For the most part they left her alone, content to write what they wanted, and in every article the beautiful, vivacious Francesca was lauded for her unwavering and loving support, while the "plain and antisocial" Theresa was criticized for her seeming neglect of her husband in his time of need.

She sighed quietly, as she stared out at the heavy downpour, missing Sandro so much it hurt and wishing that she could just talk with him. The baby moved restlessly, and she winced slightly as a tiny foot caught her just beneath the ribs. She sang a quiet lullaby and ran her hands over the mound of her stomach. She was feeling her burden more and more with each passing day.

"Theresa?" The quiet voice coming from behind her made her jump nearly out of her skin, and she yelped before turning to face Lisa and Rick, both of whom stood framed in the doorway of the den.

"God, you startled me," she gasped as they stepped into the room, neither cracking a smile, both looking relentlessly grim. "What's wrong? Has something happened?"

"Terri—we have to get you out of here," Lisa said urgently, rounding the sofa to stand in front of her.

"What? Why?"

"We'll explain once we're out of here."

"No." She shook her head stubbornly. "Tell me now. Is it Sandro? Was he hurt?"

"He *will* be once I get through with him," Rick threatened furiously.

"Rick, not now," Lisa groaned, and Theresa's eyes settled on the grim-faced man in confusion.

"I don't understand." Her confused gaze went from Lisa's frantic expression to Rick's furious one. "What's going on?"

"A story just broke in the European newspapers."

"What story?" she asked in bewilderment, and Rick swore softly.

"Sweetheart, we can discuss it later. For now, we have to leave before the vultures descend."

"No, Rick," she maintained stubbornly. "I'm not leaving my home without good reason." Rick's jaw clenched and his expression clearly gave away his frustration with her.

"Terri, they're saying that Sandro was blackmailed into marrying you. That he did so for his father. They're also saying that a *source* close to the family claims that since Sandro has no reason to be with you anymore, he'll be filing for a divorce as soon as he gets back."

"I never thought of that," Theresa half whispered to herself. "Of course he's free now. That's probably why I never heard from him, he's been busy planning this. I should have known that he would want that. I should have seen this coming."

"Theresa, don't you dare beat yourself up about it. If the divorce rumors are true, then he's a bastard for abandoning his pregnant wife when she needs him most," Rick fumed.

"No, I'm happy for him. He was trapped." She was so dazed, she barely knew what she was saying, and Rick swore in disbelief.

"My God, it's like you have battered-wife syndrome. Stop making excuses for him. He's an ass who hurt you time and again." When it looked like she was about to protest, Lisa stepped forward.

"Come on, darling, let's get you packed up and out of here." Her cousin took charge, grabbing hold of Theresa's arm and jerking her out of her stupor. Lisa steered her out of the room, tossing a warning look over her shoulder when it looked like Rick wanted to say something more.

~

After getting settled at Rick and Lisa's, Theresa decided to give the couple, who were walking on eggshells around her, a break from her presence by taking a nap. She was just slipping into a troubled doze when she heard the unmistakable voice of her husband coming from a distance. She frowned and sat upright, pushing her tangled hair out of her face. She tilted her head, not sure if her imagination was playing tricks on her, until she heard it again. It was Sandro, without a doubt, and he sounded agitated.

She got out of bed with some difficulty before padding to the door on bare feet and opening it slightly. This time she could clearly make out his voice.

"I had nothing to do with that story," he was protesting. "And I'll be damned if you keep me away from my family like this."

"She doesn't want to see you, Sandro," Rick stated firmly, and there was a moment's charged silence.

"Maybe not," Sandro conceded quietly. "But that's because she doesn't know everything. I just need to explain things to her. I need to talk with her."

"Explain what? How you've been cheating on her with that woman since nearly the day of your wedding? How you've spent every available moment with her since you returned to Italy for the funeral, while your pregnant wife waited in vain for you to call her every day?"

"I haven't cheated on her," Sandro growled after a moment's silence. "Not in deed and not in thought. Not once. She knows that."

"All she knows is that her husband left a month ago, supposedly to attend his father's funeral, but then hooked up with his mistress and started divorce proceedings once he grasped that nothing was tying him to his wife anymore."

"There's a hell of a lot tying me to my wife, Palmer," Sandro gritted. "Our baby for one."

"Oh, please, we know how little you actually *want* that baby, De Lucci."

"I want him," Sandro said quietly, so quietly she nearly missed it. "I want them both."

"Stop it." Theresa could stand it no more, she waddled into the living room, where Rick and Lisa stood on one side of the room and Sandro on the other. The atmosphere was so charged that Theresa was sure her hair was standing on end. Sandro's face tightened at the sight of her.

"Theresa," he whispered. "This was not meant for you to hear."

"It doesn't matter." She shrugged listlessly. "I'm tired . . . I'm so tired of all this, Sandro."

"I know, *cara,* but it will get better. I promise you that."

"I don't see how it can." She shook her head bitterly and he groaned, closing the distance between them in four strides before gathering her into his arms and hugging her tenderly.

"It can. It *will.* I didn't file for a divorce, Theresa. I have no reason to divorce you."

"Sandro please just—*shut up*!" she interrupted furiously, pushing him away forcefully. His face went ruddy but his mouth slammed shut. "If you won't divorce me, then I'll be the one divorcing you. I don't want a husband who feels obligated to be with me. You have no reason to stay with me anymore. I can take care of myself, and I can take care of this baby. I don't need you or your guilt. You're free to leave. In fact, I want you to go." He said nothing, merely stared down at her, with one hand squeezing the nape of his neck. His face was inscrutable, his eyes dark with an emotion that she could not read. He looked stunned, incapable of movement, and Theresa figured that he probably needed a harder push.

"For God's sake, go back to the woman you love! Go back to Francesca." She turned away from him, dismissing him contemptuously, but froze when he swore shakily.

"God, you are the most contrary little bitch!" he hissed. "I don't *love* Francesca. I don't think I've ever loved her. Maybe when I married you, for about five seconds, I believed that I did. But I was disabused of that notion pretty damned early on in our marriage. I don't love her and I have no idea why the hell you're so fixated on her." She turned on him furiously, ignoring Rick and Lisa, who were watching the exchange in morbid fascination.

"Maybe I'm fixated on her because every time you go to Italy, the papers and Internet are full of pictures of you two attending the same functions, touching, kissing, dancing, or hugging! Don't you *dare* insult my intelligence by saying that it meant nothing. I believe you when you say that you've never slept with other women while we were married. But I'm willing to bet you came pretty close with her. I mean, how the hell could *she* be the other woman? *I* was the other woman. Your entire family knew it, my father knew it. I know it."

"We're in the same social circle, Theresa. She was always at the same functions as I am. She's an old friend; naturally I hugged her or touched her occasionally. Yes, I danced with her, dropped a few casual kisses on her cheek. It meant nothing. I treated her as I would one of my sisters. I don't desire her, I don't love her, and I don't *want* her! Those are feelings reserved for you . . . only for you." His voice deepened and his face softened at the admission. His eyes were gentle as he registered the confusion on her face. Was he saying he *loved* her? And if he was . . . did she believe him? She wasn't sure of the answer to either question, and a second later she didn't really care when she suddenly doubled over in pain.

Sandro, Rick, and Lisa all surged forward in concern, but her husband got to her first. He had an arm around her waist before she could blink.

"What's wrong?" he demanded hoarsely. Theresa grabbed his free hand in both of hers and squeezed it urgently as her entire body quivered in excruciating pain. After an eternal moment, the pain lessened and faded and she pushed her way upright, meeting Sandro's frantic gaze with a panicky one of her own.

"It's the baby," she whispered in fear. "I think the baby's coming."

"No, no, no." The naked panic and fear in his eyes did nothing to alleviate Theresa's own terror. "He can't be coming now. He's nearly a month early! Are you sure?"

"I've been cramping all day but I thought it was due to stress," Theresa moaned after the pain had subsided. "But now I think I'm having contractions."

"Okay, it's okay," he soothed, automatically gathering her trembling body into a hug. "We'll be fine. We have to get you to the hospital."

~

Theresa had argued, begged, cajoled, and attempted to reason with him, but Sandro had refused point-blank to defer his position as her coach to Lisa. In the end, Lisa had declined to go in to the hospital with her, saying that it was best for Theresa to have her original coaching partner with her. Shocked and hurt by what she felt was an unforgivable betrayal, Theresa had refused to look, or even *talk*, to her cousin while Sandro shepherded her out to his car. Lisa had seemed to be cheerfully and deliberately oblivious to Theresa's pointed and rather childish silent treatment, promising that she and Rick would be at the hospital soon.

"She did what she thought was best, *cara*." Sandro tried to placate her en route to the hospital. She turned her head and stared out at the passing scenery, scared and angry and not really in the mood to be comforted by him. "She knew that I would have insisted and we'd have just wasted time arguing futilely about it."

"I wanted somebody I trusted in there with me," she said, keeping her eyes glued on the road ahead. He didn't respond to that, but from the corner of her eye she saw his hands tighten on the steering wheel and knew that she'd scored a direct hit. The rest of the journey went by quickly, and before she knew it, she was being admitted into the elite private maternity clinic that Sandro had arranged for her months ago. She'd had only one contraction en route but it had nearly sent Sandro off the road in a panic.

Still it was hours before anything more interesting than that happened. The doctor confirmed that she was indeed in labor but reassured them that it was perfectly normal for women to go into labor a few weeks early. They were taking extra precautions because of her health issues during the pregnancy, but for someone whose pregnancy had been fraught with drama, Theresa's labor was pretty boring aside from the intense periods of pain. Her obstetrician monitored her condition carefully and weathered Sandro's demanding, panicked questions with admirable calm. Her contractions seemed to leave Sandro more wrung out than they did her, and he wasn't dealing with it very well.

About five hours after her admission, Theresa found herself glaring up at her hovering husband in frustration.

"For God's sake, go and get yourself some coffee or something, you're driving me up the wall!"

"I won't leave you. What if you have another contraction? What if your water breaks and they rush you into the delivery room? What if there are complications?" he asked hoarsely, his eyes dilating more with each anxious question. Theresa rolled her eyes in exasperation.

"I doubt any of those things will happen in the two minutes it would take you to leave the room and get a cup of coffee, Sandro," she sighed impatiently.

"They could," he insisted stubbornly.

"Unlikely." He didn't respond, merely continued to sit by her bedside. They were both silent for a few minutes.

"Why are you here?" Theresa asked tiredly.

"Because this is where I want to be," he responded, and she squeezed her eyes shut.

"Why do you want to be here?" she persisted.

"You're my wife, *cara*. You're having my baby." He reached out and covered one of her hands with his. "I belong here."

"You don't belong here," she whispered hoarsely.

"I do."

"You have another life, a family that wants you to come home, a woman you love and who loves you. You don't have to be here, Sandro." She shook her head tiredly, tears seeping from beneath her eyelids.

"I have this life, with you. It's the only one that matters to me," he insisted. "I have a wife who loved me once, and who maybe . . . someday . . . would dare to love and trust me again? I don't *have* to be here . . . but I *want* to be here."

"Too many things have happened between us. More than two years of pain," she whispered rawly, and his hand contracted around hers. "I can't go back to being the naive girl who loved you with all her heart."

"But maybe . . . the *woman* who replaced the girl could find a way to love the flawed man she'd once placed on a pedestal he had no business being on?"

"You've hurt me so many times," she confessed, opening her eyes and meeting his full on. He flinched slightly beneath the accusatory glare.

"I know."

"In so many ways."

"I know."

"Why should I forgive you and love you again? Why should I open up my heart to a man who could easily crush it in the palms of his hands?"

"You probably shouldn't." He smiled bitterly. "But I wish you would."

"I can't," she whispered, tears drenching her pale cheeks, and he nodded slightly, reaching out to wipe at the tears.

"I know," he said again, before lapsing into silence.

Her water broke four hours later, and she was moved to the delivery room. She and Sandro hadn't exchanged any further meaningful conversation, he'd just continued to soothe her and coach her through the ever-increasing pain. She didn't ever say it but she was pretty grateful to have him there. Even though he was as nervous and edgy as a cat in a barrel between contractions, he was a solid rock during them.

Four intensely nerve-wracking, sweaty, and pain-riddled hours later, during which time Sandro supported her, swore at her doctors, threatened the nurses, and seemed to come close to breaking down into tears on several occasions, Theresa finally gave one last painful push. There was a rush of activity at the foot of the bed as Theresa felt an overwhelming flood of relief. Sandro's eyes remained glued to her face, bright and feverish above the surgical mask they had forced him to wear. He dragged down the mask and leaned down toward her, until his mouth was so close to her ear she could feel his hot and moist breath fanning over her overheated skin.

"You're amazing, *cara mia.* So incredible . . ."

She jerked her head away from his mouth and turned her face to stare at him in bewilderment, rocked by the emotion she heard in his voice. But his attention was now on the doctor and the squalling, naked, and tiny bundle the man held cradled in his gentle and capable hands.

"Here's the little lady who's been causing all that fuss and bother," the man said jovially. "Congratulations, Mr. and Mrs. De Lucci, you have a beautiful and perfectly healthy baby girl."

Theresa's breath hitched in her chest at the man's words, and her eyes remained glued to Sandro's face. But instead of the rapidly concealed disappointment she would have expected to see, she witnessed something she would never have believed if she hadn't seen it with her own eyes: she watched her husband fall hopelessly and helplessly head over heels in love with the outraged bundle of femininity the doctor placed onto Theresa's chest.

Theresa was overwhelmed as she stared down at the tiny, wailing infant on her chest and immediately loved her with all her heart. While at the same time, Theresa was not entirely sure what to do with this baby girl who should have been a boy.

"She's beautiful," the smitten Sandro crooned, dropping a large hand to the baby's tiny head and gently stroking the soft skin and tufts of still-wet hair. "She's so very beautiful, Theresa."

"Yes," she muttered automatically. "She really is." He frowned down at her, puzzled by her response or lack thereof.

"Theresa . . . what's wrong?"

"Your wife is exhausted, Mr. De Lucci," the doctor said brusquely. "Give her time to recover, and I'm sure she'll be fawning all over this little beauty."

"Yes. I'm tired," Theresa said remotely, and Sandro's brow furrowed. He watched as Theresa absently stroked the baby's down-soft back, without once looking down at the infant, and knew that something was terribly wrong.

CHAPTER ELEVEN

She's gorgeous, Terri," Lisa gushed, and Theresa smiled tiredly, nodding her appreciation of the comment. Lisa seemed not to notice her lack of enthusiasm, or if she did, probably dismissed it as exhaustion. Rick had been in earlier but was at work at the moment. Sandro was leaning against a wall, arms crossed over his broad chest and legs crossed at the ankles. He said nothing but Theresa was aware of him watching her every move with brooding intensity.

It was just over a day since the baby had been born, and Sandro had gone home only to shower and change and to bring her a change of clothes. He'd also packed a bag for the baby, filling it with the tiny little pink and white things he'd bought months ago while Theresa had been industriously buying toys and clothes for a baby boy.

"Have you thought of names yet?" Lisa was asking, and Theresa winced slightly at the memory of a conversation she'd once had with Sandro. He must've have remembered too because he made a caustic sound.

"Last time we talked about it," he spoke for the first time since Lisa had arrived ten minutes before, "she had her heart set on Kieran, Liam, Ethan, or Alexander." Lisa frowned at that.

"Only boys' names?" Lisa asked in confusion.

"You forget, your cousin was obsessed with having a son," he taunted. "What a pity for her that she failed so dismally at achieving her goal." Theresa's soft mouth quivered at the slight, and his eyes darkened at the sight but he kept pressing. "She's so torn up by this inability of hers to do anything right, that she hasn't even bothered to *look* at our daughter. Or hold her. Or even attempt to feed her. Why hassle with a mere girl child when it won't get her out of her miserable marriage with me? When it won't win her the affection of her thrice-damned father?"

"Theresa?" Lisa prompted gently, watching as tears spilled onto Theresa's pale cheeks. Sandro cursed rawly before levering himself from the wall and sitting down on the bed to wrap her in his strong arms.

"Don't cry," he whispered. "I'm a bastard. Just don't cry."

"You're not a bastard," she sobbed. "You're right. I can't look at her. I can't hold her. I don't understand why I feel this way. I hate myself for feeling this way. I just wanted to make this all right. I wanted to have that son and release you from your obligation to me. I wanted to finally do something right in my father's eyes. Everything would have been perfect."

"Do you hate our baby?" he asked painfully, keeping his face buried in her hair.

"Of course not. I love her so much it hurts. But I feel like such a failure."

"Oh God, sweetheart, just let it all go," he groaned. "Let yourself love her. Allow yourself to be happy."

"But what about *you*? I promised you . . ."

"For God's sake, just stop it." He shook her slightly. "I told you before, I don't *want* out of this marriage. And if you give me nothing but daughters for the next twenty years, I would consider myself blessed."

She made a muffled sound as she buried her face in his neck and wept. She so desperately wanted to believe him. He rocked her soothingly and after a long while, he released her and gently lowered her until her head rested on the pillow.

"Why don't you rest, *cara,* and when you wake up, I think it's time you meet your daughter and give her a proper welcome into this world." Theresa stared up into his dark, handsome face, barely noticing when her cousin got up and left, squeezing Sandro's taut shoulder on her way out. Her vision started to blur after a while and she fell asleep still trustingly clutching one of her husband's large, capable hands in both of hers.

~

She awoke to the sound of angry, hushed voices and blinked groggily as she tried to get her bearings.

"I don't want you anywhere near her." She heard Sandro hiss furiously and tried to concentrate on the drama unfolding in her doorway where she could see two large men silhouetted. One was unmistakably Sandro, and the other . . . she narrowed her eyes slightly, trying to focus a bit better. It looked like her father.

"She's my daughter and I'll damned well see her when I want to," the other man blustered, confirming that he was, indeed, Jackson Noble.

"So that you can damage her more than you already have?" Sandro asked, almost shaking with rage. "I won't let you get close enough to hurt her like that again. And you can forget about getting that grandson you want anytime soon. I refuse to give you the pleasure."

"Well, then stay married to her until you do, or give up the vineyard," her father sneered.

"The vineyard never meant as much to me as it did my father. You can have the damned place back. I want your grasping paws out of my business and the taint of your presence away from my marriage. You won't be getting your hooks into Theresa again, and you most certainly will not be any kind of presence in our children's lives."

"Sandro . . ." Theresa sat up slightly. "It's okay. I want to speak with him."

"Theresa . . ." His voice shook with anger as he stepped into her slightly darkened room. "No."

"It's okay." She smiled, her lips trembling. "He doesn't have the power to hurt me anymore. I want to see him."

"Theresa . . ."

"Sandro." Her voice was firm and brooked no argument, and he sighed before stepping aside to let her father in.

"Father." She nodded warily as she watched the large, handsome man whose affection and approval she had craved her entire life enter the room.

"Theresa, you look none the worse for wear," he observed in the cold, distant voice he always used on her, and she immediately went back to that insecure little girl who had never understood why her daddy didn't hug her and didn't want to spend time with her.

"Have you seen my daughter yet?" she asked, her voice strong and sure. Not betraying the little girl who still lurked somewhere inside.

"Not yet, no." He seemed uncertain in the face of the new strength in her and unsure of what to make of it.

"It's funny," she suddenly observed, "what having a baby does to you. You would go out of your way to protect that new life from anybody who would threaten its happiness. I won't allow you to hurt my baby the way you hurt me. I don't want you in her life unless you're prepared to love her in the way you were unable to love me: wholeheartedly and unconditionally." As if on cue, a nurse brought a fretting, pink-wrapped bundle into the room. She paused for a moment, sensing the tension in the room before pasting a bright smile onto her lips and bringing the baby over to Theresa.

"I think that it's way past time this little one meets her mother properly." Theresa's entire face lit up, and her heart filled with overwhelming love as the nurse placed the beautiful infant into her arms. She finally took inventory . . . counting fingers and toes, stroking downy black hair and velvety skin. She even enjoyed it when the little one opened her rosebud of a mouth and started to wail angrily.

"Hello there, sweetheart," she whispered. "You are the most beautiful thing I've ever seen in my life." The nurse brusquely proceeded to give her a crash course in breastfeeding, ignoring the way Theresa's face flamed when the older woman started talking about breast pumps and let-down reflexes. Her father shifted uncomfortably while Sandro sat down at her bedside, a mixture of amusement, overwhelming pride, and bewildered love on his face. She had never seen him look more vulnerable or more protective. He sent a warning glare her father's way, before his unsettling scrutiny shifted back to her. Theresa, in the meantime, was struggling to conceal her milk-swollen breast from them after the nurse unceremoniously yanked the bodice of her nightgown down. The woman obviously thought that Theresa had nothing to be embarrassed about in front of husband and father. She fumbled with a towel but it was Sandro who reached across and draped it over her shoulder to cover her breast and the baby's head. The baby found her nipple and latched on with enough force to make her wince. He concealed her from her father but kept the towel up on his side so that he could watch, ignoring her flustered glare.

"She's got a pretty healthy appetite, doesn't she?" he muttered in fascination, his voice alive with adoration. "Does that hurt?" Theresa shook her head slightly in response and snuck a glance up at her father, who was unused to being so completely ignored and clearly did not like it.

"Jackson, we'll discuss the details of the broken contract at a later date. You can have back the vineyard, and you're more than welcome to keep the damned money, but your daughter's mine, as is the beautiful baby she's given me. Sue me for breach of contract if you must."

"I don't want that useless piece of land back, we could renegotiate the terms . . ." Her father sounded almost desperate, and Theresa suddenly lost patience with both men.

"Stop talking about me like I'm an expensive piece of meat," she seethed. "Take your sordid business elsewhere. I want it nowhere near my baby. Father, I've given you my conditions."

"You're so brave now, aren't you?" her father sneered. "But if push came to shove, I wonder how strong you'd be?"

"I'm stronger than you'll ever know, father." She smiled serenely. "Years of constant rejection from the people you love can leave you with pretty tough skin. You can't hurt me anymore. I don't want or need your version of love. I find that I no longer want or need you in my life."

"Yes, *so* brave now that you have your loving husband's support." The man's words were laced with bitterness. "But while he may love your baby, Theresa, he'll never love *you*. He has Francesca Delvecchio, and, yes, he's Italian enough to want that baby of yours, so it's just a matter of time before he finds a way to get her away from you." Theresa blinked, her fear showing, as her father presented a scenario she had never once considered. She couldn't prevent herself from glancing over at Sandro, whose face was dark with fury, his entire body coiled with tension. He looked like he was about to tear her father's throat out.

"I think it's time you left, Father," she whispered painfully, and her father sneered one last time before he pivoted on his heel and strode from the room.

"Don't you *dare* believe what he just said, Theresa," Sandro whispered rawly, focusing his glare on her. "Don't you dare!"

"I know that you love her, Sandro," she whispered. She wasn't sure if she meant the baby or Francesca, and she could tell by the look of uncertainty on his face that he wasn't sure either and so he was at a loss as to how to respond. "Would you try to take her from me?"

"No!" he practically shouted, and the baby startled. Theresa soothed her with slight rocking motions until she started suckling again. He reined in his temper and gentled his voice with visible effort. "I wouldn't do that to you. I'd *never* hurt you like that."

"But you want her . . ." Again the ambiguity and his frown deepened.

"If you mean *the baby*, then yes, of course I want her. But it's a package deal for me. I want *both* of you. You're my family. I don't want a life separate from yours. I want *our* life. The one we've been building together these last few months."

"What do you mean? All we ever talked about was divorcing," she asked in confusion.

"I'm referring to all those nights together. The movies, the games, the great conversations . . . What the hell was that if not relationship building? We know that we're great in bed. But we'd never really tried all the other stuff that couples do. The last few months, we did do those things. We may have done things a little backward, *cara,* but that doesn't mean that we can't have a solid marriage like Rick and Lisa's. The only one of us who'd ever mentioned divorce was you. I don't bloody want a divorce. I want *us*. Together."

"I think," she whispered so softly he could barely hear her and had to lean in closer to make out her words, "I think that you're a wonderful man, Sandro. A decent man, and because of that, I know that you'd do anything to make things right. You'd make any sacrifice to give the baby and me a normal life. But I can't let you do that. I can't let you keep forfeiting the things you want just because you think it's the right thing to do."

"This again," he muttered impatiently. "I went from demon to saint in pretty short order, didn't I? I want you to listen to me very,

very carefully, Theresa, because I won't be saying this again. I'm not a saint. I'm being very selfish when I say that I want you and our baby with me and when I say that I want us to be a family. I have duties back in Italy, people I love and need to take care of. But right now I don't give a damn about any of that because I want to spend my every waking moment with you and this baby. This life I've built with you, it's the only one that matters to me anymore. So please stop telling me what *you* think I really want and try listening to me for a change."

Theresa stared up at him uncertainly. Dare she believe that he meant this? That it wasn't just a really good act? She cleared her throat, trying to formulate a response, but he leaned over and kissed her gently, stilling the words.

"Don't say anything, Theresa. Just give me a chance." He looked like a man perched on a ledge with her as his last chance of redemption. How did she resist that? How *could* she? "I know I'm asking you to make yourself vulnerable again, and I'm so sorry for that. But I want you to trust me. Just one more time . . . allow yourself to trust me." She bit her lip before taking a deep breath and stepping out onto that ledge with him.

"We need to name this little one before we take her home," she said lightly, ignoring the way he released the breath that he'd been holding for countless moments. She felt the tension drain out of him, and his relief was so overwhelming it was an almost tangible thing.

"Any ideas?" he asked huskily, reaching over to stroke the top of the baby's soft head with his thumb, somehow managing to brush the sensitive skin of her breast too, and she shivered at the contact. "Well, since she has all this fuzzy black hair, we should probably stick with Lily." His face lit up with pleasure, and he dropped a quick kiss on her smiling mouth. "I only hope she has the temperament of a Lily and not that of a Sofia."

"If she takes after you, we're in for a bumpy ride," he joked, and she rolled her eyes.

"Please, you're no angel yourself," she retorted without any heat. "Let's just name her Lily and hope for the best."

"Hmm, if she *does* have your stubbornness and fiery temper, I'll adore her even more," he admitted. "It'll certainly make life interesting."

"Why did you keep buying girl's toys and clothes, Sandro?" she asked after a short silence, and his thumb paused its stroking for an infinitesimal second before continuing on. "I mean, I'm grateful for them now, of course. But why?"

"Why?" He shook his head and hesitated again before raising his eyes to meet hers. "I was just . . . hoping for a girl." Her jaw dropped as she gaped at him for a few moments. That thought had never once crossed her mind.

"You were *hoping* for a girl?"

"Yes. Very much," he staggered her by confirming, his eyes remaining steady so she was in no doubt as to his sincerity.

"I don't understand." She shook her head slightly. "Why?" He didn't respond, dropping his eyes to the suckling infant at her breast.

"Sandro?" She prompted, and he raised his eyes to hers once more. He smiled cryptically before shrugging.

"This is neither the time nor the place to be having that particular conversation, Theresa," he frustrated her by saying.

"But . . ."

"We'll discuss it soon, but right now I think Lily is ready to be burped." He pointed to the infant whose tiny mouth had slackened. She awkwardly dragged her bodice back up and then clumsily repositioned Lily until the baby was draped over her shoulder.

"Could you get the nurse?" she asked Sandro, putting his previous comment from her mind for now. "I'm not sure how to do this."

"Rub your hand on her back in a circular motion." He noted the surprise in her eyes before shrugging. "The nurse showed me how to do it last night. You were out cold, but they managed to get her fed and handed her over to me for burping."

Theresa complied with his instruction and was soon rewarded with a tiny burp. The sound was adorable in a way that only a new parent could appreciate, and they grinned at each other when they heard it. In that one glorious moment of solidarity, Theresa started to believe in the possibility of a happily ever after again, and it frightened her to death.

The thin sound of a distressed infant's wail jerked Theresa from a restless sleep. She sat up and fought her way out of bed before groggily trudging to the nursery. When she got there she blinked up at the already-present Sandro who was cradling his crying daughter tenderly in his strong arms. He was wearing only a pair of boxers and held the tiny baby up against his strong, naked chest. He was crooning gently to her and Theresa was transfixed by the sweet picture they presented.

He looked up and saw her standing in the doorway. His hair was messy and standing up in spikes.

"Hey." He smiled over at her. "I was hoping you'd sleep through this. You looked exhausted earlier. I don't think she's hungry. Just cranky. I think her wet nappy woke her up. I changed her and she's all dry and comfy now, but she hasn't worked the bad mood out of her system yet." Theresa walked over to them and peered over one bulging bicep into Lily's scrunched-up little face and smiled in amusement.

"*Very* cranky." She leaned over to drop a kiss on the baby's damp forehead and felt Sandro tense when her cheek brushed against his chest in the process. They both paused awkwardly before Theresa cleared her throat and stepped back. She dropped into the padded rocking chair and tucked her feet up beneath her and watched as Sandro continued to pace and gently talk to the crying baby.

He eventually sank down into the second rocking chair beside Theresa's, while continuing to soothe the baby. Lily's wailing eventually decreased down to a few sad sniffles before she dropped back to sleep. Theresa looked over and smiled when she saw that Sandro had fallen asleep too. Lily was firmly anchored to his chest and held in place with a broad hand on her tiny back.

She looked from the man to the infant and smiled at the similarities between them. Lily had his mouth and something about the set of her brow was one-hundred-percent Sandro. Theresa got up quietly and went over to pick up the baby. Sandro's brow furrowed when she tried to move his hand and instead he tightened his grip slightly.

"Sandro," she whispered, "let me put her to bed." His eyes fluttered open, and he smiled when he saw her leaning over him.

"Theresa," he murmured, and in that unguarded moment, Theresa saw a depth of emotion in his liquid brown eyes that staggered her. She blinked and in that split second he came fully awake and his eyes shifted back to neutral and slightly distant. Theresa wasn't sure if she'd imagined the intensity of the emotion or not. He relinquished his hold on Lily and ducked his head to drop a loving kiss on top of her downy soft black hair.

Theresa was aware of him getting up and following her to the crib. He stood directly behind her and watched over her shoulder as she put the infant to bed. Theresa was intensely aware of him and of the fact that all that stood between them and total nudity was her nightgown and his boxers.

"She has your nose," he whispered into her ear and she jumped, surprised and disturbed to feel his hot breath on her skin.

"Do you think so?" she asked casually. "I can't tell."

"It's an unmistakable nose . . ." His hand came to rest on her shoulder, and she tensed at the feeling of his warm hand on her bare skin. Her breathing went shallow. His hand swept down her shoulder in a gesture that couldn't be mistaken for anything other than a caress and shackled her upper arm loosely. He brought his other hand up to grip her free arm in a similar fashion. He gently dragged her back until she was leaning against his hot, hard chest, and he released his grip with a rumble of satisfaction. His strong arms encircled her waist, and he held her as they both watched their sleeping baby.

The tension eventually left her body as she allowed herself to relax against him and tilt her head back to rest against his shoulder.

"Look at what we did," he murmured into her ear, his low voice brimming with love and pride. "She's perfect." Theresa smiled at the awe she heard in his voice.

"It's been said that any fool can make a baby," she teased, and he snorted.

"Yeah, but have any of them made a baby as absolutely perfect as this one?"

Theresa looked down at the sleeping baby, with her wrinkled face and the slight milk rash that pinkened her cheeks and her patches of soft spiky hair. She looked like a wrinkly, grumpy little old lady . . . but she was *their* wrinkly, grumpy little old lady, and she was adorable.

"No . . . I don't think any of them has," she concurred smugly.

"Theresa . . ." His voice took on a serious tone and she tensed again. "I just . . . I wanted . . ." he seemed at a loss for words, and Theresa frowned, wondering if they would actually have that promised conversation. It had been more than a month since Lily's birth, and they hadn't yet discussed his claim that he'd hoped for a girl.

"Thank you," he finally said, and she turned slightly to look up into his face, visibly surprised by his words.

"For what?" she asked.

"For giving me everything I never knew I wanted," he said after a long pause. His voice was thick with emotion, and he met her eyes directly. *His* eyes were burning with intensity as he willed her to believe him.

"What have I given you, Sandro?" she asked, turning fully in his arms.

"A life." The two words frustrated her because they told her nothing. She was about to ask him to elaborate, when more words came tumbling out. "Happiness, contentment, and a beautiful daughter."

"And are happiness and contentment all you ever wanted from life?" she asked after giving his words some thought. He smiled.

"No. I want more than that. But it's a good start."

"What else do you want?" she asked.

"You," he said without hesitation.

"You have me."

"No, I don't. Not the way you were before, back when we first married before I stupidly proceeded to trample your heart and ego into the ground."

"I've changed since then, grown up. I won't ever be the same woman I was back then."

"Yes, you've changed—in so many wonderful ways—but you've also become more guarded. And I don't blame you, I really don't. But I want you to trust me again."

"I do," she whispered.

"No, I want you to trust me with your heart, Theresa. I want you to allow yourself to love me again. I won't hurt you."

"Why should I trust you that way again, Sandro?" she whispered, and he smiled before cupping her face and staring levelly into her eyes.

"Because I love you, Theresa." The words staggered her. She should have expected them, should have known he would say them, but for some reason she hadn't and now had no idea how to deal with them or how to process them, or worse, how to believe them.

He smiled bittersweetly.

"I know you don't believe me yet," he whispered. "But I'll make it my life's work to convince you." He bent his head and kissed her gently, his lips moist, gentle, and sweet on hers. He raised his head much too quickly, and Theresa went up on her toes to prolong the contact.

"Sandro . . ." She didn't know what to say, but he shook his head and smiled gently.

"It's okay. I just wanted you to know." He kissed her again, a little bit more urgently this time, and she could feel his erection straining against her stomach. It startled her because she hadn't really felt him in so long. Her dormant hormones sprang to life in an instant, and she pushed closer to him, deliberately rubbing herself again his hard penis. He deepened the kiss, his tongue plunging into her mouth in clumsy desperation, and his lack of finesse made her even hungrier for him.

"The doctor gave me the all-clear for sex last week," she reminded him, and he groaned at her urgent words.

"I didn't tell you how I felt because I was trying to get you into bed." His voice was thick with desire, and she smiled up into his flushed face.

"I know that, Sandro. Now hurry up and take me to bed, will you?" He shuddered and lifted her into his arms before carrying her out of the baby's room, into hers next door.

He gently deposited her onto the bed and watched as she dragged the nightgown up over her head and tossed it aside, his dark eyes going slumberous with desire. Suddenly self-conscious, Theresa remembered that she'd gained weight and acquired some stretch marks during her pregnancy. She wasn't the same slender, smooth-skinned woman he'd had sex with last. She lifted her hands to cover herself, but when Sandro swore reverently, she paused and looked at him. He couldn't take his hot eyes off her; he looked like a starving man staring at a feast while wondering which dish to start with.

She watched in fascination, her shyness forgotten, as he fumbled with his boxers and kicked them aside. He was so hard it looked painful, and she could see how his heart was racing with every throb of his gorgeous penis.

"God," he groaned slightly, his voice awed and a little disbelieving. "Oh God, oh God, oh God . . . you're more beautiful than I remembered." He stumbled to the bed and gathered her into his arms, kissing her hungrily. His usual finesse was gone; the hungry kiss was almost adolescently awkward with bumping noses and clashing teeth. But neither of them cared as they went at each other with a ferociousness that bordered on animalistic.

Theresa had one brief moment of lucidity, when she asked him to wear a condom. In the past, Sandro would have been infuriated by the request. This time he stumbled from the bed in a daze and made his way to the en suite, where they stocked a new box of condoms every six months, in case their guests needed any. He was back in seconds, box in hand, but was shaking so badly that the packaging defeated him.

"I can't . . ." he growled in frustration, and she took the box from him with slightly steadier hands. She managed to extract a condom, tossed the box aside, and ripped open the foil package. She held up the little rubber circle with a questioning glance and his pupils dilated even further.

"You do it," he urged huskily, and she smiled before, with agonizing slowness, rolling the condom down his length. She gave him one more stroke for good measure, but he arched himself away from her touch.

"Don't . . . baby . . . I'm going to come."

She lifted her hand to the nape of his neck and dragged him down for another urgent kiss. Without breaking the kiss, Sandro flipped her onto her back and parted her thighs with his own. Despite his obvious desperation, he entered her slowly and with infinite gentleness.

"Am I hurting you?" he asked against her mouth, and she murmured a negative, pushing back up into him, to make it clear that she wanted more of him inside of her. It was all the invitation that Sandro needed before he sheathed himself completely. They both groaned, and he tilted his head back, his eyes closed in ecstasy.

"Oh God . . . Theresa . . . so long! It's been so long," he whispered. "I've missed this. I've missed *you*." He began to move, and she gasped at the feeling of fullness inside of her. He knew her body very well and shifted his position slightly until every stroke hit her in exactly the right spot. It didn't last long—barely five minutes—and for the first time in their marriage, Sandro lost all control and came before she did. Theresa watched his face contort, as his body clenched and his back arched. A desperate sound was ripped from his throat as he tried to hold back and couldn't. Theresa followed seconds later, his orgasm triggering hers. She clenched around him, squeezing him tightly and prolonging his pleasure as she took her own.

For a few moments they both hung suspended in stasis after their powerful mutual orgasms, and time seemed to freeze until

Sandro collapsed onto the bed beside her moments later, breathing heavily as he gathered her into his arms.

"Theresa, love of my life," he whispered into her hair, as they fought to catch their breath, and Theresa smiled before snuggling into his chest with a contented moan and falling asleep in his strong arms.

CHAPTER TWELVE

It was three weeks later and Theresa headed down to the kitchen for breakfast and found her husband already seated at the table, newspaper in hand. He'd already dressed Lily and had her little baby carrier placed on the table in front of him. Lily was asleep and Sandro was so absorbed in his paper that he didn't notice her at first. It was Phumsile's day off, so he'd fixed himself a bowl of cereal, toast, and some coffee. She smiled at the sight of them, her heart overflowing with love for them both.

"Good morning," she greeted cheerfully as she headed over to the breakfast nook. She dropped a kiss on the baby's cheek and then, after the briefest of hesitations, one on her husband's lean cheek. While Sandro was a lot more affectionate these days, she still felt a certain reserve around him, not sure if she could touch and kiss him as freely as he did her. She knew she was being silly, but she seemed unable to overcome her emotional barriers. He told her he loved her every day, but she still couldn't quite bring herself to believe him. She often cynically caught herself wondering if he meant the words or merely said them because he thought they were what she wanted to hear. She didn't understand herself, on the surface it looked like she had everything she'd ever wanted but she still didn't quite believe it was real.

"Good morning." He smiled up at her and put his newspaper aside as she got herself some cereal and sat down opposite him. He did that all the time now. She seemed to have his undivided attention: the business section was set aside, the television switched off, phone calls terminated, and stock reports carelessly tossed away whenever she walked into a room. He wanted to know how she was feeling, how her day was going, what her plans were. They talked all the time, they spent companionable evenings together, and he was a hands-on father. They'd had a quiet family Christmas and had both delighted in buying hugely impractical toys for Lily, things that she wouldn't be able to play with for years. Sandro had surprised her with an emerald pendant and earrings, and she'd given him a silver Montblanc pen with Lily's and her names engraved on it. Their New Year had been equally quiet as they'd invited only Rick, Lisa, and Rick's brother over for a poolside barbecue. They made love every night and he worshipped her body during those long, dark hours. They had a great life. So why couldn't she trust him?

She knew that her reserve was frustrating Sandro . . . hell, it was frustrating her, but she needed something more. She just didn't know what.

"I thought I'd let you sleep in," he was saying as he sipped his coffee. "Between Lily's and my demands last night, you didn't get much sleep." She blushed and averted her eyes to her cereal.

"Thank you," she mumbled. Her cell phone rang and she retrieved it from the kitchen counter where she had left it to charge the night before. A quick glance at the screen told her it was Lisa.

"Hey," she greeted.

"Hey yourself, Birthday Girl," her cousin greeted, and Theresa started. It was her birthday. She'd completely forgotten. "Rhys and I are taking you and Lily out to lunch. Our treat. But we're doing some serious birthday shopping first."

"I'm not sure . . ."

"No arguments, cuz. I'm sure Sandro will understand. He won't expect you to spend your birthday by yourself while he goes off to work . . . and he can have you this evening." Theresa glanced over at Sandro, who was playing peekaboo with a slightly groggy Lily. A helpless smile tugged at her lips as she watched him earnestly play with their daughter. Lily looked confused, but at least she hadn't started wailing yet.

She refocused on her conversation with Lisa, certain that Sandro had no clue that it was her birthday, and she wasn't about to inform him, not when she knew how angry this new Sandro would be with himself for never bothering to discover that information.

"Uhm . . . okay, what time do you want to meet?" She and her cousin quickly worked out the logistics of their meeting, and she hung up shortly after they'd finalized their plans.

"You are meeting Elisa?" It was a question more than a statement. Sandro had lifted Lily from her carrier and was cuddling her to his chest while she suckled on one of his knuckles.

"Yes, some shopping and lunch."

"Do you want me to take Lily to the office while you enjoy your girls' day out?" She smiled at the inherently selfish offer, knowing that he would *love* showing his daughter off at work.

"I appreciate the offer, Sandro, but while she's still breastfeeding, I don't think having her away from me for that long is a good idea." He grimaced at that logic. She knew he missed Lily while he was at work. After a month of paternity leave, he had very begrudgingly gone back to work, but he called every day, claiming to miss "his girls." It was sweet.

She watched him go back to muttering sweet nothings to his daughter between sips of coffee.

"Sandro, do you know who leaked that story about our marriage to the press?" She surprised herself by asking, and she could tell by the way he jerked that the question had thrown him. He lifted his eyes to her, absently rocking Lily as he tried to gauge her mood.

"My oldest sister, Gabriella, had indiscreet conversations about our private family business with one of her friends. When my father died, the family was in the news for weeks, and this 'friend' saw a golden opportunity to make some money. Our marriage wasn't the only thing that was dragged out for public scrutiny. My sister Rosalie's teenage abortion hit the news, my other sister Isabella's cheating husband . . ." He shook his head in disgust. "Ours was just the *biggest* news because of your father's involvement. It made a bad time for the family even worse. I was so busy doing damage control after the news of Rosalie's pregnancy and subsequent abortion that when the story of our marriage first hit, I wasn't even aware of it until my mother brought it to my attention. I dropped everything and flew home to you. I couldn't stand the thought that you'd think it was true . . . that you'd think I valued our marriage so little that I would file for a divorce without even talking to you about it."

"What happened to the friend?"

"She sold our secrets for a pittance but the status she had in our society has diminished to nothing. She is no longer welcome in the circles she once ruled. Trust me, there's no greater punishment for someone like her. Gabriella has learned a valuable lesson in discretion, and a few Italian publications are currently being sued for libel when they completely fabricated a lot of the so-called 'facts' to back up the already juicy story they'd been handed. Like the 'fact' that I was filing for a divorce."

"Also . . ." She paused.

"Also?" he prompted.

"Why didn't you call? You promised you'd call every day," she whispered.

"*Cara*, my father had just died. My sisters, mother, and *Nonna* were emotional wrecks . . . I had so much to take care of but, every time I spoke with you, all I wanted to do was get the hell out of there and come home." That was the second time in as many minutes he'd referred to their house as "home," and the word warmed her down to her soul. "Trust me when I tell you, the urge to come back was so strong that I actually ordered a car to take me to the airport after one of our awkward little conversations. I was torn between following my heart and honoring my responsibilities. But if I hadn't strictly rationed our phone calls, I *would* have abandoned those responsibilities."

"You wouldn't have," she said with an incredulous little laugh.

"Don't underestimate your allure, sweetheart. I would have . . . in a heartbeat. I know it was selfish of me not to call, but it was the only way I could think of to control the impulse to just hand the whole mess over to my sisters and come back to you. At the same time, our very stilted conversations weren't helping matters. I was worried about you, though, so I called Phumsile practically every day for updates on how you were doing. I swore her to secrecy and practically gave her the third degree every time we spoke. When you and I spoke, I was so frustrated and hated how emotionally distant you sounded. I was also afraid of saying the wrong thing and alienating you even further. It was driving me into the wall."

She laughed slightly.

"Up the wall," she corrected.

"What?" He looked baffled.

"It was driving you 'up the wall' . . . not into it."

"Into the wall, up the wall, over the wall, whatever." He flicked a dismissive hand. "It was driving me crazy." Charmed by his failure to grasp the English idiom, Theresa laughed again and decided to let the matter go. His explanations had gone a long way toward dispelling some of her lingering uneasiness with their relationship. Lily started to fuss and Theresa reached for her before quickly and efficiently baring a breast, she winced slightly when Lily latched on hungrily. Sandro dropped his jaw into the palm of one hand and watched them possessively. He enjoyed watching her feed Lily. In fact he was so completely fascinated with the new shape and size of her breasts that he handled them with gentleness and a bit of reverence whenever they made love.

"Thank you for answering my questions," she said after a few moments of silence, broken only by the snuffling sound of the hungrily feeding infant.

"I'm happy to answer any others." His voice trailed off in invitation and she nodded.

"Good to know." She needed to ask him about Francesca, about their future . . . but she was meeting Lisa. *Later*, she promised herself. She would ask him later. She ignored the tiny voice in the back of her head that called her a coward.

~

"So what are the plans for tonight?" Lisa asked curiously as Theresa enjoyed the decadent slice of chocolate mousse cake she was having for dessert.

"We'll probably have a quiet evening." She shrugged. "Sandro doesn't know it's my birthday."

"Oh." Lisa glanced away for a long moment before turning back to Theresa. "Do you want me to tell him?"

"No, he'd feel awful if he knew." Lisa's lips tilted at the sides.

"Well, at least he wouldn't be indifferent," Lisa said. "Which is probably what he would have been a year ago."

Theresa nodded.

"I know." She paused. "He told me he loved me . . . about a month ago. And he's said it every day since. But, I can't *quite* seem to bring myself to believe him."

"Theresa, it's been pretty obvious to me for a while now that he's in love with you," her cousin startled her by saying.

"It has?"

"Yes . . . I think I started to see it when he tried to forgive my debt for no good reason and then when you fainted after your amniocentesis and started crying when I got there. Rick was right, the man looked devastated when you burst into tears. I think you should start believing in him. I know that he hurt you badly in the past, but it's time for you to decide if you can forgive him or not. Because if you can't, then there's no point in staying in this marriage, but if you *can,* then I think this man is going to do his damnedest to make sure that you're happy for the rest of your life."

~

Lisa went home with Theresa that evening deciding that they should have an impromptu birthday dinner for her. But when they got back to the house and Theresa got a phone call from Sandro telling her that he had to work late, Lisa grimly bullied Theresa into a pretty dress, called Rick, and said that they were taking Theresa and Lily out to what she called a "fancy" restaurant.

Theresa was in no real mood to celebrate, and when they got to the restaurant, she dragged her feet to the entrance, where Rick stood waiting. He looked quite dashing in a tuxedo and was well matched with Lisa, who was wearing one of the pretty evening gowns she had bought on their shopping expedition that afternoon.

"Look, guys, this is too much fuss," Theresa protested. "Why don't we just head back to my house and have a nice dinner or something?"

"Too late now, sunshine, we're here, so you're going to have to deal with it." Rick grinned before dropping a kiss on her cheek and then reaching over to taking Lily's carrier from her. "Happy birthday, Theresa, you look ravishing."

The knee-length silk slip dress was a little too low and made her swollen breasts look slightly too voluptuous for her liking. She felt a little uncomfortable in it, but Lisa had chosen it, saying that the ice green color did wonderful things for her hair and eyes.

"I mean, did you guys even think to make reservations?"

"Theresa, with your dad and husband being who they are, do you really think getting into any restaurant you want is ever going to be a problem?" Lisa scoffed, and Theresa wrinkled her nose, conceding the point. Lisa flounced through the door, and Rick stood aside to let Theresa in.

The maître d' smiled and led her through without question. Surprised, she followed him with a little frown on her face. He led her through double glass doors. The place was packed with people, and for some reason no one was sitting down. She squirmed uncomfortably when everyone turned to stare at her, not quite sure what on earth was going on.

"Surprise!" She nearly jumped out of her skin at the collective shout, and then finally noticed that she recognized most of the faces in the room. Rick, who had stood outside of the room until after the surprise, in case it scared Lily, moved to stand beside her.

"What's going on?" she whispered in panicked confusion.

"It's a surprise birthday party, you ditz," he teased, dropping another fond kiss on her cheek before heading off to find his wife in the throng. People were milling around her, kissing her and shaking her hand. She recognized Gabe Braddock and all of Sandro's Friday night buddies along with their significant others. Rick's brother, Bryce Palmer, came up and gave her an unceremonious pat on her back and a gruff "happy birthday" before disappearing back into the woodwork. The man hated crowds. She could imagine this scene wasn't really to his taste, but he was here and she was so utterly confused by that. Why was he here, why were any of them here? How did Lisa even *know* to invite Gabe Braddock and that lot?

"Happy birthday, my love." A familiar pair of strong arms wrapped around her waist, and she was tugged back against a broad chest. Sandro dropped a kiss on her neck. She turned in his arms and stared up at him in bemusement.

"*You* did this?" she asked in disbelief. "But I thought you didn't—"

"*Cara*," he interrupted with infinite patience. "I'm not a stupid man, I wasn't about to repeat my past mistakes. I love you and I wanted to show you how much."

"How long have you been planning this?" she asked.

"God, since before my father died. The plans were put on hold until after I returned, and then with Lily's birth they stalled a bit, but I wanted to do something special to make up for all the times your birthday was neglected or forgotten over the years." She knew he meant by her father as well as himself and was helplessly touched by the gesture.

"Thank you." She smiled and stood up on her toes to kiss him. He cupped her face and kissed her hungrily.

"You look beautiful," he told her.

"You don't look too bad yourself," she said, stepping back to take in his tailor-made tuxedo.

"Hey, break it up you two." A brash male voice intruded into their intimate little cocoon, and they both turned to see Gabriel Braddock's smiling face. "Sandro, it's like every time I see you with this gorgeous thing, you have your hands all over her. Share the wealth, bro." He stepped forward to envelope Theresa in a warm hug.

"Happy birthday, gorgeous. We've missed you." Considering how they'd met her only once, months ago, Theresa initially doubted the veracity of that statement, but the sincerity in his face led her to believe that he actually meant his words.

"Thank you." She smiled. "I'm sorry I never came to any of your other football nights."

"You had a difficult pregnancy, perfectly understandable," he dismissed with a careless flick of the hand. "And congratulations on your beautiful daughter, by the way. Sandro's been flashing pictures of her at us for weeks. It'll be nice to see her in the flesh. Where is the little darling?"

"My cousin's husband has her." She glanced around for Rick and saw him showing Lily off to his business partner, Vuyo, and his brother, Bryce. The little group was soon joined by Bryce's business partner, Pierre de Coursey, and Pierre's wife, Alice. They were all fussing over the sleeping baby.

De Coursey and Palmer had recently offered her a year's internship at their prestigious company DCP Jewellers, after she finished her jewelry design course at college. Sandro had sent a copy of her portfolio to the men and they'd been impressed with her "raw talent." It was yet another example of Sandro's commitment to making her as happy as he could. He knew how much her designing meant to her and had believed in her enough to approach the jewelers on her behalf. At first she hadn't been comfortable with the blatant nepotism, but both Pierre and Bryce had convinced her that they genuinely saw value in her work.

"Looks like she's not wanting for attention, so I'll take her beautiful mother out for a spin on the dance floor in the meantime," Gabriel said, and whisked a laughing Theresa away from Sandro before the other man could protest, twirling her around to some upbeat music.

He'd had her for barely two minutes before someone cut in, and after that she was passed from partner to partner for the next half hour before Sandro finally claimed her.

"Think you can spare some time to flirt with your husband, *cara*?" he asked grumpily, and she blinked up at him uncertainly until she recognized that he was a little jealous. The fact boosted her confidence and brought a delighted smile to her face.

"I have a few minutes to spare between dances." She nodded after a considering pause, and he growled before dragging her closer and tucking her head onto his shoulder. They swayed together slowly, and he started nuzzling her neck. She sighed and melted into his hard body, enjoying the warm, spicy scent of him. They were so wrapped up in each other that they didn't notice anybody standing beside them until a voice penetrated the fog of desire.

"Sandro?" He made a protesting sound before raising his head and blinking at someone standing behind Theresa. She watched his face light up and a smile grace his lips before he launched into rapid Italian. Baffled, she turned in his arms and froze.

"*Cara*, this is my mother and two of my sisters. They flew over to meet you and the latest addition to our family. Mama, Isabella, Rosalie, this is my wife, Theresa." The four women eyed one another warily, none of them quite certain what to expect. Finally, the youngest of the trio of gorgeous brunettes stepped forward with a smile. Theresa guessed that she had to be Rosalie.

"I'm very pleased to meet you at last, Theresa," she said in lightly accented English, and to Theresa's utter shock gave her a warm hug. "I'm Rosalie."

"I . . . nice to meet you," Theresa muttered helplessly in response, her eyes desperately seeking Sandro's. He looked anxious but smiled reassuringly when he met her gaze.

"I was expecting them to arrive next week but they flew in late last night, just in time for your birthday." She could see the apology in his eyes, as if he feared their presence would diminish her pleasure in the birthday party. She shook her head, the gesture so slight that only he caught it, and smiled at him.

"Well, what a doubly wonderful surprise then." She shook off her shock and bestowed a genuinely warm smile on the small group of Italian beauties. Sandro's sisters were receiving a lot of speculative male looks already.

"My daughter Gabriella couldn't make it. She's having some trouble with her oldest child," Sandro's mother said. "And of course, my mother-in-law is too old to travel. But they both send their best." Theresa very much doubted that, remembering how particularly hostile those two women had been to her during the video conference.

"Mrs. De Lucci." Theresa reached out to grip the other woman's hands in both of hers. "I'm so sorry for your loss, and I'm sorry that I was unable to attend the funeral."

"Don't be silly, Theresa," the older woman scoffed, doggedly blinking away her sudden tears. "You were heavily pregnant. Traveling in that condition would have been foolish. You did the right thing. Now, where is this granddaughter of mine? I've seen photographs of course but I'm ready to meet her." The imperiousness in her tone brooked no disobedience, and Theresa grinned when Sandro practically saluted before abandoning them in search of his daughter.

She tensed when she realized that he'd left her alone with his intimidating family and braced herself for whatever would come next. She was under no illusions that they liked her or accepted her, knowing that they would all pretend to get along just fine for Sandro's sake but that what went on behind his back would be another story entirely.

"I owe you an apology," Sandro's mother shocked her by saying, and Theresa dared a glance into the elegant older woman's face. The woman no longer looked intimidating. In fact, her face had softened completely, and Theresa blinked up at her in surprise. "I was less than . . . gracious, when you called to speak with my husband. After the funeral, Sandro told us the truth about your marriage, about the way both he and your father had treated you, so I now know that you would have been completely justified in not wanting to speak with my husband. But you showed a greater depth of character than the rest of us combined when you agreed to meet him. You made a dying man very happy in his last few hours. He was so worried about Sandro and what he'd sacrificed for our family, but talking to you eased his mind considerably, and he was at peace when he passed away that night. I have you to thank for that."

"I was happy to meet him," Theresa responded, a little blown away by this turn of events.

"Well, this is nearly two years too late, but I am *very* happy to meet you too, Theresa." Her mother-in-law engulfed her in a totally unexpected and very awkward hug. Theresa returned it in bemusement before both women stepped back a few seconds later, looking equally flustered. Rosalie and Isabella were both grinning. Rosalie introduced Theresa to Isabella, explaining that the other woman spoke little English

"But she wanted to meet you," Rosalie confided cheerfully. Theresa could see that she and Rosalie were going to get along just fine. The other woman was an irreverent bundle of laughs, and they were both giggling conspiratorially over the way Sandro had practically jumped earlier to do his mother's bidding, when he finally returned carrying Lily. The baby was awake and wailing, not happy with the crowd of unfamiliar people surrounding her. Her little face was wet and scrunched up, but her aunties and grandmother immediately started fussing all over her.

Sandro handed Lily over to his mother for a moment before turning to Theresa.

"You okay?" he asked in a low voice that only she could hear. She nodded, smiling reassuringly up at him.

"I'm sorry. I didn't expect them to show up so soon. I hope they haven't spoiled the party for you. I wanted this night to be perfect."

"And it has been pretty near perfect so far," she assured him. "They've been lovely, Sandro. All of them."

"Good, because I would have bounced them the hell back to Italy if they'd said anything at all to upset you," he told her.

"Don't be silly. They're your family."

"Wife trumps all," he retorted, and she rolled her eyes.

"I'm going to rescue Lily from the Kissing Brigade over there. She's probably hungry." She went over to do just that, practically floating on air as she felt Sandro's eyes still on her. *Wife trumps all?* She very definitely liked the sound of that.

In the end, Theresa got her dream birthday party, complete with singing, a huge cake, and dozens of floating balloons. The evening couldn't have been more perfect. After making sure his family was loaded into a taxi that would take them to their hotel, he called their driver to come and pick them up. Lily had been put to bed in a quiet room equipped with a professional nanny the staff had provided for her and Rhys. She stirred restlessly when her parents collected her, and they both tensed, knowing that it was close to her regular feeding time.

"I'm knackered." Theresa yawned once they were all snugly ensconced in the backseat of the car. He had his arm draped around her shoulders, and she had her head tucked against his chest. Lily was contentedly suckling at her breast, and both of them were in danger of falling asleep on Sandro.

"I had a wonderful evening, Sandro," she muttered sleepily.

"I'm happy to hear it, *cara*," he whispered into her hair.

"All those balloons." Her voice faded, and the last thing she heard before dozing off was the sound of his indulgent chuckling.

~

Theresa woke up some time during the early hours of the morning when she felt Sandro leave the bed. She blinked in confusion, not sure how she'd gotten to bed. She was stark naked, and she didn't remember getting undressed or even coming upstairs for that matter. She could hear Lily fretting through the baby monitor and was about to get out of bed when she heard Sandro's gentle voice crooning to the baby. Lily calmed down a little, and Theresa smiled as she listened to him sing to the baby, his sleep-roughened voice slightly off-key. His voice faded and she sat up, switching on the bedside lamp and adjusting the pillows behind her back when she discerned that Sandro was probably bringing Lily into the bedroom for her feed. He appeared moments later, looking completely rumpled and wearing nothing but white boxer shorts. He smiled when he saw her sitting up in bed.

"Your daughter's hungry." He nodded down at the fussing baby, and Theresa reached up for her. He transferred the wriggling bundle gently before rounding the bed to climb in next to Theresa. He watched raptly as Theresa fed the baby.

"I don't remember getting home," Theresa whispered after a few minutes.

"Yeah, you were wiped out. I brought Lily upstairs and then went back down for you."

"You *carried* me? Sandro, I weigh a ton . . ."

"Hardly," he scoffed.

"Well, that explains why I'm totally naked."

"I felt I deserved a reward after all that hard work." He grinned wickedly, and she rolled her eyes.

"Sandro, I'm moving back into our bedroom tomorrow," she told him quietly. He said nothing at first and instead reached over to toy with one of Lily's closed fists. It was something she'd been thinking about since Lily's birth. He spent every night in the spare bedroom with her anyway, so insisting on separate bedrooms was a bit of a moot point. The master bedroom was a lot more comfortable and closer to the nursery.

"That's good," he said, keeping his eyes on the suckling baby. "I'm happy to hear that, Theresa."

An awkward silence descended, and Theresa wasn't sure what had caused it. His response to her news had been lukewarm at best.

"You do *want* me to move back, right?" she asked after another long silence, and was surprised by the flash of fury she saw in his eyes when he looked up at her.

"Of course I want you to move back, Theresa. I also want you to trust me, to forgive me . . . to *love* me," he seethed, sitting up abruptly and leaving the bed to pace the room like a menacing cat, all feral grace and power. Theresa watched him in helpless fascination.

"I don't know what to say or do anymore, Theresa," he said quietly, running agitated hands through his hair. "Then again it doesn't seem to *matter* what I say or do . . . you're determined to keep an emotional distance between us. Do you think I haven't noticed? How much longer are you going to punish me for my stupidity?"

"I'm not trying to punish you." She was appalled that he would think that. "I'm really not. I just . . ." she didn't know what to say, because now that she thought about it, she wondered if she hadn't been subconsciously punishing him after all.

"I have something for you," he muttered. "It's your birthday present. I was going to give it to you in the morning, but since you're up . . ." He left the room abruptly and returned a couple of minutes later with a thick envelope in his hand. He reached over to take the sleeping baby from her and dropped the envelope into her lap. She stared at it uncertainly for a long time, while Sandro continued to pace with Lily cradled in his arms. Finally, hesitantly, she reached for it and turned it over in her hands. But the plain brown exterior of the A4-size envelope gave no clue as to its contents. She glanced up at Sandro, but he was now standing at the floor-to-ceiling windows, presumably staring out at the stormy predawn sky.

"It won't bite you." His deep voice startled her, and she realized that, because of the glow from the lamp, he could see her reflection in the window. She ran a finger under the flap of the envelope to open it and reached inside to extract a thick sheaf of legal-looking papers. Her stomach plummeted at first when she saw their names printed on the top sheet, and for a brief awful moment, she thought he was serving her divorce papers. Then she looked closer and frowned.

"Sandro . . . what did you do?" she whispered in shock. "You can't do this."

"I can . . . I have." He shrugged, still watching her reflection in the glass. "It's yours."

He had given her the vineyard. His *father's* vineyard.

"But it's your father's."

"And when he died, it became mine. I suppose technically your father could snatch it back at any moment, but it's a gesture, Theresa."

"Why?" she asked helplessly.

"I didn't want you to doubt my reasons for wanting to be with you. I didn't want it hanging between us anymore."

"But your mother and sisters . . ."

"They know about it, and for the most part approve of my decision. Not that it would have mattered if they didn't. This isn't about them; this is about us. It's about fixing what I broke." He turned around to face her and stalked back to the bed. "The vineyard is *yours*, Theresa, and if you don't want it, you can burn it to the ground or transfer the deed to Lily. You can hand it back to your father on a platter. It doesn't matter to me. The only thing that matters to me is you. You're the sun I revolve around, and without you . . ." He shook his head as his voice broke.

"I think it's time you told me about Francesca," Theresa said, and he inhaled deeply before sitting down next to her. Theresa reached over and took Lily from him. Thankfully the baby continued to sleep peacefully.

"Francesca . . ." He shut his eyes as he tried to gather his thoughts. "She's the kind of woman I always pictured myself marrying. Poised, sophisticated, beautiful . . . She keeps all her emotions locked up tight, which suited me fine because I never appreciated messy emotional scenes. We dated and got along pretty well. I fancied myself in love with her. It was a very neat, clinical, and uncomplicated version of love. I thought that we were perfectly suited." Theresa tried to keep her expression neutral, but it hurt so much listening to him talk about the other woman in such terms. "Then I came here to meet your father and saw you for the first time. Your quiet beauty drew me immediately. I don't think I ever told you that. I couldn't keep my eyes off you that first time, and I wanted you with a violence that shocked the ever-loving hell out of me. If your stupid father had left things alone, I'm pretty sure I wouldn't have been able to keep my hands off you. But when he forced the issue, he did the one thing that guaranteed I would keep my distance from you. I don't *like* being told what to do, *cara*. And even though you were exactly what I'd wanted, I very perversely kept you at a distance.

"I resented you and I resented your father for messing up my life and my future plans. I went into our marriage determined to grab that damned divorce with both hands as soon as you had a son. But things got messy . . . and emotional. I tried so hard to keep you at a distance. I refused to kiss you, I pretended to want other women, and all the time I couldn't stay away from you. I could see how much I was hurting you and . . ." She watched him struggle to find the right words before he shook his head and broke eye contact. "At first I didn't care. I rationalized that it was nothing more than you deserved. But the more distant and closed off you became, the more frustrated I became with you. I told myself that it was because I wanted to *see* you suffer, but when I gave it any serious thought, I knew it went deeper than that. I hated not having your attention. When we first married, you showered me with attention. You knew something was wrong, but you were always so determinedly affectionate and loving. Seeing that affection and that *trust* fade from your eyes . . . it was so much harder than I'd ever anticipated."

He got up and started to pace again. Theresa watched him prowl aggressively around the room and felt the ice around her heart melting with every word he uttered. He was being so brutally honest with her, some of his words were ugly and hurtful, while others sent her heart soaring.

"Every time I returned to Italy I spent time with Francesca," he confessed roughly, stopping his pacing abruptly to pin her with his intense glare. "I *never* touched her. I want you to know that. Not in any sexual way. I never wanted to. My mother and sisters kept arranging these little get-togethers with her family and ours; they tried to push us together more often than not. I very rarely sought out her company. I saw her at parties and family gatherings but never felt the need to contact her at any other time. You were never far from my thoughts while I was out of the country. I found myself wondering what you were doing, who you were with, if you were happy . . . if you missed me." He cleared his throat self-consciously. "I *really* wanted you to miss me, Theresa. I told myself it was because you would suffer more, wondering what I was up to . . .

"What a joke! I wanted you to miss me because I missed you. The few times I called home you were so distant, and it drove me out of my mind. All I could think of when I was away was getting back to you. I fantasized about the things I would do to you when I had you naked beneath me again. Why else do you think I was always so damned horny when I got home after those trips?" Theresa blushed as she recalled a particularly memorable homecoming; Sandro had returned on a Friday and hadn't let her out of bed until Monday morning. The man had been insatiable.

"That morning when you said you wanted a divorce." He shook his head. "You shocked the hell out of me. Up until that point you'd been so passive and accepting of the situation."

"The quintessential doormat you mean?" she inserted drily.

"I don't think you were ever a doormat, Theresa. I think you were trying to make the best of a bad situation, and in the end when you no longer could, you showed me who you truly were. I was fascinated with you before, but once I started seeing the real you, I fell hard and fast. I was horrified when I discovered that you knew nothing about your father's sick arrangement. I hated what I'd done to you, how I'd made you suffer for his mistakes. I tried to make it up to you, but by then you clearly despised me and with good reason. I wanted to get to know you, I wanted us to have a real marriage, but you insisted that you wanted nothing to do with me . . . and, Theresa, if you ever wanted revenge for the way I'd treated you, you got it in spades when it felt like nothing I was doing or saying was making any difference to the way you felt about me.

"And then when you told me you were pregnant." He knelt on the bed and stared down into their sleeping baby's face before raising his eyes to hers. "Suddenly it felt like there was a ticking time bomb in the house. I didn't have all the time in the world to make you love me again; I had only a few short months. The one thing I'd wanted above all else in the beginning was now a noose around my throat, tightening with every passing day. I loved the baby with everything in me, but I feared it too because I was terrified that it would eventually take you away from me. I didn't want you to exclude me from the pregnancy; I wanted to show you what we could be like if we operated as a solid family unit, but you were so depressingly obsessed with having a son that it felt like a constant uphill battle. I started praying for a girl because I knew a girl would buy me more time. A girl would keep you with me longer; it would also prove to you, once and for all, that your father's ridiculous contract meant nothing to me anymore. That I wanted our marriage to last forever."

He finally seemed to run out of words, taking in a deep breath of air and exhaling it shakily. His eyes searched hers desperately but she kept her expression neutral, despite the joy bubbling up inside of her. This vulnerable and naked passion was what she'd been waiting for. He'd finally bared his soul for her, and it was almost blindingly beautiful.

"So you want our marriage to last forever?" she asked after a long silence.

"Yes."

"And you love our baby?"

"Yes, of course."

"And you love me?" Her voice shook a bit at the enormity of that realization.

"God, *yes*!"

"Good."

"Just good?" he asked in disbelief.

"Well, what else do you want from me?" she asked innocently, and he growled. She laughed at the feral sound before reaching up her free hand to cup his tense jaw. "Sandro, you gorgeous idiot . . . I *never* stopped loving you. I just got much better at hiding it from you. I was too afraid of being hurt again."

"I'll never hurt you again," he promised vehemently.

"Don't make promises you can't keep, Alessandro," she warned.

"Okay, I'll try my *best* not to inadvertently hurt you again," he rephrased carefully, and she smiled, the old affectionate smile that she used to shower him with in the beginning of their marriage. She heard Sandro's breath catch at the sight.

"Much better," she approved, and he growled again. This time the sound was more a sexy purr than a warning. He swept both her and Lily up in a fierce hug, but when Lily made a high-pitched sound of protest, he let them go reluctantly.

"I love you with all my heart, Theresa, and I want to marry you," he said huskily, and she started.

"I love you too, Sandro, but the last time I checked, we were already married."

"I want to give you the wedding you should have had, *cara*. I want to say my vows again and mean them with all my heart."

"You don't have to do that, Sandro." She shook her head. "I know you love me. You don't have to prove anything to me."

"I don't have to do it, Theresa, but I *want* to do it. I want my family there to see me marry the woman who holds my heart in her hands. Please marry me again, Theresa, and make me the happiest man in the world."

She wound an arm around his neck and dragged his head down for a long kiss.

"Yes. With my entire heart, yes, Sandro."

EPILOGUE

The weather on the late spring day in September was perfect. The sun was shining and the sky was a gorgeous shade of blue, with not a single cloud marring its perfection. The string quartet struck up "The Bridal March," and the small gathering of people who were seated on the wrought-iron chairs in the beautiful garden all turned in unison, craning their necks to see the bride.

Theresa clung to the arm of her maid of honor as she regally made her way down the flower-strewn red carpet. Her eyes were fixed on the tall man standing beneath the rose bower with his hands solemnly folded in front of him. His eyes were devouring her as she walked toward him. He looked gorgeous in his simple black suit. His hair had been cut close to his scalp, and as she got even closer, she could see the nick on his jaw where he'd cut himself shaving that morning. She could see the appreciation in his expression as he took in her simple ivory chiffon slip dress, with its lightly beaded sweetheart neckline, to its dropped waistline and the ankle-length flowing skirt. Her gleaming hair was topped with a simple coronet of white roses, and in her hands she held an equally simple bouquet of creamy white roses.

She stepped up beside him, and Lisa, her maid of honor, offered Sandro his bride's slender right hand. He smiled down at his wife's cousin and dropped an appreciative kiss on her cheek before focusing his attention on his beautiful bride. Theresa handed her bouquet over to Lisa, who stepped back to stand beside Gabriel Braddock, Sandro's best man. Theresa had eyes only for her husband, who looked absolutely stunned at the sight of her.

"You look . . ." He shook his head. "There are no words, *cara*. Beautiful doesn't begin to describe you."

She lifted her free hand to his jaw and stroked his skin tenderly, with all the love in the world reflected in her eyes. The pastor cleared his throat and they stepped apart. Theresa sent a quick glance over to her ten-month-old daughter, who was sitting on her elegant grandmother's lap. Theresa smiled at her mother-in-law and Sandro's sisters, all three of whom were present. A smiling Rick sat beside Isabella De Lucci with a sleeping Rhys cradled in his arms. Her father had made an appearance and sat in the row behind the De Luccis. Things were still very strained between him and Sandro, but he had begrudgingly released Sandro from their contract and hadn't tried to take the vineyard back, saying that he wouldn't contest Theresa's ownership. Theresa still hadn't decided what to do with the contentious plot of land but was leaning toward deeding it over to Lily. Theresa often took Lily to visit Jackson, and while he was still cold toward his daughter, he seemed to love Lily in his own gruff way and spoiled her rotten. Theresa had invited him to the wedding, never expecting him to show up, and now sent a small, appreciative smile in his direction, and he nodded slightly in acknowledgment.

She turned her attention back to her groom; this strong, beautiful man was her whole world and she loved him with all that was in her, secure in the knowledge that he felt exactly the same way about her. In that moment her life could not be any more perfect. The pastor smiled and began to speak.

"Alessandro and Theresa have both opted to write their own vows. Alessandro, would you like to begin?" Sandro smiled down at his beautiful wife and, in a voice that shook with emotion, began with the five words that had become his new mantra.

"Theresa, love of my life . . ."

ABOUT THE AUTHOR

Natasha Anders was born in Cape Town, South Africa. She spent the last nine years working as an Assistant English Teacher in Niigata, Japan, where she became a legendary karaoke diva. Natasha is currently living in Cape Town with her temperamental and opinionated budgie, Sir Oliver Spencer, who has kindly deigned to share his apartment with her. Please feel free to contact her (or Oliver) on Twitter at @satyne1.

Printed in Great Britain
by Amazon